# When Angels Cry

*MaryLu*
# Tyndall

# When Angels Cry

© 2017 by MaryLu Tyndall
Published by Ransom Press
San Jose, CA 95123

ISBN: 978-0-9971671-4-6
E-Version ISBN: 978-0-9971671-5-3

Library of Congress Cataloging-in-Publication Data is on file at the Library of Congress, Washington, D.C.

This book is a work of fiction. Names, characters, places, incidents, and dialogues are either products of the author's imagination or used fictitiously. Any similarity to actual people, organizations, and/or events is purely coincidental.

Unless otherwise indicated, all Scripture quotations are taken from the New King James Version of the Bible. Scripture quotations marked NKJV are taken from the New King James Version®. Copyright © 1982 by Thomas Nelson, Inc. Used by permission. All rights reserved.

**Cover Design** by Ravven
**Editor: Lora Doncea at editsbyLora.com**

Ransom Press
San Jose, CA

*Because thou hast kept the word of my patience, I also will keep thee from the hour of temptation, which shall come upon all the world, to try them that dwell upon the earth. Behold, I come quickly: hold that fast which thou hast, that no man take thy crown.*
*Revelation 3:10-11 (KJV)*

## Foreword

Dear readers, this book is not meant to be a study in theology. It is a work of fiction, an adventurous, romantic story that I hope will both entertain and enlighten you. Based on many years of personal research into the Scriptures and end-times prophecies, I have presented one possible scenario of what the future might look like. I realize there are a variety of opinions and theories regarding these important times. I also realize that there are many different viewpoints on predestination, free will, the gifts of the Holy Spirit, and eternal salvation. However, the Word of God that is quoted and emulated by the characters is meant to be as close to the truth as possible. If you have questions or even objections, I encourage you to search the Scriptures for yourself and ask God to reveal His truth to you personally. Having said all that, if you're ready for an intense spiritual ride, then turn the page and let's get started!

*But know this, that in the last days perilous times will come. For men will be lovers of themselves, lovers of money, boasters, proud, blasphemers, disobedient to parents, unthankful, unholy, unloving, unforgiving, slanderers, without self-control, brutal, despisers of good, headstrong, traitors, haughty, lovers of pleasure rather than lovers of God, having a form of godliness but denying its power.*
2 Timothy 3:1-5 (NJJV)

# Chapter 1

*Mid-July, Fort Lauderdale, Florida - In the near future*

"No, Father God, I can't. I won't! Not him. Anyone but him." Angelica heard the defiant words flow from her mouth, though she could swear she was still fast asleep, safe in her bed. Yet the vision of the angel remained—all glowing brightness and peace, instructing her with an authority and a gentleness she'd never experienced from anyone on earth. She shook her head, desperate to wake up, not wanting to hear the angel's message again.

A salty breeze spun around her, followed by the squawk of a seagull, and she pried her eyes open to find her bedroom forming out of the shadows. "Just a dream," she breathed out. Like the many that had come before it.

Tossing off the sheet, she swept her legs over the side of the bed, dragged a hand over the perspiration on her brow, and dropped her head in her hands. "Father, are You sure? You can't possibly..." But of course He was sure. She'd managed to ignore the first two dreams, pushing them from her thoughts, shrugging them off as products of her wounded heart. But this one had been more real, more demanding. All saying the same thing.

Struggling to her feet, she moved to the open window and knelt with arms atop the windowsill. Across the street, a half-moon lingered above a charcoal sea, flinging ribbons of silver onto the water. A warm breeze stirred her hair and brought the scent of salt and life. She glanced at the clock. 3:00 a.m. No wonder Ocean Blvd beneath her second-story window was deserted—except for a single car slowly swaying over the yellow line.

The lap of waves soothed her, and she raised her face toward the sky sprinkled with thousands of stars. "Father, why me? Can't you send someone else?"

Moments passed as she settled her chin on her hands and stared at the sea.

*I have chosen you.* The soft voice floated from within her, sparking her spirit to life and reaffirming the source.

"Drat." She frowned, but then gazed up at the sky once again and sighed. "I am your servant."

"I don't have all day, Mrs. Clipton. I told you I needed that document by five." Daniel forced back his anger as the older lady shuffled through papers on her desk.

"I'm sorry, Pastor Cain. I had it right here a moment ago. I've just been so busy with Marie and Jason away on missions this week. I hope you can forgive me…"

The woman rambled on while Daniel glanced at the Rolex on his wrist. "Do you have any idea how important this meeting is? If I can get the city council to agree, we can add another twenty acres to our property, open up a women's shelter. Think of the souls we could save!"

"I do, Pastor." The woman fumbled as her eyes started to well with tears. "Here." She breathed a sigh and handed him the folder, hands trembling.

One thing Daniel couldn't stand was incompetence. He liked Mrs. Clipton, he did. She was a widow with no children who loved everyone she met. However, despite her extensive resume, she was often forgetful and unorganized. He supposed it was old age. But she had no other source of income, so out of the kindness of his heart, he had employed her as his executive admin. He just wondered how far God expected him to go with his charity.

Grabbing the folder, he shoved it beneath his arm, then turned and nodded to his security detail. Falling in on either side of him, the two men escorted him from the administrative offices of Fort Lauderdale Church of Grace out into the massive foyer. Chandeliers hung from arched ceilings, sunlight streamed through stained glass windows that depicted scenes from the life of Christ, while a life-size wooden cross made from Jerusalem olive wood took up the entire east wall. Crossing the plush royal-blue carpet, he headed out a set of thick wooden doors into the searing Florida sun.

He'd hired the two burly ex-marines after some nutjob fired a shot at him last year during a rally at the FAU Stadium. If he admitted it, he rather liked being flanked by armed men in black suits. They made him feel important, valued. Someone worth saving. Something he could never have imagined just ten years ago when he'd started this church with a rock band and ten homeless people on the beach. Now, look at him. Nearly twenty thousand people attended FLCG every week. He employed a staff of over two hundred and owned the fifty acres on which the sanctuary, office, and school buildings stood.

All in just ten years.

His associate pastor, Thomas Benton, met him at the bottom of the stairs where a limo idled, ready to take him to his meeting at town hall. With light blond hair perfectly styled and slicked back, Thomas bore little resemblance to the wild, insecure pastor's kid Daniel had befriended in seminary.

"We're late." Thomas adjusted his three-piece Hugo Boss suit and stared at Daniel through Gucci sunglasses.

"Mrs. Clipton again," Daniel spat out, just as he spotted a beautiful woman walking over the front steps toward him—a beautiful, *scantily-dressed* woman. His security goons immediately started for her.

Something about her—the way she walked and held herself—made Daniel stop and stare. Not that she wasn't stare-worthy. Shapely legs flowed out from a black miniskirt while a sequined halter top clung to curves in all the right places. No way she was hiding a weapon in *that* outfit.

"Daniel…Pastor Daniel," she said, halting before his guards, one of whom held an arm out to stop her from proceeding. "A word, please?"

"Come now, gentlemen." Daniel nudged the men aside. "Surely, this woman is no threat. What may I do for you, Miss?" Honey-blonde hair hung in a short bob around an attractive face that was plastered with far too much makeup. But it was her eyes that mesmerized him—green like jade, studying him from within thickly-mascaraed lashes and glittering green eye shadow.

She continued to gaze at him as if she expected him to say something. Sweat broke out on the back of his neck, and for the first time in many years, he felt uncomfortable in the presence of a woman.

Thomas gripped his arm. "We have to go. *Now.*" He arched an incriminating brow, and Daniel nodded and turned to follow him.

"You're not ready," the woman finally said.

Daniel faced her. "I beg your pardon?"

"You're not ready," she repeated. "Your light has gone out."

That voice. Where had he heard it before? It whisked around him, stirring something deep within him...something from a lifetime ago.

Thomas cleared his throat. "Alright. Thank you very much, Miss." He tugged on Daniel and gestured toward the security guards to keep her at a distance. "Church services are Sunday at 9:00, 11:00, and 1:00."

But she had already turned and was walking away.

"Odd." Daniel commented as he adjusted himself in the plush limo seats, thankful for the air conditioner.

"Just some crazy prostitute, no doubt. You really shouldn't stop to talk to these people. It doesn't look good."

The security guards took their seats, one up front with the driver and one back with them, and the limo sped on its way.

"Aren't I supposed to help the lost find salvation?" Daniel eyed his friend.

"Of course. And you do. In your sermons every week."

Daniel sighed. "Maybe she needed help. A word of encouragement."

"Then she can come to church. Although, I would hope in more modest clothing." Contrary to his judgmental tone, Thomas' stare latched upon the woman through the shaded window.

Daniel poured himself spring water from the mini bar and sat back, trying to shove the woman from his thoughts. "What did she mean by my light going out?"

"She's probably high." Thomas snorted. "In fact, I think I recognize her. She works at a local nightclub, the Mermaid Den, a cocktail waitress or something. Definitely not someone you should be associating with."

"And how would you know about this nightclub?" Daniel raised a teasing brow.

Thomas chuckled and looked away. "One of our members fell off the wagon and called me from there to pick him up."

Daniel studied his friend. Good explanation. Perhaps a little *too* good.

"Listen, Daniel." Thomas leaned forward on his knees. "You can't risk yourself for someone like that. You are far too important. The people of Fort Lauderdale need you. Heck, Washington D.C. needs you, and soon the entire world. If that isn't enough, then God needs you."

Daniel smiled and sipped his water. Thomas was right, of course. He needed to look at the bigger picture, concentrate on the entire ocean and not on the little fish swimming around in it.

Baliel and Nazare stood side by side on the steps of the Fort Lauderdale Church of Grace. Nazare watched the limo head down the driveway while Baliel kept a keen eye on Angelica as she opened her car door and got inside.

"So, they have finally met again," Nazare said, unable to keep the excitement from his voice.

Baliel folded arms over his massive chest. "Yes. She obeys the Father."

Nazare, the taller of the two angelic warriors, gripped the hilt of his sword and descended one step before facing his friend. "I am thankful for that. Do you think she can reach him?"

Baliel's gaze shifted from Angelica to Nazare. "If he listens."

"If *she* continues to obey," Nazare returned.

"She will."

Nazare turned his attention to the retreating limo. "He is stubborn. I fear for him."

"Do not fear. It is not from the Creator. Trust and do your job."

Nazare took another step down, tightening the grip on his blade. "If only I could—"

"You cannot." Baliel spoke with the authority of his station. "Now go and protect."

With one final nod to his friend, Nazare disappeared.

Baliel did the same, his gaze fixed on Angelica's car.

"Okay, Father, I did it." Angelica repeated for the third time that morning since she'd dragged herself from bed after only four hours of sleep. "I spoke to him, just like You asked."

Rubbing the sweat from her neck, she closed her bedroom window, followed by the living room windows, before flipping on the AC from the controller mounted on the wall. 7:00 a.m. The earliest they were allowed to use their air conditioning, and even after that, they could only run it on two-hour segments with one hour off in between. After 11:00 p.m., it had to be shut down for the night—all part of some state mandate to conserve energy. But in the heat of Florida summer, it was unbearable.

Opening the fridge, she grabbed the egg carton, bacon, milk, OJ, and bread, and spread them across the kitchen counter. She would make everyone a rare breakfast this morning. For once they had real bacon, and she didn't intend to let it go to waste. Opening her Bible on the counter, she flipped on the small TV screen and switched to the Internet station for the morning news—as was her habit. Watch and pray. Didn't the Lord command them to do just that?

Two newscasters were discussing the recent world economic collapse while the camera panned in on food lines that had become a normal sight in most cities. Drowning them out for a moment, Angelica read a passage from 1 John. The holy words settled a cloak of peace on her as she prayed for God's provision for those in need and thanked Him for always taking care of her and her son Isaac. Reading the Bible had become such an important part of her morning that she found she couldn't do much else until she had absorbed the words of life.

Now, as she busied herself with cracking eggs into a bowl, the news story turned to a meteor that had just crashed into Southern Russia.

"Father, I pray no one was hurt," she whispered, watching a home video of the fireball speeding toward earth.

Next, the scene switched to people looting and rioting in the streets of Chicago, some of them hungry, others just plain mad. All of them devouring everything in their path like an army of locusts, all while tossing rocks at local police. Before she could even pray for them, the story switched to a terrorist attack in Spain that killed fifty-one civilians on a train, and then to rising tensions in the Middle East between Iran, Russia, and the U.S., along with continued civilian casualties in the attacks on Damascus.

Angelica lifted up a series of prayers for all involved as she put a pan on the stove to heat.

The newscaster continued, "UN peacekeepers have not been successful at stopping the recent violence on the Temple Mount in Jerusalem. Last week alone, twenty Israelis and two Palestinians were brutally stabbed in continued altercations over who owns the world's most holy site."

"You own the holy site, Father," Angelica said. "Please help them to see that."

"On a happier note," the news continued. "Soon we all will be able to purchase food and other necessities by simply swiping our wrist over a scanner. LiberateTech has announced that over 100,000 Americans have already received the implanted chip, which will not only put a halt to identity theft and petty thievery, but will contain your entire medical and financial history in case of emergency."

Breathing out a sigh, Angelica stared at the screen. "Oh, dear Lord, it's beginning." Heart heavy, she added slices of bacon to the hot pan, the sizzling preventing her from hearing the remaining stories. Perhaps that was a good thing. There was no end to bad news. Every day, new crises occurred, and every day, they fulfilled the prophecies that were foretold in the precious book lying open before her. She whipped the eggs and then dropped bread in the toaster.

Yet so few people were even aware how close they were to the end.

She flipped the bacon over as her thoughts drifted to Daniel. He had aged, of course, but the years had been more than kind to him. He'd filled out quite nicely—thicker, more muscular. But his hair was the same, that gorgeous chestnut brown with a dusting of trimmed whiskers along his chin and jaw. And those eyes—deep blue like indigo. He had looked at her as if she were a stranger. Yet... she thought she'd seen a hint of recognition flicker behind his gaze.

Of course, more than a decade had passed, and she'd changed a lot herself. She was no longer that dreamy-eyed college girl—thin, bubbly, and looking for a good time. And he was no longer the shy boy who thought he'd never amount to anything. No, he'd become a world-famous pastor with his own kingdom to rule.

Yet...at what cost? Shock had stiffened her when she'd first seen him, when she'd drawn close and saw the darkness that surrounded him—all shifting shadows and chains. Where there was darkness, there were always chains. But there'd been so many. Perhaps she shouldn't have been surprised after what she'd read about him, after the few sermons she'd seen him preach on TV. But still, to see him trapped in such thick darkness had jolted her.

The toast popped, she buttered it, and put in two more slices.

Regardless, she had delivered the message and her task was done.

Then why did she feel the Spirit telling her that she had only just begun?

"No, Father, I can't." She transferred the last of the bacon onto a paper towel. "Don't ask me to." Still, the pinch in her spirit remained. Maybe it was just the jolt to her emotions, residual feelings she hadn't yet dealt with. What else could she do for Daniel, anyway? "Okay, Father, if You want me to go see him again, show me his face today." She smiled, knowing she would not be in a position to see Daniel, either in person or on TV. She would be busy with the kids and errands and chores before she went to work again tonight.

"Hi, Mom."

Angelica looked up and smiled as Isaac entered the living area, dragging his backpack behind him. Dressed in his usual jeans and T-shirt, his hair looked like it had been tossed in a dryer.

"Bacon!" His eyes lit up as he entered the kitchen. "What for?"

"'Cause I love you." She drew him into a hug. His head still fit neatly beneath her chin, but she knew that wouldn't be the case for very long. He was growing up fast, too fast for her liking.

"Did you finish your homework last night?"

"Yeah," he mumbled. "But it was dumb." He plopped down in a chair at the table.

"Why?" Angelica poured eggs into the pan.

"Dumb stuff they are teaching us in Science. Stuff about aliens from other planets coming here and creating our world."

"Hmm." She grabbed a spoon and stirred the eggs. "But you know better."

He nodded. "It's just hard 'cause I gotta read the book and answer questions. And then take a test."

"Just do your best." Angelica wished she had better advice, but there was nothing she could do. Homeschooling had been outlawed, and she couldn't afford private school. Although they weren't teaching anything different due to state laws. Ten was such a tender age, and she hated that her son was being filled with lies and deception.

"Look who's making breakfast!" Wearing sweats and a pink Victoria Secret nightshirt, Leigh appeared from the hallway, hand in hand with her seven-year-old son, Joel.

Even with her long black hair a mess, Leigh's tall, shapely figure and exotic face made her look more like a model than a checker at Walmart. She and Angelica had met at a single parents' club and became instant friends. Moving in together made good sense since Angelica watched Joel during the day while Leigh worked, and at night, Leigh watched Isaac while Angelica worked.

Joel ran to sit beside Isaac who was playing a game on his phone.

Leigh frowned and pointed to Angelica's open Bible. "What's this?"

"Yikes." Angelica winced. "I'm sorry. I got up late and hadn't done my reading yet."

Leigh groaned. "Do you want us all to be arrested?"

"I'm sorry." Angelica dried her hands on a towel, silently chastising herself. "I'll keep it in my room like I promised."

"Who knows who's watching us?" Leigh glanced over the room, her eyes landing suspiciously on the TV.

It was hard to imagine anyone would be spying on two single moms barely making ends meet, but the way the world was going, who knew?

"Why don't you toss it and get the accepted version?" Leigh yawned and poured herself some coffee.

"Because the NWLV version has been changed."

"All they did was take out the bad parts, the offensive, archaic stuff." Leigh sipped her coffee. "You mean the truth?" Angelica smiled. Oh, how she prayed for God to open her friend's eyes. "No arguing today, 'kay? Let's enjoy a good breakfast." Grabbing a plate from the cupboard, she handed it to her friend. "Not watching this horrid news." Leigh grabbed the remote and began switching stations. A familiar voice made Angelica nearly drop her plate. Heart plummeting, she lifted her gaze to the TV where Daniel Cain's face appeared larger than life on the screen.

*Pure and undefiled religion in the sight of our God and Father is this: to visit orphans and widows in their distress, and to keep oneself unstained by the world.*
James 1:27 (NASB)

# Chapter 2

Angelica spread her Little Mermaid towel under a palm tree, set down her beach bag, and turned to rub sunscreen over Isaac.

"Mommm," he complained. "I'm not a baby anymore. I can do it myself." He pushed her hand away.

"You always miss spots and you know how you burn." She continued lathering on the cream until she was satisfied, then cupped his chin and kissed his forehead. "Now, go have fun. But come back when you see Anna."

Grabbing his surfboard, he darted off, kicking up sand as he went.

"Watch the undertow!" she called after him, then said a prayer for his safety as she quickly switched to the spirit. The being of light appeared, strolling beside Isaac, shorter than other angels she'd seen and wider in girth, but fully armed and always by her son's side. *Thank you, Father.* If there was one thing that made a person pray more, it was having a child. And if there was one thing that had helped Angelica realize God's love for her, it was the love she had for Isaac. She always told the Father that if He loved her even half as much as she loved Isaac, she had nothing to fear. To which He always replied, "I love you much more than that."

She smiled. She'd not had an earthly father, and the resulting insecurity and search for love had cost her dearly. If only she had embraced God as Father earlier in life…if only she had received His unconditional love, she could have avoided so much pain—to herself and others.

But then she wouldn't have Isaac. His laughter drew her gaze back to him, sitting atop his board several yards out from shore. He waved, and she waved back, thanking God for turning her mistakes into such a glorious blessing. Now, if she could only raise Isaac knowing God as Father, he could avoid making those same mistakes.

Lowering to her towel, Angelica put away the sunscreen and watched as her son caught a wave and stood, weaving his way through the foamy surf to shore. Living so close to the ocean, he had become a proficient swimmer and a fairly good surfer. So much so, that many of the kids frequenting the beach had befriended him. His outgoing, charming personality naturally attracted people—so like his father. Yet, thankfully, their similarities ended there.

Clouds moved aside, and the sun's full glare made Angelica slip on her sunglasses. Though early in the morning, the beach was already getting crowded. Families set up their umbrellas and coolers, kids dragged pails and shovels to the wet sand, teenage girls wearing string bikinis lathered on suntan lotion, giggling at boys who ogled them from a distance. A volleyball game started yards to her left. Behind her, the hum of traffic on Ocean Blvd buzzed, accompanied by the creak of shopping carts pushed along the sidewalk by the homeless.

Saturday was not the best day to go to the beach if one wanted peace. In a few hours there'd hardly be an empty spot on the sand to lay a towel. But it *was* the best time to help others see the light of God's truth. Something she wasn't particularly good at herself, but with the support of other believers, God had blessed their Saturday meetings. Already a few people she remembered from last week waved at her and began assembling in their normal spot.

Taking off her sunglasses, she made her way to the water before the leaders, Anna and Clay, arrived. As a child, she'd spent many hours at the beach—snorkeling, swimming, and body surfing—and she never grew tired of the warm salty water, the smells of the sea, and the horizon that seemed to stretch to eternity. Battling incoming waves, she waded out to her waist then dove beneath the water. Warmth soothed her body like a liquid massage, easing away her tensions and muting sounds of the world above, luring her deeper to a tranquil place where violence, sorrow, and evil could not exist. Kicking her feet, she sped downward, embracing a few precious moments of peace and calm before lack of air forced her to surface.

After spotting Isaac several yards to her left teaching a young boy how to surf, she swam to shore and headed for her towel.

"Oh!" She bumped into a column of brick…no, a man. "I'm sorry." Raking back her wet hair, she stared up at him, blinking water from her eyes. *No! Can't be!* But it was. Daniel Cain—bare-chested, muscles rounding his chest and arms, six-pack stomach—staring at her as if she were a mermaid emerging from the sea. Ever since he had appeared on her TV screen three days ago, she'd tried to put him out of her mind. Surely, that incident hadn't counted as actually *seeing* his face, had it? So, she had ignored it, along with the nagging twinge in her spirit. But she couldn't very well ignore the hunk of man now standing before her.

*Good one, Father.* Sometimes she didn't find God's sense of humor funny at all.

Great. Why was he just standing there staring at her as if she'd sprouted horns? Pushing past him, she started up the sand.

"Angel?"

She closed her eyes. *No, no, no!* Swallowing, she turned around.

"It *is* you!" He smiled—that brilliant, charming smile of his—as he removed earbuds from his ears and scanned her from head to toe. Did he really need to study every inch of her to confirm it was her? Though she wore a modest swimsuit, she suddenly had the urge to cover up the extra pounds she'd gained over the years.

"How have you been?" he asked, sincerity in his eyes.

"Fine." She gave a plastic smile, hoping to dissuade him. "Busy." She turned to leave, knowing it was the wrong thing to do, that God had put this man in her thoughts—in her path—for a reason.

He gently grabbed her arm, chuckling. "That's all I get after *twelve* years? Busy?"

She pulled from his grip and continued walking. He fell in beside her. *Drat!*

"I can't believe you're still in Fort Lauderdale," he said cheerfully as if he hadn't destroyed her life. "I'd love to catch up."

"I'd rather not, if you don't mind."

This seemed to confuse him immensely. "Do you know who I am?"

Halting, she faced him. "Is it so surprising that I want nothing to do with the great Pastor Daniel Cain?"

An ember of unexpected sorrow burned in his eyes. "I guess it shouldn't. I just thought…I thought after all these years…"

"Where's your entourage?" She glanced behind him.

"What?"

"Your bodyguards? Aren't you too important to be left alone?" Turning, she kept walking, kicking up sand and battling the gentle tug within her to speak to him. But she didn't want to speak to him.

"I only need them for public events—wait." He leapt in front of her. "That was *you* at my church the other day." He fingered the stubble on his chin. "I didn't recognize you behind all the makeup. But I should have with those *eyes*."

Skirting around him, she proceeded. *Please, God, make him go away.* One glance over her shoulder showed her Isaac was still happily surfing. Good.

"What did you mean by what you said?" He followed her. "Why did you come to my church?"

"I had a message to give you. That's all." Relief swept through her as she saw Clay and Anna setting up chairs beside her things, where a small crowd was already forming.

She hoped that would dissuade Daniel from following her.

It didn't.

Anna and Clay's eyes widened at the sight of him, then shifted inquisitively to her.

Grabbing a towel from her bag, Angelica began drying herself, doing her best to ignore him, while shaking her head in a not-so-subtle hint toward her friends. They didn't get it. Instead, they eagerly approached, no doubt wanting an introduction.

"Daniel Cain, these are my friends, Anna and Clay," Angelica spat out quickly.

"Pleased to meet you." Daniel stretched out his hand and shook both of theirs, his gaze taking in Anna's tattoo sleeve on both arms—a relic of her past. Yet, despite *that* past, at forty-five, she maintained a youthful glow that made her look much younger.

"How do you two know each other?" Anna asked.

"We don't," Angelica said at the same time Daniel said "Old friends." Which made for an awkward moment.

A moment that was thankfully interrupted by Isaac, who dropped his board and burst into the middle of them, hair dripping and a wide grin on his lips.

"Clay, Anna!" he squealed, and the two embraced him, not caring that he was soaking wet.

"You're that big-time pastor." Isaac stared up at Daniel. Angelica's heart shriveled, even as Daniel seemed to grow taller. "I am, and who might you be?"

"I'm Isaac. This is my mom." He smiled at Angelica, and she handed him her towel.

Daniel gaped at her, his brow crinkling. "You have a son?"

"Yes." She avoided eye contact and was thankful for the additional people who crowded around them—Hank, a homeless man; Sarah, a drug addict; two Cuban gang members; an off-duty fireman; JoAnn, an elderly woman they called Crazy Jo; and Mercy, a young mother.

Clay pulled his guitar from its case, sat down, and began to tune it. "We share God's Word here on Saturdays," he said to Daniel. Though Clay looked like a rock star from the eighties with his long curly brown hair and skinny physique, he was the most Spirit-filled musician Angelica had ever heard.

"Preaching?" Daniel snorted and ran a hand through his hair, making it stand up in all directions. "I've been jogging on this beach for years, and let me tell you, this crowd does not respond to having Jesus shoved in their faces."

"Good thing," Anna said. "'Cause we don't shove Jesus on anyone. We just recite God's Word and love on people."

"You know what I mean," Daniel said. "Besides if the city gets wind of this, they'll drag you all to jail."

Clay jerked hair from his face and smiled. "Until then, we will do what God calls."

"Pastor Dan, can I call you Pastor Dan?" Anna said, a bit too glibly. "We are just loving people and praying for them. Angelica has a wonderful gift of discernment. She can pinpoint someone's exact spiritual need. Then we pray for them—for healing or whatever. And if they need deliverance, my husband, Robert handles that." She glanced around. "He'll be here soon."

"Deliverance, as in demons?" Daniel laughed. "You guys are kidding, right? That stuff doesn't happen anymore."

Anna shared a knowing smile with Angelica as Clay began to sing "Amazing Grace." Isaac sat at his feet and joined him.

"I need to speak to you, Angel." Daniel tugged on her arm.

"Please don't call me that. And I'm busy right now."

"How about meeting me for coffee later?"

Couldn't the man take a hint? "I can't. I'm sorry." Even though she felt the Spirit nudging her within, felt God telling her to agree. *I cannot do this, Father. Please.* "It's been nice seeing you again, Daniel. Now, if you'll excuse me."

Daniel's heart felt as though it had been stomped into the sand by a herd of elephants. Certainly not because he still had feelings for Angel—after all these years and what she had done to him, that would be ludicrous—but because he was simply unaccustomed to rejection. Backing away from the group, he retreated to the shoreline, then turned to watch her one last time.

By now, a group of at least twenty people sat listening to the music. Much to his surprise, Angel began kneeling before each one, laying her hands on them and closing her eyes. After a minute or two, she would say something that seemed to have an impact on each person. Some shouted for joy. Others appeared to be crying. Anna followed in Angel's wake, touching each person and mumbling prayers that he could not make out from where he stood. One elderly lady began to praise God so loudly, it drew the attention of others on the beach. An older man who looked like a Hells Angel, joined them and laid hands on a young man who began to shake and tremble like a tree in a hurricane. Two homeless men parked their carts by a nearby palm tree and joined the group, listening to Anna, who was now saying something that had them all riveted.

Impossible. *Charlatans.* How had Angel gotten mixed up with this group of false prophets? She hadn't even believed in God when he'd known her before. Pivoting on his heels, Daniel shoved the earbuds in his ears, turned on the music, and jogged down the beach.

Yet, later on, as he was showering at church, he couldn't stop thinking about Angel. Why wouldn't she at least have coffee with him? After all, she was the one who broke *his* heart. She was the one who'd approached him after all these years with her cryptic warnings—warnings of which he certainly had a right to an explanation. Besides, after meeting her friends, he felt an obligation as a pastor to warn her about entangling herself with some crazy cult. Maybe Thomas had been right, and her mind was addled by drugs. It saddened him to think of how far she had fallen from the girl he once knew.

But wait. Her eyes had been clear and sparkling, those lustrous sea-moss eyes he remembered so well. Her hair was still blonde but shorter, and she'd gained some rather alluring feminine curves. Plus, she had a son! Wow. She'd always been a wild spirit, carefree and untamable. But also naive. Apparently, she was still that way.

After dressing in his casual Saturday jeans and T-shirt, Daniel passed through the sanctuary and stopped to gloat at the enormity of it—the hundreds of rows of cushioned pews extending as far as he could see and then up into two levels of balconies. How far he had come. Movement turned him around to see Rubio, his music director, walk out onto the stage with the band.

"Hey, Daniel." He nodded toward him. "We're practicing for tomorrow."

Daniel ground his teeth. When would the man grant him the respect he deserved and call him Pastor Daniel? "How's the play and the light show coming?"

"Good." Rubio approached as the band set up their instruments. One of the singers—Kathy, Daniel thought her name was—stared at him, smiling. Drawing female attention was the curse of being a single pastor, but it was a curse he rarely complained about. The difficult part was resisting the many temptations constantly flung his way.

"The show will blow them away, Dan. And the play, it's as good as anything on Broadway."

"Good. Senator Tames will be in attendance, and I want it perfect."

"You can count on me." Rubio pointed his finger at Daniel and clicked his tongue. He was the best music director in the business, but Daniel always got the feeling the man would stab him in the back if given half a chance.

Leaving the sanctuary, he made his way past the administrative wing to his office. He needed to go over his sermon for tomorrow. They'd picked up coverage on another national station, and he wanted it to be perfect for his new listeners.

"Pastor! Pastor!" Harold Jake's voice sent ice down Daniel's spine. What was the man doing here on Saturday?

Pasting on a smile, he turned to face him.

"Pastor Daniel, I've been meaning to speak to you about something." His tone was so urgent, you'd think the roof was caving in. Daniel knew better.

Drawing him to the side of the hallway, Harold leaned closer, the wrinkles on his face tightening. "It's the music. Several members are complaining. It's far too modern. Really, it sounds like heavy metal and sometimes too close to that rap stuff those African Americans sing. I really don't think it's acceptable in church, do you?"

Daniel maintained his smile, though it pained him to do so. "Our goal is to attract young people who don't know God. Having music they can relate to is a great way to do that, wouldn't you agree, Harold?"

"It just doesn't seem very respectful. Or holy. I mean why can't we sing those good old hymns, you know? At least some of the time."

*When hell freezes over.* Daniel had no intention of risking losing the younger crowd, as well as a possible lawsuit for the lyrics in some of those *old* hymns. "Tell you what, Harold. Send me a list of hymns that haven't been outlawed, and I'll see what I can do."

"Thank you, Pastor. I knew you'd see things my way." Harold winked as if they shared a big secret before turning and walking away.

With a sigh, Daniel proceeded to his office. Last week it was the bathrooms that didn't measure up. The month before that, it was the bulletin that wasn't quite right.

But Harold Jakes was a wealthy widower and one of the church's biggest tithers. Daniel could handle him. Shoving aside thoughts of the annoying man, he smiled as he entered his office at the end of the hall. As big as a small apartment, it was elegantly furnished with the best leather sofa and chairs money could buy. Oil paintings of Old Testament saints lined the walls, while a huge mahogany desk stood in the center like a podium of power. An extensive library reached from floor to ceiling on his right and a small kitchenette stood on his left.

He was about to close the door when the sound of heels click-clacking echoed down the hall, and Kimberly Monroe, the college-group pastor appeared. She looked up and smiled as she approached. Was it his imagination or did her body sway a little more when she knew he was watching?

"Pastor, sorry to bother you on a Saturday." She pushed past him and entered his office.

"No problem. Have a seat." Daniel wove around his desk, keeping the thick wood between them. And for good reason. With a shapely figure, a cherub face, and long blonde hair, Kimberly was a constant temptation. Not only to him, he imagined, but to most of the men who worked at the church.

"What can I do for you, Miss Monroe?"

"Well, as you know you are officiating John and Mike's wedding next Saturday, so I wanted to make sure you knew to be here an hour early before the ceremony at 2:00. Oh, and the reception will be in the East Chapel, so be sure to be there, as well."

"Thank you, I am aware." He stared at her, knowing there must be more.

She swept hair back over her shoulders and sighed. "But the real reason I'm here is that one of my college students is complaining about the neutral bathroom again. She says there are men in there, ogling women."

"She's free to use the women's bathroom."

"But she actually identifies as a man... you know that. You counseled her."

Ah yes, Georgiana or George, whatever. Nice enough girl. Polite, well-mannered, loved God. He did remember her...him. Ugh. Why did things have to be so confusing?

Thomas, his associate pastor, strolled in wearing shorts, a T-shirt, a smile, and his eyes all over Kimberly. "Tell her to take care of business before she comes to church."

She waved him away playfully. "I can hardly do that."

"Still." Thomas shrugged and leaned on the corner of Daniel's desk, dangling a foot. "We have accommodated all gender identities. What else can we do?"

Kimberly cocked her head. "She's asking for a one-room bathroom with a lock. And you know what would happen if she took this to the press."

Daniel squeezed the bridge of his nose. "I'll see what I can do."

"Thank you, Pastor." Rising, she smiled sweetly at them both and walked out the door, swinging her caboose as she went.

Staring after her, Thomas rubbed the back of his neck. "Wouldn't you like a piece of—"

"Remember *who* we are," Daniel interrupted sternly. "And Who we serve."

"Ah, lighten up, Dan. You're still living by those archaic rules from the old Bible. That was just the culture at the time."

Was it? Daniel wondered. He glanced at the picture of his mother on his desk, framed in oak. She had not thought so, nor had they taught that in seminary just a decade earlier.

"God can hardly expect us to go against the natural impulses He gave us, right?" Thomas arched a plucked brow. "You gotta get with the times, or you're gonna lose church members."

Daniel nodded, knowing his friend was right. "Listen, I need to work on my sermon. Is there something you need?"

"No need. But I have good news." Thomas' eyes flashed. "Word among evangelical circles is that your name is at the top of the D.C. list."

"Seriously?" Daniel grinned, elation sweeping through him. Only thirty-three and in line to be the next spiritual advisor to the President.

"Who knows where you could go from there, bud? Run for the Senate, VP, who knows?"

Daniel smiled at his friend's enthusiasm. Thomas had always been in Daniel's corner, always celebrated Daniel's successes. How many people could say that about a friend? "Yeah. Just not sure I'm cut out for politics."

"Who you kidding, man? Think of the power you'd have. Making laws and policy that protect Christian rights. Who's to say God doesn't want you in a seat of power for such a time as this? Besides." Thomas pointed at him. "People love you. You have a way about you that makes them feel at ease."

Nodding, Daniel kicked back and crossed his ankles on top of his desk. *Senator Cain.* It definitely had a ring to it. "You may be right. I guess we'll see. Hey, you know who I saw today? Angelica Smoke."

Thomas coughed and pushed from the desk. "Smokes? Wow. How long has it been?"

"I can't believe you still call her that. Twelve years."

"Twelve years...Is she still hot?"

Daniel cringed. Was that the only thing Thomas remembered about her? Daniel's memories were filled with so much more...her zest for life, her carefree spirit, her kindness and love for those in need...the way she made him feel. He had truly loved her. Once. He pictured her in her one-piece swimsuit that clung to curves in all the right places, wet hair slicked back, water beading on her long lashes. "Yeah. And you'll never guess this, but she was that crazy girl who came up to me the other day on the steps?"

"Naw. Really?" Thomas walked away, suddenly interested in one of Daniel's paintings.

"Yup."

"So I'd guess from her clothes, she's still a cocktail waitress." Thomas' tone was biting. "Incredible. Did you ask her what she meant?"

"Didn't get much of a chance. She turned me down for coffee."

Chuckling, Thomas faced him. "The great Daniel Cain, one of *Newsweek*'s top ten most eligible bachelors, rejected?"

"Stop it." Daniel tossed a pen at his friend. "You know, I wouldn't mind seeing her again."

"What? Are you nuts?" Thomas barked. "She's a cocktail waitress! And probably a druggie. You can't be seen with the likes of her."

Daniel cocked a brow. "I thought we got rid of those archaic rules?"

Thomas planted fists at his waist. "Not the kind that have to do with reputation and status. And yours has to be pristine. Especially if you want to continue in this business and eventually make it to D.C. Stay away from Smokes. She was bad news twelve years ago, and she's bad news now."

Daniel knew he was right. Angel had always been the crazy one, the throw-caution-to-the-wind type. She had nearly gotten him expelled from seminary. If that had happened, where would he be now? Probably working down at the docks with his drunken father.

Yet, after Thomas left, Daniel struggled to focus on his sermon. Angel's words haunted him. He had to know what she'd meant. He had to see her again.

And if she wouldn't come to him, he would go to her.

*A little while longer the light is with you. Walk while you have the light, lest darkness overtake you; he who walks in darkness does not know where he is going.*
John 12:35 (NKJV)

# Chapter 3

Baliel and Nazare stood together at the far end of the long bar in the Mermaid Den. Two bartenders hustled back and forth, pouring drinks for patrons while waitresses carrying trays hurried about the dark room. Tables made to look like ship wheels littered the area, full of people laughing and drinking. Music blared from massive speakers, the *thump thump* of the bass pulsating through the chaos. Thick glass covered one entire wall, giving view to a pool beyond where women dressed in mermaid tails and tiny bikini tops swam around, smiling and waving at the crowd, luring lonely men like the Sirens of old.

A typical Saturday night at the Mermaid Den. Men and women numbing their pain and their consciences with alcohol until they gave into every wicked impulse, opening the door to a multitude of demonic hosts lurking in the shadows around them. Baliel knew all the dark spirits too well. There was of course, Lust, a slimy-looking fellow, skittering about from table to table. Immorality and Homosexuality stood beside a group of college-age humans who were deep in conversation. Greed licked his lips by the bar, alongside Alcoholism. Then there were Jealousy, Envy, Strife, Depression, and Hopelessness, all pacing, eyeing the throng, ready to pounce at the first hint of an opening. Even Suicide had shown up tonight.

And though they all cast spurious glances at Baliel and Nazare, they remained at a distance from the two warriors.

Nazare adjusted the sword at his side and uttered a deep sigh. "When is the Father going to put an end to this wickedness?"

"When every last soul He has called responds."

"We should fight these dark spirits now, kill them all, and put an end to it." Nazare seethed, gripping the hilt of his blade. Though he stood seven feet tall, he was still dwarfed by Baliel, who gazed down at him in disapproval.

"Patience, my friend. The time is not right. All humans must be given a choice between darkness and light. And they must do it soon, before it is too late."

A dark-haired burly man sold drugs to young woman in the corner, drawing the attention of the warriors. Nazare shook his head, his heart heavy. "The Father has told me that she will be dead by morning."

Baliel crossed arms over his chest. "Yes. And lost forever. But He gave her every opportunity, and she has made her choice."

"At least I don't have to frequent such places as you do."

"I don't mind. My job is to protect *her*." Baliel gestured toward Angelica Smoke, delivering drinks to one of the tables. A column of light surrounded her wherever she went—the only light shining in the dark place. "See how she spreads the love of the Father wherever she goes."

They watched as she stopped before a table, casting a glow on the patrons. She spoke, and golden sparkles shot from her mouth and poured over them, disturbing the darkness and shoving it into retreat. But as soon as she left, it returned.

"Why does the Father keep her here?" Nazare asked.

"For such a time as this. She does much good, though she doesn't know it. Last year, she helped three people find their way to the Father."

"You are fortunate to be assigned to such a one. Mine is on the way."

"Which is why we must be diligent tonight. She must make the right decision. She has been fighting the Father. You see how Fear circles her, looking for an opening?"

Nazare nodded as his gaze locked onto the tiny gray shadow with the huge red eyes that hovered over Angelica. "Such a small demon for how great a torment he invokes."

"Indeed. If only humans knew that it takes but a word of faith to defeat him."

Angelica's feet hurt. And it was only 11:00. Three more hours to go. Just three hours. *You can make it, girl.* She halted before a table of men in their twenties, all mesmerized by the swimming mermaids, all drunk after three shots of vodka each. Two of them were singing to the song blaring from the speakers, one was face down on the table, while three more started to argue over which drink was theirs as she placed them on the table. Taking a moment, she sought God's Spirit, looking for a spark of light, something she could use to start a conversation.

Instantly, a dozen demons appeared slithering about the men, wrapping their tentacles possessively around their heads and chests. Fiery eyes shot her way. The spirits trembled when they noticed she could see them—not only see, but she could scatter them with a single Name. Yet they clung to their hosts, baring their fangs, knowing that if she did, these men would invite them back within a second.

She shook the vision away and set down the last drink, hating that she'd given even a speck of attention to the devilish beings. They were mere shadows to her, wisps of emptiness. As long as she walked in the light, they couldn't touch her. But she hated what they did to others. She hated the way they controlled unsuspecting victims and bound them in chains.

One of the men faced her, his glazed eyes landing on her chest. "How's about going out with me after work, babe?"

"Sure." She smiled. "I could tell you all about Jesus and how you don't have to waste your life away on empty pleasures."

He gaped at her, mouth so far open she expected drool to spill out. But then he chuckled. "Good one."

"Honey," his friend said. "I'll let you talk to me about Jesus or anything you want if you'll come home with me."

"Tempting." She pasted on a smile. "But no thanks. Will there be anything else...*from the bar?*" she clarified.

"Naw. She's serious." One of them pointed at her with his glass. "She tried to shove that religious junk on me last time I was here. Told me I shouldn't drink so much." He snorted.

"Waste of good looks, if you ask me." Another one sneered at her. "You religious freaks are holding society back from progress."

Angelica gave a sarcastic smile. "I agree, that is if you consider sitting here getting wasted every Saturday night and taking strangers home to your bed 'progress'."

Before they could respond, she spun on her high heels and left. *Well, there goes another tip.*

And for what? Was she doing any good at all here? She seemed to bumble every opportunity God gave her to speak. And when she did, she was insulted, jeered at, and once even spit on.

Making her way to the bar, she sensed Sal Romero staring at her before she ever saw him. Too late to avoid the man, she smiled and approached the forty-something owner of the club, who looked out of place in the expensive business suit that hung impotently on his spindly frame.

He gave her an incriminating look. "I told you not to spread your Jesus crap here, Angelica."

"It's not crap, and I was merely suggesting a topic of conversation for my first date with the man."

He shook his head and motioned for Greg the bartender to pour him a shot of tequila. "I don't know why I keep you on."

"'Cause I'm your best waitress." She raised a brow. "The only one who shows up on time, doesn't call in sick when I'm not, and doesn't steal money from the till."

He snorted and gave her a half smile. "But you're scaring away the customers, and I can't have it. No matter how much I like you. I don't need the cops coming down on me."

Angelica handed Greg the order for table three. As he went off to prepare the drinks, Sal leaned toward her.

"I've told you a thousand times, you don't have to work so hard. I'd be more than happy to take care of you and your son." A waft of spicy tequila coupled with too much aftershave nearly made her choke.

She took a step back. "Yes, I know Sal, and I appreciate the offer, but I don't want to owe anyone." *Nor pay the price you would expect.* Sal was a decent boss who offered a fair wage and kept the rowdy customers off her. He was even understanding when she needed to take off work when Isaac was sick. But his constant salacious offers made her sick to her stomach.

Growling, he marched away. "I'll be in my office."

Greg gave her an understanding look as he placed drinks on her tray. "You should report him for sexual harassment."

"And lose my job? I can't do that. I have a son to support." She picked up the tray. "Did you ever read that book I gave you?"

He shook his head and started wiping down the bar. "Nope. Too busy working as many extra hours as I can to

save for college. You know I wanna get out of here
someday."

Angelica nodded. So did she—desperately. She hated
wearing this skimpy outfit and being constantly ogled and
propositioned. She hated serving alcohol to people who
abused it. But she'd been sending out resumes for years.
Since the economic crash, no one was hiring, and especially
not someone without education or skills. God must want her
here for a reason. Still, she wouldn't stop trying.

Nor would she stop hoping—and praying—for Greg to
find the hope he had lost in Jesus. The young bartender
wasn't particularly good-looking, so most women shunned
him, not exceptionally bright, so people dismissed him. But
he truly cared about others. He had nothing this world
valued, but he had a huge heart. "My invitation to come meet
my friends on Sunday is always open."

He began mixing another drink. "Not much for church,
either." He smiled.

"It's not so much a church as it is just people loving on
people."

Melody darted up, out of breath, and spouted off a list of
drinks to Greg. "Crazy crowd tonight." She glanced over her
shoulder at a group of college kids doing shots and getting
louder by the minute. Though there wasn't a dance floor, two
couples started dancing, if you could call it that. Bumping
and grinding was more like it.

"Hang in there, Mel. Just three hours to go." Angelica
patted the girl on the arm.

Her lips slanted. "Yeah, but then I work the breakfast
shift at the pancake house."

Greg set a drink on her tray. "I don't know how you do it
all with two kids at home."

Neither did Angelica. In fact, the normally gorgeous dark-
skinned lady looked more tired than her thirty-seven years
warranted. She received no child support for her two kids due

to one father missing and another in jail for abuse. But she was a hard worker, and a mama tiger who would do anything for her kids.

On that point, Angelica could relate. Lifting up a prayer for the lady, she headed back onto the floor, praying silently for each person she passed, for God to protect them from evil and to open their eyes to the truth.

She delivered the drinks without incident, took another order, and was passing by a table when a hand reached out for her, halting her in her path. Turning, she braced herself to fight off yet another immoral proposal. What she didn't expect was to see Daniel Cain, sitting there all handsome in his T-shirt and jeans, a glass of sparkling water in his hand.

"What are you doing here?"

"I need to talk to you." The appeal in his eyes would soften Genghis Kahn.

"You shouldn't be here. Go home." Turning, she walked away—anger, frustration, and fear all battling for dominance.

Following her, he turned her about. "Please, meet me for coffee after work."

Was he kidding? She stared at him. She had the perfect excuse—a child to get home to. But she couldn't seem to say the words. The music switched to some techno tune, shaking the floor beneath them. Drunken laughter bombarded her from all directions. The odor of alcohol, cheap perfume, and sweat filled her nose. And in the midst of it, she sensed light and goodness. Her angel appeared behind Daniel and another angel she'd not seen before—there one second and then they were gone.

"Okay. Denny's on Sunrise Blvd. 2:30."

Before giving him a chance to respond, she spun around and wove through the crowd, instantly regretting her easy acquiescence.

Daniel tapped his spoon on the table and glanced out the smudged windows of Denny's into the darkness. The smell of stale coffee and grease made him think twice about having ordered a salad, wondering what condition he'd find it in. But he'd skipped dinner. And Angelica was late. He glanced at his Rolex again—2:45—and then looked over the mob that had swamped the restaurant as soon as the bars closed. He felt sorry for the poor waitresses, scrambling around delivering food and enduring lurid invitations for probably no tips. These were the exact people he had originally wanted to reach for Christ—the drunks, the downtrodden, the poor, and hopeless. They had been the reason he'd entered seminary and why he'd started a church on the Fort Lauderdale strip. He smiled, remembering those carefree days with Thomas, Brian, Joe, and Mindy as they shared the gospel with anyone who would listen. Just a group of young dreamers who thought they could change the world. They *had* saved a few. But the money had run out, dreams faded, and they split up in search of greener pastures. Thomas—along with his head for business—had convinced Daniel to rent a nearby warehouse and lure the people from the beach to an actual church service every Sunday where they felt obligated to tithe.

"We can't keep doing this for free," he had said. "You have a gift, bro, and you shouldn't give it away. Neither of us went to seminary to end up homeless."

So, Fort Lauderdale Church of Grace was born. Daniel was the charisma and Thomas the business mind. And the two of them had become unstoppable.

His thoughts drifted to Angel and her friends witnessing to people on the beach that morning. Watching them had stirred a longing within him for the good ole days, the powerful sense of God's presence, the excitement at yanking a person from the grip of hell. But those days were gone. They lived in a different era now with a government hostile to Christians. Especially nutty ones.

Besides, Daniel could do more good from the pulpit of a huge church than anywhere else. And quite possibly from D.C. in the near future.

He smiled as the bell at the door jangled, and Angel entered and glanced around. Only then did he realize he'd expected her not to show. As she'd done twelve years ago when she broke his heart. Still dressed in her alluring waitress get-up, several men turned to stare. But upon spotting Daniel, she ignored them like a pro and headed his way. Man, she was an attractive woman, even after all these years, even after having a kid. That last thought sobered him.

Sliding onto the seat across from him, she set down her purse and let out a huge sigh as if this was the last place on earth she wanted to be. "So, I'm here."

Ignoring the pang in his heart, Daniel sipped his coffee. "Thank you for meeting me."

She pursed her lips and waited.

The waitress brought his salad and slapped it on the table before turning to Angel.

"Just coffee, please," she said before noticing his food and laughing. "I can't believe you're eating a salad. From Denny's!"

He had forgotten how beautiful her smile was and how the sound of her laughter soothed the tension from his neck and shoulders.

"Yeah, I keep to a pretty strict diet now. Can't eat cheeseburgers forever."

"I don't see why not." She shrugged playfully. "And, if I remember, you always added fries and a chocolate milk shake."

He smiled. "So you *do* remember me."

"How could I not?" She shot back as the waitress returned with her coffee.

He tried to regain her smile. "You're still as beautiful as I remember."

Tearing a packet, she dumped sugar into her cup. "Give me a break. I'm not twenty anymore. Your charm won't work on me."

"If I recall, it never did. You always saw through me."

She poured cream into her coffee and stirred it, and he noted no ring graced her finger.

"So, you have a son?"

"As you saw," she answered without looking up.

Why did the thought disturb him so? "You must have met his father shortly after we…" He hesitated, seeking the right words.

Her eyes met his, a flash of anger, followed by sorrow. She looked away. "I was a different person back then. I was heartbroken and needed comfort."

*Heartbroken?* He huffed. "How quickly you moved on…within weeks." While he was drowning in agony.

"What did you expect me to do?" Spite filled her tone, and he stared at her, confused.

He had expected her to return his calls, answer his emails and letters, show up at their favorite haunts. But none of that had happened. "Where is his father now?"

"I don't owe you any explanations, Daniel." She cupped her coffee and stared out the window.

He dove his fork into the salad. He was botching this. Although he had no idea what "this" was. "No, you don't," he finally said, unsure how to proceed. Which baffled him. Famous, charismatic Daniel Cain always had an answer, always knew what to say to charm people and persuade them to his way of thinking.

But suddenly in this woman's presence, he felt like a twenty-one-year-old boy on his first date.

He watched her as she fingered her dangly earrings, a gesture that brought back memories of that first date so long ago. He'd taken her to the *Oceans Grille* on the beach. Nothing fancy, but it was all he could afford. She had been delighted. He could still picture her sitting at a table on the patio, gazing at the ocean, her long sun-bleached hair blowing in the wind, her skin tanned and golden, her green eyes mesmerizing. But it was her smile, her laugh, her love of life and everything in it that had captured his heart. Time had drawn a few lines around her eyes and mouth, but she was still stunning. Life and love sparkled in her eyes. Yet there was sorrow there, too, and worry he'd not seen before.

"Honestly, it's just good to see you again," he said.

She sipped her coffee. "What do you want, Daniel?"

Her abrupt tone sliced. What *did* he want? He wanted to run his fingers through her hair. He wanted to apologize for whatever had come between them. He wanted to start over. "You always were so bluntly honest. I loved that about you."

Drunken laughter blared over them from a table across the way, drawing her gaze, those eyes of hers, so bright and intelligent, even masked by all the makeup. Yet, there was no judgment in them. Another couple in a table next to theirs stared at them curiously.

"I always felt safe with you, Angel, like I could tell you anything and you would never condemn me."

"It wasn't my place to condemn you, Daniel. I was just as lost."

Humility. Another of her qualities he had loved.

"Listen, Daniel. I'm tired. I want to go home. Either tell me what you want, or I'm leaving."

*If you were of the world, the world would love its own.
Yet because you are not of the world, but I chose you out of
the world, therefore the world hates you.*
  *John 15:19 (NKJV)*

# Chapter 4

Angelica cringed at the pain on Daniel's face, but it couldn't be helped. If he thought he was going to charm his way into her life again…if he thought she'd fall at his feet—like she was sure so many other women did—he had another thing coming.

Though she could see why any woman would do such a thing. With his thick chestnut hair and the stubble on his chin to match, those deep blue eyes, and an incredible physique…well, put a kilt on the man and he could pass for a hunky highlander. Add to that the way he lifted one side of his lips to form that sexy dimple she remembered all too well, his perfect teeth, and his success and fortune, she imagined he had left a string of broken hearts after hers.

"Sorry to keep you. I'll be brief." He shoved away the salad he'd barely touched, instantly stiffening. "I have a question and a warning. First the question. What did you mean by I'm not ready and my light has gone out?" He stared at her as a business man would awaiting a report.

"I don't know." Though she could guess—as he should be able to, as well. "God gave me those exact words. Why don't you ask Him? You're the pastor." She regretted her flippant tone yet again, but talking with Daniel, sitting so close to him, was stirring up things she'd long since buried.

And she couldn't allow that to happen. *Wouldn't* allow that to happen.

His forehead wrinkled. "Yeah, right. God speaks to you in specifics."

"He doesn't to you?"

He looked perplexed for a moment, then he leaned his arms on the table and grinned. "Perhaps it was your inner self simply wanting to see me again."

She pressed into the back of the booth, putting as much distance between them as she could. "I've known where you've been since you started your church, Daniel. Why would I all of a sudden want to see you?"

He shrugged. "We were friends once. *Good* friends."

She gazed out the window at the few passing cars. *No, we were so much more than friends. I was in love with you. Deeply and madly.* So much so, that it had taken her years to get over him. *Father, what do You want from me? I can't bear to reopen these wounds.*

The answer came swift, deep, and without words. *He must return to me. Soon.*

*Why me?* She wanted to ask, but didn't. God knew what He was doing, right? And it was always for the good. Taking a moment, she shifted her focus into the spirit realm and saw Daniel sitting in a fog so dark and thick, she could barely make out his features. Chains wrapped around his chest and arms, while a speck of light barely flickered from inside his soul. She shook off the vision, sorrow clamping her heart. She wanted to help him, she truly did, but nobody listened to her or did what she said, least of all an important man like Daniel Cain.

"Daniel, listen. God doesn't give me a message unless it means something and is important. I suggest you pray about it, seek Him, and remember your first love."

"Me? Remember my first love?" He snorted in disbelief. "Do you know how many people come forward a week in my church to accept Jesus?"

"That has nothing to do with it."

Shock followed by annoyance claimed his handsome features.

"You were so on fire for the Father back then," she said. "So ready to serve Him. Even though I didn't believe in God at the time, I loved your zeal." And now it was gone. Just a spark remained. But how could she tell him that?

Anger fumed in his eyes. "I serve God every day. My whole life is serving Him. How do you—a cocktail waitress—presume to tell *me*, a man who pastors twenty thousand souls each week, that I'm not on fire for God?"

Grabbing her purse, she slid across the seat. "You know. You're right. I should leave."

She heard his "wait" behind her as she stormed out the door into the humid night air, more angry than she'd been in a long while. But that was Daniel. He always caused her emotions, both good and bad, to vault off the scale. Groaning, she fished for her keys in her purse and made her way to her car. All she wanted to do was go home, take a hot bath, slide under the covers…

And forget Daniel Cain.

Glass shattered and she looked up to see three men surrounding her car. Her back window was scattered over the asphalt in glittering pebbles in the street light. One man was spray-painting something on her door.

Without thinking, she marched toward them. "Hey, that's my car!"

All three men faced her. Two wore hoodies that hid their faces, the other approached her. Tall, skinny, and dark, he looked her up and down contemptuously. "You the Jesus freak?" He gestured toward her bumper sticker with the sledgehammer in his hand.

Angelica swallowed, her first thought to run. Instead, she lifted her chin. She would not deny her faith. "Yes."

The other two men finished their paint job and stood back to admire their work. *Bigot Hater* was sprawled in white across the side of her black Toyota.

That would cost her a ton of money to fix. Along with the window. Money she didn't have.

"What makes me a bigot?" she asked, rage fueling her courage.

The man, who could be no older than twenty, sneered at her. "You think anyone who's different from you is going to hell, anyone who don't believe like you do."

"Hey, ain't you supposed to be dressed more proper?" One of the artists said as he and his friend approached. "Not showing so much skin?"

The third man licked his lips. "I say we show this bigot what's what. Ready to party, Jesus freak?"

Angelica's blood pounded through her veins. *Lord?* She tried to switch her vision to the spirit realm in order to spot her angel, but her mind spun in terror. Still, she managed to spit out, "There's a difference between bigotry and the *truth*, gentlemen. One will lead you to hell, the other to heaven."

The first man grabbed her shoulders and started to drag her off while another one took her purse. "We'll show you heaven, whore."

The fist came out of nowhere, striking the man's jaw who held her. He released her, and she stumbled back, tripping on her ridiculous high heels. Out of the corner of her eye, she saw Daniel kick the next guy and then charge the third one, barreling into him like a bulldozer. The first man spit to the side, wiped blood from his mouth, grabbed the sledgehammer, and swung it at Daniel.

Angelica tried to scream but nothing came out.

Daniel ducked, then gripped the man's wrist and forced the hammer from his grasp. It fell on his foot, and he shouted in pain.

"Come on, Nick. Let's get outa here!" one of the men yelled as he scrambled away. After one last seething glare at Daniel, the one called Nick limped into the darkness.

It had all happened so fast, Angelica could only stand there and stare as Daniel picked up her purse and handed it to her. "You all right?"

Taking it, she nodded.

He glanced at her car and ran a hand through his hair. "Why would they do that?" Then his eyes landed on her bumper sticker. *Jesus, the Way, the Truth, and the Life.* He swung to face her. "What were you thinking?"

"How can you ask me that?" She started toward her car, but her legs wobbled, and he wrapped his arm around her— an iron band of strength and warmth. The scent of that cheap aftershave he'd always worn filled her nose. What was it called? Aqua Velva. That was it.

Unwanted emotions played havoc with her insides, and she pushed away from him and leaned against her car. "I guess I was more frightened than I thought."

"Of course you were. If I hadn't come along…" He grimaced as if he really cared. "Do you know what would have happened?"

She did, but she didn't want to think about it. "Where did you learn to fight like that?"

"Jujitsu classes." He crossed arms over his chest. "Listen, I know you believe in God now and all. I think that's great. But you can't broadcast it like that." He nodded toward her bumper sticker. "Not on the beach and not on your car. You're just asking for trouble."

She didn't know whether to laugh or cry at such a thing coming from a pastor's mouth. Nor did she have the energy for either.

"Why were you even talking to them? You should have run back into Denny's." He gestured toward the restaurant where several people now stumbled out the door.

Her head grew light, and she reached up to rub her eyes. "They asked me about Jesus, and I wasn't going to deny Him. Besides, maybe I was supposed to tell them the gospel."

"Are you serious?" Sighing, he squeezed the bridge of his nose. "Those crazy people at the beach have infected your brain. I know it's hard to accept, but GIFP has forbidden open evangelism. I'm surprised the cops haven't dragged you and your friends to jail yet."

Angelica finally found her keys, clicked them, and her car beeped. "I'm too tired for this. Thank you for coming to my rescue."

Opening her car door, she turned to face him one last time. Though she couldn't make out his expression in the darkness, his frustration crackled in the air.

A loud noise echoed down the street. No, not a noise, the sound of a trumpet. Deep, bellowing, and long.

Daniel glanced over the parking lot.

The people who had left Denny's stared up at the sky.

Then as quickly as it had come, it stopped.

"I've heard that sound before," Angelica said. "Last year. People have been hearing strange sounds all over the world."

"Hmm." Daniel drew a big breath. "Probably just a factory starting up its machines or a ship horn."

Other sounds emanated from down the street, where most of the nightclubs were. Screams followed by the eerie *pop pop pop* of gunfire. All too-familiar sounds in Fort Lauderdale at night.

"I have to go." Sliding into her car seat, she pressed her foot on the brake and pushed the start button. The engine cranked slowly...slowly... until it finally sputtered out.

Angelica dropped her forehead on the steering wheel. *No, I cannot be stuck here with Daniel!*

Daniel sped around the front of her car. "Looks like your back window wasn't the only thing that sledgehammer struck."

Great. Dragging herself from the seat, Angelica stared in shock at what was left of her front grille and the puddle of fluid on the asphalt that used to be inside her radiator.

"Probably tangled up your belts, is my guess," Daniel said.

"Drat." Angelica swung her purse over her shoulder, locked her car, and started walking.

"Let me drive you home." His voice followed her.

The last thing she wanted was for him to know where she lived. "No. I'm fine."

"Don't be so stubborn, Angel." He appeared beside her. "No ill intentions. I'll just drop you home. It isn't safe for you out here and you know it."

He was right, of course. She probably wouldn't make it home in one piece. And if she didn't have Isaac, she wouldn't give a flip. But she did have Isaac, so she finally agreed.

After a brief and silent drive to her place, he insisted walking her to her door, and now stood beside her, waiting to ensure she got inside safely. One thing about Daniel, he'd always been a gentleman in a world where chivalry had become a lost art.

"Thank you again, Daniel. Good night."

"If you need a ride tomorrow, I'm available."

"No thank you. I'll manage." Turning, she fumbled with her keys.

"I have AAA and can get your car towed."

"I'll take care of it, thank you." She found the key and inserted it.

He chuckled. "I don't have the plague, you know."

*Yes, you do. A plague that had already destroyed her heart once.*

"Can I see you again?"

She stared at him for a moment, street light angling over his stiff jaw. The distant sound of gunfire competed with the soothing lap of waves in the background. And she knew deep in her spirit—against her own heart, against her own will—that God wanted her to see him again. That she was supposed to help Daniel somehow…someway.

"Why?" she asked.

"I don't know. I miss our friendship."

*Then maybe you shouldn't have broken my heart.*

Opening her door, she slipped inside and faced him as a glorious idea occurred to her. "Alright. On one condition."

He smiled.

"I pick the place and time."

His dimple reappeared. "Deal."

*They exchanged the truth about God for a lie, and
worshiped and served created things rather than the
Creator—who is forever praised. Amen.*
   Romans 1:25 (NIV)

# Chapter 5

"So you see how much God loves all of us!" Daniel
smiled wide for the camera, happy to see from the
teleprompter that he had only a paragraph left of his sermon.
"He wants us all to prosper, to be in good health, and to be
happy. Just reach out"—he raised his hand and grabbed the
air—"in faith, and take what God is offering. He is your
greatest advocate, your best friend, and He wants only the
best for His children."

Someone in the audience shouted, "Praise the Lord!"
which elicited a round of applause as Daniel picked up his
Bible and went to sit in his cushioned chair to the side. He
wished people wouldn't shout out in service like that. Or lift
their hands during worship. What did that look like to people
watching on TV? The last thing he wanted was people
thinking he was some religious fanatic. Thomas nodded from
his seat beside Daniel's as the band began playing and two
singers came forward.

Daniel proudly scanned the massive sanctuary where
every seat was filled. Last week, he'd been told that even the
overfill room had been stuffed to capacity. All here to listen
to *his* wisdom. Cameras sped about on rolling tripods,
panning across the crowd, while the one up front remained
on him.

A lady, who always sat in the same spot in the front row, stood and began clapping and singing along to the worship song. Then lifting her eyes to heaven, she raised her hands, her face aglow as tears streamed down her cheeks. Other people stood and did the same, and Daniel squirmed in his seat. He'd have to ask the ushers to seat this particular lady toward the back where the cameras wouldn't see her.

The song finished, and Marley Jones, the dark-skinned youth pastor, sprang to his feet from the other side of the stage and took the podium. He cast a smile at Daniel and gave him a thumbs-up before he read announcements and said the closing prayer. Was it just Daniel or was the prayer especially long today? He would have to speak to Marley about that. Wouldn't want to bore people. Finally, Marley said his "Amen" and sent the crowd off with a blessing.

Thank God. Daniel rubbed eyes that felt like lead as the cameras shut down and the people began filing out. After he'd dropped off Angelica, he'd only gotten three hours of sleep, and he hoped the camera hadn't picked up the shadows beneath his eyes. But seeing her had been worth every second. How could he have forgotten how special she was, how great it felt to spend time with her? He knew if she gave him half a chance, he could charm his way back into her life. With that thought lightening his step, he made his way to his office, longing to lie down on his couch for a couple hours of shut-eye.

He wasn't so lucky. Before he could close the door, Thomas and Marley appeared in the hallway.

"Can't it wait until tomorrow, gentlemen?" Daniel complained as Thomas pushed his way past him into the room. Marley waited at the door with a smile until Daniel bade him entrance.

Thomas slammed a newspaper on top of Daniel's desk.

"What's this?" Daniel moved to the other side and focused on the article in the religious section of the *Sun*

*Sentinel*. A large picture of him and Angelica sitting in the booth at Denny's took up half the page with the headline, "Famous Pastor Steps Out With Cocktail Waitress." Unfortunately, the picture revealed quite a bit of Angel's skimpy outfit as well as a look of longing on Daniel's face. He cringed.

"So, this is why you look like a zombie this morning!" Thomas raged. "Have you gone insane? What do you think you're doing?"

"Listen." Daniel sank into his chair and rubbed his eyes. "We were just having coffee. That's it. Nothing scandalous."

Marley started for the door. "I'll come back later."

"No, Marley—stay," Daniel said. "This won't take long." Besides, Daniel could use a friend right now, and Marley had a way of seeing things clearly.

"No, it won't take long if you come to your senses." Thomas shook his head. "Innocent or not, this sort of thing could ruin you. Not only as the pastor of this church, but for any chance at public office."

Marley sank into a chair.

"She's an old friend, as you well know. We were just catching up."

"You can't play catch-up with the likes of her. Don't you get it? Not in your position!"

Daniel stared at his friend, dark eyes flashing, a strand of his perfectly styled hair falling over his forehead. And he knew Thomas was right. Hanging out with the wrong type of people, whether it was innocent or not, would definitely roadblock the career path he'd been planning for so long.

Thomas must have sensed his compliance, for he took a deep breath that softened the lines on his face. "Do you know you've been invited to participate in the World Religions Conference in Brussels in two months? I was trying to get in touch with you last night to tell you. It's a huge honor."

"Aren't they trying to blend all the religions into one?" Marley spoke up.

"Yes." Thomas cast a glance his way. "And why not have our own Daniel Cain there to represent the protestant branch." He leaned his knuckles on the desk. "It's such an incredible opportunity and a huge honor. But something like this"—he jabbed his finger at the article—"could ruin everything."

Daniel squeezed the bridge of his nose. "You're right." He glanced at the picture. "I was only curious about the meaning behind her message."

"Who cares what a loser cocktail waitress has to say?"

Normally Daniel would agree, but why then did he suddenly have the urge to punch his friend for saying so?

A knock on the door brought their gazes up to see Harold Jakes and Mrs. Brinkenburg, both looking as though they'd eaten a jar of pickles.

Great. Daniel huffed. Could his day get any worse?

Mrs. Brinkenburg stormed in, Harold at her heels like a lusty lap dog. A spinster at fifty-eight, she'd finally caught the eye of a man—the perfect man for her. How much fun they must have on their dates complaining about the church.

Thomas made an effort to turn the paper over when Mrs. Brinkenburg said, "Oh, I've seen it, Pastor Thomas. That's why we've come. Plus, there's another matter regarding today's service." She glanced at her cohort Harold, who gave her a sheep-like grin.

"I can assure you, the situation is resolved." Thomas approached the two busybodies and wrapped an arm around each of their shoulders. "It was just a misunderstanding and a doctored-up photo. It won't happen again."

"I should hope not." Harold jutted out his chin.

Thomas turned them both around and herded them to the door. "Let's not disturb Pastor Daniel any more. Come to my office and I'll be glad to hear your concerns." He winked over his shoulder toward Daniel.

Thank God for Thomas. Daniel sat back in his chair, nearly forgetting Marley was still there until the man cleared his throat and stood.

"I should leave you to rest."

"No, Marley. Forgive me. What can I do for you?"

The black man approached, his face a vision of calm and kindness. He'd been a gang member in Miami who'd had a vision of Jesus one night as he was heading to kill a rival gang member. Or so he said. Whatever it was, it changed his life, and he began preaching to young people on the Miami strip. Which is where Daniel had found him ten years ago. Marley was the real deal. And he had a way with young people.

He halted before Daniel's desk and pointed at the newspaper. "For one thing, I don't see what the problem is with you hanging around with sinners. Isn't that what Jesus did?" He glanced over his shoulder at the door. "And didn't the Pharisees come down on Him about that too?"

Daniel smiled. "He means well, Marley. Thomas just wants the best for me."

Marley flattened his lips as if he were trying to keep from saying something.

"Sit," Daniel said. "What's on your mind?"

"I won't keep you, Daniel. I wanted your take on something. Some of the kids are asking about polygamy. They are saying since it's okay for two men to get married, why not three men or two women and a man." Marley rubbed the back of his neck. "Honestly, after they reformed our Bibles, I don't know what to say to them, or where to point them to find the truth."

Daniel laid a hand on his Bible, the NWLV—New World Love Version. "This is our truth now. At least if we want to bring as many people to Christ as possible." Rising, he made his way to his coffee bar and poured himself a cup, then glanced at Marley to offer him some, but he shook his head. Cupping the warm mug between his hands, Daniel turned to face his friend. "Besides, there was lots of polygamy in the Bible. And if the Supreme Court has ruled that marriage can be between any willing parties, then who are we to go against the rule of the land? The Bible also says we should obey our civil laws."

"It just doesn't seem right. I know God frowns on these perversions. I feel like we are leading them astray."

Stiffening, Daniel glanced at the open door. "For one thing, don't ever call them perversions, not where anyone can hear you." Daniel approached his friend. "You have to keep the big picture in mind, Marley. Saving souls. If we started condemning these things, they will shut us down. And what good could we do then?"

Marley stared at the ground, saying nothing.

"Come on, Marls." Daniel leaned back on his desktop. "Have I ever led you astray? We've done great things here."

"You mean God has." Marley looked up at him.

"Yes, yes. Of course. And if God has blessed us, we must be doing His will."

"I'm gonna pray about this," Marley said, rising.

Daniel slapped him on the back. "Good. I'm sure God will help you see things clearly."

After saying their goodbyes, Daniel closed and locked his door, then lay down on his couch. After a few moments of fidgeting restlessness, he flipped on his flat-screen mounted high on the wall. Tanks and military men with rocket launchers filled the screen as a woman's voice spoke in a British accent.

"War makes strange bedfellows. In an unpredicted turn of events Turkey, Russia, and Iran have formed an alliance with Libya and the Sudan in an effort to squash ISIS and form their long-awaited Muslim Caliphate. Recent bombings have killed more than one million civilians and demolished much of the city of Damascus." The camera panned over miles and miles of ruins, then shifted back to tanks positioning along the border of Iraq. "Recently, over a hundred Christians were crucified by ISIS, their corpses left rotting on crosses in the desert. The Middle East is on the brink of World War III."

Daniel flipped it off and closed his eyes. Who cared what happened thousands of miles away. Not his problem.

Nazare lowered his head, a sudden despondency coming over him. What would it take to wake up Daniel from the deception that kept him enslaved? Day after day, Nazare reported back to the Father on Daniel's status, and each day the news grew worse. Now, having just witnessed him *yet again* rejecting the truth for a lie—in both cases with Marley and Thomas—Nazare dreaded his next report. Not to mention Daniel's disinterest in the signs of the times and his cavalier attitude toward his brothers and sisters being slaughtered. In truth, things didn't look good for this man who had once been one of the Father's most promising evangelists.

If only Nazare could do something—appear in Daniel's dimension and warn him, instruct him, show him the right path. But he couldn't. The Father's strict orders were to watch, protect, and never interfere. And that's just what he had been doing since he'd been assigned to Daniel at his birth. Not an easy assignment by any means. Daniel's childhood had been a difficult one—filled with fighting, divorce, and an unloving, disapproving father. The enemy had been strong back then, invading and controlling Daniel's father, forcing him to destroy not only his marriage but his only son's confidence and hope. Yet, Daniel had made the right choice. He had clung to his mother and the light within her. And instead of allowing the enemy to crush him, he'd risen out of the ashes to love the Father with all his heart.

Nazare had rejoiced over this victory, along with all of heaven and its many witnesses. And through the years, he had done his part keeping the darkness away. Until bit by bit, compromise after compromise, deception after deception, Daniel had invited the evil in himself. Even now, the demons holding him captive taunted Nazare with malicious grins from where they'd infiltrated Daniel like enemy spies, slithering and snaking around his soul, encompassing him in darkness.

And he couldn't do a thing about it, save watch…and cry.

He'd begged the Father to reassign him to another. This post was far too painful. And lonely, Nazare might add, for most of the people Daniel dealt with had no angels with them at all. Except for Marley's angel, Campana, who had come in earlier with Marley. The two of them had spoken briefly as they watched the proceedings, and Campana was quick to point out what Nazare had already noticed—Marley's light was growing brighter.

"This is good news, indeed!" Nazare had said.

"I agree. Marley is beginning to see the truth, to think for himself, to spend time with the Father. It is good."

"You are fortunate to be able to watch such wonderful progress."

"Yes, and we all hope Daniel will soon follow."

Nazare drew a deep breath as he now watched Daniel sleep, the light within him barely flickering. Indeed, he must soon turn back to the Father, for time was growing short.

*And he said, "Go your way, Daniel, for the words are
closed up and sealed till the time of the end. Many shall be
purified, made white, and refined, but the wicked shall do
wickedly; and none of the wicked shall understand, but the
wise shall understand.*
*Daniel 12:9-10 (NKJV)*

# Chapter 6

Angelica pulled up in front of Franklin Elementary
School and parked, keeping the car running and the
AC on. It had taken a week and three grand, but she finally
had her car back in one piece—the window, radiator, belts,
and front grille replaced, plus a new paint job. The three
grand went on her credit card, that evil monster she kept
trying to defeat—the one who, just when she thought she'd
delivered the final death blow, rose up again with a mighty
growl. Oh well, she thanked God she at least had credit she
could use during an emergency. And a roommate willing to
share her car while Angelica's had been in the shop.

All because of a Jesus sticker.

Which was still happily displayed on her bumper. She
didn't know if it did any good, but she prayed every day that
when people saw it—even just the name of Jesus—that it
would pique their curiosity and draw them to investigate why
He was the truth, the life, and the way. After all, there was
great power in that name. Something she had experienced
firsthand.

So what if she'd been persecuted? It wasn't the first time and wouldn't be the last. Jesus had warned His followers that the world would hate them, and she hadn't suffered anything yet compared to her brothers and sisters across the globe.

Glancing behind her, she smiled at Joel buckled up in the back seat, fast asleep. That kid never failed to pass out in the car. If only Angelica could do the same in her own bed, but her visions had returned. Not the same one about Daniel, but others full of violence, war, riots, and hatred—pure evil growing darker and darker covering the earth like a massive fog bank. Yet sprinkled among the darkness, beams of light shot up to heaven. Some dwindled, flickered, and were swallowed up by the encroaching darkness, but others grew brighter and brighter, shoving the evil back. She knew the lights were God's people protected by His holy angels, some not committed enough to withstand the battle, others growing stronger each day. What she didn't know was what to do with these visions. She'd spent the morning walking along the beach, seeking an answer to that very question, while also praying for Isaac's safety and salvation as she did each day.

The school bell rang and within seconds, kids dashed out of the buildings like a prison break. She couldn't blame them. Under the new GIFP Education rules, kids only got the month of June off. Then it was back to school in July when, in her opinion, children should be swimming, riding their bikes through puddles, playing baseball...and just being kids. Angelica exited the car and stood by the door, squinting for a view of Isaac. There he was, talking with another boy. He saw her and ran toward the car, school papers in hand.

She embraced him like he was the most precious gift in the world—which he was, an unexpected gift that had come at a huge cost. But one she would gladly pay a thousand times over.

"How was your day?" She scruffed his hair and ushered him into the car, thankful that he still allowed her such public displays of affection.

"Okay," came the usual reply as Angelica slid into the driver's seat.

"Isaac!" A shout of exuberance reverberated from the back.

"Hi Joel." Isaac gave his friend a huge grin. "Hey, Mom, my friend Chris wants me to come over after school tomorrow. He's got the new micropulse laser Soldier of Mars game and a huge backyard that looks like a jungle. Can I go?"

Angelica's heart shriveled at the excitement in her son's voice. "No, I'm sorry, honey. I don't know anything about Chris' parents or how safe his home is."

"But you talked to his mom once," he whined.

Angelica sighed and turned to face him. "Yes, but she couldn't assure me of your safety." In fact, she had been annoyed at Angelica's questions about keeping an eye on the kids, not having pornography visible, and not using bad language. Simple requests, weren't they? Angelica would have thought another mother would have understood these things. But once it became obvious that Chris' parents had very few restrictions, Angelica could in no way allow Isaac to go to their house.

"Aw, Mom. I never get to go anywhere." Isaac kicked the back of the passenger seat, a scowl dragging down his normally cheerful face.

She turned back around and shifted the car into gear, angry at herself...angry at the world.

"Wanna play *Commando* when we get home?" Isaac asked Joel.

"Yay!" the little boy squealed.

"After your homework." Angelica pulled into traffic.

"Aw, Mom. I don't have much."

"Then it won't take long to finish." She smiled at him through the rearview mirror. "What did you learn today?"

He was still frowning. "Lots of things. 'Bout something called communism."

Angelica cringed. "Really? What about it?"

"That it's a type of government where everybody gets to have a house and nobody goes hungry or doesn't have food."

Lovely. Angelica tried to shove down the fear rising within her. "Did they also tell you that because the government takes care of you, you have no freedom to speak out against them or live your life as you choose?" *Or that Communism has claimed the lives of millions of people?* But she wouldn't frighten him with that fact.

Isaac shook his head and stared at her with innocent eyes.

"We'll discuss it later."

"They also said that the Global Initiative for Peace is trying to unite the world and bring peace to all the people."

The GIFP. Of course they were uniting the world—under their greedy, power-hungry leadership, in the guise of peace, prosperity, and fairness for all. In truth, their goal was to rule over the ignorant masses, to be philosopher-kings who decided where people lived, what work they were suited for, and even who was worthy of life or death. The worst part about their ideology was that they were anti-Christian. Not anti-religion, just against Christianity, because it upheld beliefs of individual freedom, the value of human life, and that people should worship and depend on God, not the State.

She pulled into her apartment driveway and parked in her spot. "Isaac. You mustn't listen to your teachers. Not about everything. From now on, you will tell me each day what you learned at school, and I want to see all your homework assignments, too."

He nodded and smiled. For now, he was compliant. For now, she could counter the false propaganda with the truth.

But what about when he became a teenager and his peers and girls became more important than his mother?

*You will have to trust Me,* the voice whispered deep within her, and she nodded, tears burning her eyes.

"Mommy, why are you crying?" Isaac asked.

"Unbuckle me," little Joel said from the back seat.

"I'm fine." Grabbing her purse, she gathered the boys and headed upstairs.

Two hours later, she started dinner for Leigh and the boys, the least she could do for her friend who spent the day on her feet. However, due to rationing, all she had was pasta, tuna fish, and a little bit of cheese, so she decided to make a tuna casserole. It may not be gourmet food, but it would fill the little ravenous bellies who hovered around the TV screen playing video games.

The lock clicked, the door opened, and in walked Leigh, looking like she'd run a marathon.

And lost.

"Rough day?"

"You have no idea." Locking the door, she dropped her purse and keys on the table and spread her arms wide for Joel who was making a mad dash toward her.

"Mommy!"

Picking him up, she twirled him around and showered him with kisses. "I love you so much it hurts." She set him down, and he ran back to join Isaac.

"Hmm. What smells good?" She sniffed the air.

"Soufflé de poisson," Angelica replied with pomp. And when Leigh stared at her, confused and slightly horrified, she added, "Tuna casserole. Poisson means 'fish'."

Laughing, Leigh headed toward the bedroom to change. "I'm sure it will be delicious! Thank you so much, Ange."

Angelica checked the casserole and turned down the oven temperature, then began setting the placemats and silverware on the table. The doorbell rang. A peek out the tiny hole revealed a delivery man with flowers in his hand. "Yes?" she said through the door.

"Delivery for Miss Smoke."

Odd. She hesitated for a moment but finally worked through two locks and the door chain and opened it to a huge bouquet of pink roses and gardenias—her two favorite flowers.

Too shocked to respond, she grabbed them, signed the man's paper, thanked him, and closed and locked the door again.

"Whoa. Flowers!" Leigh entered the room in sweats and a T-shirt. "Expensive ones. Who are they for?"

"Me, I guess." Angelica set them down on the table and snagged the card.

"Oh, do tell? A secret admirer?" Leigh peered over her shoulder.

"No." She said absently as she read the card.

*Looking forward to seeing you again....you name the time and place.*

*Daniel Cain*

"Daniel Cain, the world-famous pastor?" Leigh giggled. "I had no idea you knew the man."

"I don't. I mean I used to. Long ago." Angelica tossed the card onto the table, a frown tensing her forehead.

"What's the problem, Ange?" Leigh bent down to smell the flowers. "I wish some rich, famous guy would send me flowers."

"He's not just some rich famous guy. He's—" She bit her lip. "Never mind." Sighing, she left to get dressed for work, all the while begging God, as she'd been doing all week, to remove Daniel from her life—and more importantly—from her heart.

Of course, even though it was a weekday night, the Mermaid Den was packed. Probably due to Sal's two-for-one drink special. Which only made Angelica's job all the more difficult, carrying more glasses on her tray, making more trips around the bar, and enduring more complaints about the watered-down drinks. Still, amid all the slurred propositions, drunken shenanigans, loud music, and general misery and darkness, Angelica did her best to cling to God's peace within her. On occasion, when her feet ached, her spirit waned, and the night seemed to stretch into eternity, she spotted her angel standing guard at the far end of the room. He said nothing, merely stood still with eyes straight ahead and hand resting on the hilt of his sword. Nearly as tall as the ceiling and as wide as two men, he wore a white tunic that hung to his knees. Thick belts, embedded with jewels, sat upon his hips and strapped across his chest, embedded with jewels and housing all manner of weapons—swords, knives, axes, and other items she'd never seen before. Metallic boots covered his feet to his knees, and a helmet made of the same material sat upon his head. From beneath it, hair as light as the sun hung to his shoulders around a strong, angular face. His entire being shone from a light source all its own.

Five years ago, when she'd first seen him, she'd fallen facedown to the floor, trembling uncontrollably. But now, whenever she was privileged to have a glimpse of him, she took great comfort knowing God had sent him to protect her.

Even so, she didn't seem to be making any headway tonight in sharing God's love. Mentions of the futility of alcohol and the love and mercy of God had only gotten her insults and no tips. Finally, grabbing a soda from the bar, she headed to the break room to sit down for her allotted thirty minutes. Removing her high heels, she rubbed her feet and drew in a breath of stale air that smelled of greasy food and alcohol. The music, barely muted, thumped the walls like some angry giant trying to bust in to disturb her few moments of peace. Sitting back in her chair, she sipped her soda and began to silently pray. Sensing her angel in the room, she thanked God for His protection and then proceeded to ask for wisdom and discernment to reach the lost.

But her thoughts drifted to Daniel and the gorgeous bouquet he'd sent. After all these years, he remembered her favorite flowers. The thought warmed her, though she tried desperately not to allow it. What did he want from her, anyway? *Father, I don't understand. He won't listen to me. He thinks he has Christianity by the tail.*

*Go see him.*

"But Father, I don't want him near my son. Isaac has enough deception to deal with at school. Daniel will only influence him negatively, and he's such a tender age." Fear began to buzz around her. She could sense the demon grinding its teeth and drooling, waiting for an opening in her armor, waiting to take a bite out of her heart. The enemy knew her weakness all too well.

*Trust Me.*

"I'm trying, Father." She bowed her head. "I'm placing Isaac in Your hands as I do every minute of every day."

*I've got him.*

She nodded. And Fear abandoned her. But he would return. He always did.

*Go see Daniel. As you promised.*

Angelica didn't have time to respond before the door opened and in walked Greg. He smiled when he saw her, took a seat, and opened a bag from In-N-Out Burger. "Aren't you eating?"

"Not hungry."

The smell of sizzling meat and grilled onions captured her nose and made a liar out of her as she watched him unwrap the burger and take a bite.

"Crazy out there tonight," he commented.

"Yeah." Angelica rubbed her feet again, seeking the Father's wisdom on what to say to this man to help him see the light. She'd already told him the gospel, gave him a Bible, another book on God's love, and invited him to her church.

*Lord, give me something.* She sought the Spirit within as Greg continued eating. A vision flashed through her mind of a little boy, a Golden Retriever, and a woman at a park. The woman and the boy were tossing a Frisbee back and forth, trying to keep it from the retriever, who leapt up and caught it from time to time, making them both laugh.

Greg offered her a French fry. She took two and shoved them in her mouth. "When you were a boy, you had a Golden Retriever," she began cautiously.

His forehead wrinkled as he stared at her. "How did you know that?"

"And you and your mom and your dog would play Frisbee at the park."

He set down his half-eaten burger. "I hate it when you do this. You're freaking me out, Angelica."

"Your dog's name was Puddle."

He closed his eyes for a moment before shaking his head. "How do you know that?" His tone was angry.

"God told me." Angelica swallowed a lump of emotion. "He loves you, Greg. As did your mother. I'm sorry she died so young."

By the mixture of horror and agony on his face, Angelica thought she'd overstepped her bounds, and he would bolt out the door. But instead, he sank back in his chair and released a heavy sigh. "Maybe my mom loved me, but I don't know about this God of yours."

She wanted to tell him more about God, but all she was hearing now was *love him.*

So, she did. She spent the remainder of her break asking about his life, his childhood, his friends, and his dreams.

Some of it made her laugh, some made her cry, but through all of it, Greg seemed to grow a bit cheerier just having someone listen to him. And care.

Back out on the floor, Angelica's own spirits were lifted as she prayed for Greg and then continued praying for each patron she passed.

Until from a small table in the shadows, she caught a familiar face grinning her way.

She halted before him, empty tray in hand. "Why, Thomas Benton. This is the last place I'd expect to see you."

"Been a long time, Smokes," he returned with that fake smile of his. He ran a finger around the rim of his glass. "Couldn't believe my eyes when you wandered up to Daniel's church. Not after you gave me your word."

"I gave you my word to let him get through seminary and start his church. That was all."

"Hmm. So now that he's rich and famous, you hope to worm your way back into his life, is that it?"

"You know me better than that." She eyed him.

"You may not have taken my money back then, but look at you now. You're still just a cocktail waitress." His nose wrinkled as if she disgusted him.

"Is there something you want? We're having a two-for-one drink special tonight." She smiled sweetly.

"Yes, there is something I want." He leaned forward, arms on the table. "I want you to stop seeing Daniel."

"Believe me, I've been trying."

He gave a snort of disbelief. "All you have to do is say no. Although"—he scanned her with a salacious grin—"I suppose that's something you were never good at."

"Listen Thomas, I have no intention of reacquainting myself with Daniel. Now, if that is all, I have customers."

He grabbed her wrist. *Tight.* She tugged from him. "Stop seeing him or else." Releasing her with a snap, he tossed a twenty note onto the table and stormed out the door.

*But the manifestation of the Spirit is given to each one for the profit of all: for to one is given the word of wisdom through the Spirit, to another the word of knowledge through the same Spirit, to another faith by the same Spirit, to another gifts of healings by the same Spirit, to another the working of miracles, to another prophecy, to another discerning of spirits, to another different kinds of tongues, to another the interpretation of tongues.*
*1 Corinthians 12: 7-10 (NKJV)*

# Chapter 7

Daniel was elated when Angel called him and invited him to a gathering at a friend's house. That she was introducing him to her friends was a good sign, wasn't it? A sign that she intended to keep him around awhile. Whatever her reasons, he was thrilled he was going to see her again. He had not stopped thinking about her during the past two weeks. And despite Thomas' warning, he couldn't turn her down.

When he reached the house, he was forced to park several doors down. After climbing out of his Porsche, he clicked the key lock and glanced around, hoping it would be safe in this neighborhood. Music and singing blared from the address Angel had given him. A party? Now, that was more like the Angel he remembered.

After several rings of the doorbell, a plump, middle-aged woman with curly short hair and a kind face opened the door and smiled. "You must be Daniel."

Before he could respond, she took his arm and dragged him inside to what could only be described as pure chaos.

Several adults stood talking in the modest living area, while at least a dozen kids, from toddlers to teenagers, ran about the house shouting and chasing each other. One man sat on a stool, playing a guitar and singing as several others surrounded him and joined in, some raising their hands to heaven, while others danced, all seemingly oblivious to the clatter all around them. Wait. He knew that guitarist. From the beach that day. Not a good omen for the sanity of the rest of the crowd. He smelled a trap. Along with a spicy, rich scent coming from the back of the house that made his mouth water.

"I'm looking for Angelica Smoke," he shouted over the mayhem to the woman.

"Yes, yes, I know. I'm Misty." She shook his hand. "That's my husband Scottie over there talking with ...oh well, you'll meet everyone soon enough. Angelica!" she shouted before turning to him again. "Make yourself comfortable. We'll get started soon." And off she went before Daniel could ask exactly *what* would get started soon.

He took the opportunity to look around. Modestly furnished with low ceilings, small rooms, and wall-to-wall stained carpet, the house was barely larger than his office at church, yet it was packed with people. None of whom seemed to notice him...many of whom looked to be gang members or druggies. Uncomfortable, he shifted his feet and regretted his agreement to join Angel here.

He was about to turn and leave when someone squeezed through the jostling crowds and headed toward him. Angel, dressed in jeans and a black T-shirt, her sun-bleached hair bobbing around her face, her eyes devoid of makeup and shining as green as jade in the sunlight. She was mesmerizing.

"You came," she said. "I didn't think you would."

Instantly, relief and joy swept away all his discomfort. "Why wouldn't I?"

She shrugged. "Maybe you'd figure out what this was about."

A throng of children darted into the room, laughing and toppling over each other in an effort to tag the leader. A young toddler holding a lollipop lost his footing and barreled toward Daniel, running smack into his legs and plastering his candy onto Daniel's thousand-dollar pants.

Instead of gasping in horror, Angel giggled and knelt, pried off the lollipop, and handed it to the young boy. "Here you go, Seth. No harm done."

*No harm done?* Daniel's pants had a circle of spitty red syrup on them that would cost a fortune at the dry cleaners to remove. The little boy, who could be no older than three, stared up at Daniel and smiled. "Sorry, mister."

How could he resist that? "It's okay. Just be more careful."

Nodding, the toddler darted off and disappeared.

"So, what's going on here?" He raised an incriminating brow.

Angel cocked her head and grinned. "This is my church."

Church? Daniel swallowed and glanced over the room again, noticing that people were settling into seats, some on couches, others on the chairs that had been brought in from another room, and others on the floor.

"You go to a home church?"

"Yes. You've already met some of my friends. Let me introduce you to the rest." She started to lead him away, but he grabbed her arm.

"You told them I was coming?"

"Of course."

Then why were they totally ignoring him? How often did average Christians get to spend time with such an important religious leader? You'd think they'd be clamoring to meet him, anxious to ask him about theology or how best to run a church. He had, after all, started out much like this, with only a handful of people. And look what he'd accomplished.

"Looks like everyone is getting seated," Angel said. "I'll introduce you later. But you remember Anna from the beach." She pointed to a woman lowering to sit on the floor with two teenage girls by her side. "And that's Robert, her husband, over in the dining room."

Covered with tattoos and leather, the man looked like he should be in a biker bar, not a church. Not far from him stood two teens who looked equally threatening. *Who were these people?*

"You remember Clay, our musician, playing the guitar."

Yes, the skinny man with the long brown hair.

"And there's little Seth's mom, Elisa." She pointed to a thin lady with long brown hair in her twenties. "She's a single mom. Oh, and here comes Scottie. He's the group leader and Misty's husband. This is their home."

Daniel would never remember all these names, nor did he want to. What was the point of having church when you didn't have a real pastor who knew the Bible and had been trained to give sermons…when you didn't have a band or singers to inspire and lead worship? How could God be pleased with a group of disorganized, loud people who let their children run about without supervision?

He wasn't even sure he should be here at all. In fact, he knew he shouldn't. He pulled Angel aside. "Why did you invite me here?"

But she merely smiled and shushed him as she led him toward a couple of empty chairs. Her son—what was his name?—hurried up to her, smiled at Daniel, and sat on the other side of his mom. Daniel scanned the motley group, a mismatch of ethnicities, ages, and status. Several glanced his way in what he assumed was anticipation.

Ah, yes. Now, he knew why Angel had invited him. He leaned toward her. "Listen, if you want me to give a sermon, I have nothing prepared."

She didn't answer him. Instead, the man called Scottie took a seat in a big comfy chair and gestured to Daniel. "Everyone, please welcome our special guest, Daniel Cain, a friend of Angelica's."

Everyone turned to smile his way, tossing out, "Welcome…Glad you're here…God bless you."

Daniel returned all their greetings, preparing in his mind what to say when this Scottie person asked him to speak.

Instead, Scottie opened his Bible and began reading. Daniel knew the Word of God better than anyone, but these words didn't sound familiar at all. He glanced down at Angel's Bible, opened to Luke 21.

"And there will be signs in the sun, in the moon, and in the stars; and on the earth distress of nations, with perplexity, the sea and the waves roaring; men's hearts failing them from fear and the expectation of those things which are coming on the earth, for the powers of the heavens will be shaken. Then they will see the Son of Man coming in a cloud with power and great glory. Now when these things begin to happen, look up and lift up your heads, because your redemption draws near."

His pulse ratcheted. Heat swamped him. Wait. This wasn't the NWLV. This was the original, uncut Bible. These verses had been deleted in the new version. He whispered in Angel's ear. "This is the illegal version."

She nodded and smiled as if he'd said it was a nice sunny day.

Was she crazy? He glanced around the room at the people following along in their Bibles as if the words were made of gold. Using this version made this gathering illegal. They could all be arrested for this. *He* could be arrested. How dare Angel bring him here. Risk his life and career! He glanced at her as she followed along in her Bible, lips silently moving, thick lashes splayed across her cheeks like a silk fan. He should get up and leave. But if he did, Angel would probably never speak to him again. She definitely wouldn't want to see him anymore. He couldn't risk that.

So he listened.

"But take heed to yourselves, lest your hearts be weighed down with carousing, drunkenness, and cares of this life, and that Day come on you unexpectedly. For it will come as a snare on all those who dwell on the face of the whole earth. Watch therefore, and pray always that you may be counted worthy to escape all these things that will come to pass, and to stand before the Son of Man."

Daniel had not heard those words in a long, long time. Not since his mother had been alive, and not since seminary. He and his classmates had been so excited about the Lord's second coming. They had studied it, pondered it, preached about it, and kept watch over world events, especially what was happening in Israel. But then one of his professors had chastised them, saying they weren't to focus on such things, that Jesus would come back when He was good and ready— it wasn't their business to wonder about it or watch for it. So, they had stopped. And if Daniel were honest, many of them had gone on to lose that innocent zeal for the Lord.

Scottie glanced lovingly over the group of people. "Brothers and sisters, hear the words of our Lord and don't be concerned with the things of this world and all that it offers. Don't even be concerned with the evil around you. Time is short."

Someone shouted, "Hallelujah," which elicited a chorus of "Amens."

"For those who are caught up in this world, His return will come like a thief in the night, but for us who have made ourselves ready, we will know the season of His return as the

Apostle Paul tells us in 2 Thessalonians. And I can tell you all. It is soon." He smiled.

Nonsense. Daniel shook his head.

Everyone began shouting and praising God.

"But heed the warning." Scottie's words brought the clamor to a hush. "We must watch and pray and ready ourselves so that we may be worthy to escape the tribulation coming on the world. Not all who call themselves Christians will escape." He scanned the room. "Otherwise why would both our Lord and the Apostle Paul say we should pray to be counted worthy?"

*Blasphemy!* Daniel shifted in his seat and repressed a groan. If not for Angel, he would have already left. But at least now he knew what he was dealing with and could warn her.

Who was this egotistical man who spoke with assumed authority about the Scripture? Daniel doubted he had any education at all. He stared at him as he droned on for the next hour. Not uninterrupted, mind you. No, people took the liberty to ask questions, comment on what he was saying, even argue with him while he was giving his talk. Others brought up different passages to complement his. Adding to the clamor were constant shouts of "Hallelujah! Amen! Praise the Lord!" which made Daniel wonder how anyone could think clearly. And all the while in the background, some of the kids were still running around creating havoc, pots and pans were clanging from the kitchen, and a group huddled in the back corner praying out loud. What kind of church service was this? He'd never seen such unorthodox disorder and confusion.

After the message, Clay strummed on his guitar and people began singing. Angel joined in clapping her hands and singing so loudly, Daniel smiled at her off-key voice. He'd forgotten that about her. The girl could *not* sing. A lady got up and lifted her hands to the ceiling, another joined her and started dancing and clapping. More did the same, and before too long, half the people were acting like a bunch of clowns cheering for their favorite sports team. Daniel shook his head, feeling embarrassed for them. *And* for himself. What an uncomfortable place to bring people who want to learn about God. He turned to give his enlightened opinion to Angel, but she had her eyes closed and her face turned to heaven, and there was such a glow upon her, it stunned him. Beside her, her son was doing the same.

He glanced at his watch, then crossed arms over his chest and continued observing the hysterical display. Someone started shouting in gibberish. On and on she went, speaking what sounded like baby-talk for several minutes before she finally quieted. Then after a few moments, someone else spoke in English, saying he just received a message from God.

Daniel squeezed the bridge of his nose. *Yeah, right.*

"The Father says He is sending the Bridegroom soon."

People shouted praises.

"Get ready, my precious children. Make yourself holy as I am holy. Fear not, for I am always with you. My angels watch over you. Be strong and courageous. You have just a little more time left. But there is still work to do. Go out and love others. Tell them of me. Warn them that time is short, that I am coming soon and my reward is with Me. Tell them that I will not receive those who are not ready. Let your light grow ever brighter and brighter. Keep your oil lamps lit by walking in the Spirit. Love others as I have loved you."

You would have thought that God himself had spoken from heaven in an audible voice the way these people reacted—jumping, clapping, shouting, singing, and praising. It went on for what seemed like an eternity. Daniel just sat there, feeling awkward and uncomfortable, wishing—no, praying—that Angel would snap out of whatever trance she was in and leave with him.

Finally, the people settled down, and after several moments of weeping and laughing, Scottie grabbed a bottle of what looked like oil and called three men to come stand with him. He then asked for those who needed healing to come forward. One by one, a few of the crowd rose and stood before the men, then Scottie spread oil on their foreheads while the three men prayed.

*Come on, really?*

Angel leaned toward him. "You see that lady there." She gestured to an elderly lady with a scarf wrapped around her head. "Two weeks ago, God healed her of cancer."

Daniel repressed a groan as his anger rose at Angel's naivety. She had obviously joined a cult—been bamboozled into believing all this spiritual nonsense.

The lady across from Daniel handed him a basket full of New World Order notes and coins.

Angel took it from him. "We're taking a collection to pay Elisa's rent this month," she said as she reached in her purse, added a few notes to the basket, then passed it on.

Daniel glanced at the single mom Angel had pointed out earlier. They were paying her rent—these people who, by their clothing, appeared to barely have enough of their own? Daniel remembered an older lady who had come to his office asking the church to pay her mortgage that month. She had begged him to help, said she was losing her home, and she'd been a faithful member of the church for seven years. He had wanted to help her. He really had. But church policy was not to pay members' personal bills. If they did it for one person, then everyone would come begging. And there wasn't enough money allocated for such things, particularly when the church didn't have the resources to verify the validity of each need.

Scottie looked up at Angel. "Got anything for us, Angelica?"

"Nothing this week." She shook her head. "Just more visions of wars, riots, violence, and darkness. But always the light. Just like the message we received. As the darkness grows, the light grows stronger."

"Praise God!" someone shouted. "God always confirms His message."

This seemed to be the end of the crazy service, for people began standing and chatting amongst themselves. Several came up to meet Daniel, and Angelica introduced him around. Though they all seemed genuinely pleased to meet him, not one of them acted as if he were anyone beyond an ordinary person. So odd, when routinely he got stopped in grocery stores and restaurants by people dying to meet the famous pastor.

Of course, what did he expect from a bunch of crazies?

Finally, Angel and he stood alone in the center of the room, the scent of spicy chicken wafting around them. At least Daniel could get something out of this colossal waste of time. "That smells wonderful. What's for lunch?"

"Oh, that's not for us," Angel replied with a smile. "It's for the people standing in the food line down on Sistrunk Boulevard. One Saturday a month, each of us brings goods to distribute among the hungry. We also collect cans of food, rice, flour, and whatever else we can find to divide up."

"How many people do you feed?"

"Depends. Normally at least fifty."

"Fifty?" He whistled. "Impressive for such a small group." Of course, Fort Lauderdale Church of Grace had its own homeless kitchen that served hundreds each week.

"Come out to lunch with me," he finally said.

"It's too late for lunch."

"Early dinner?"

"I have Isaac."

*That was his name.* "He is welcome."

At that moment, Isaac dashed up with two boys his age and an older lady. "Mom, Mom, can I go to Brian's house for dinner?"

"I don't know." Angelica frowned, staring at the lady.

"It's fine with me, Angelica. We're having a BBQ and the boys can swim in the pool."

"Pleeeeeease," Isaac pleaded, tugging at her heart.

She so rarely let him out of her sight, but Mary was a godly woman with a godly husband and a beautiful home.

As if sensing her angst, Mary laid a hand on Angelica's arm. "I'll take good care of him."

Nodding, Angelica smiled. "Thank you, Mary. I'll swing by and pick him up by seven."

Isaac and the boys squealed with glee.

"That's perfect." Mary turned to Daniel and greeted him warmly before she dragged the three boys away.

"Well, I guess a late lunch is on," Angel said with a tone that lacked enthusiasm.

Daniel would take what he could get. Besides, it would give him a chance to warn her about these fanatics. If she didn't break off with them, she and her son would end up in jail.

*For all that is in the world—the lust of the flesh, the lust of the eyes, and the pride of life—is not of the Father but is of the world.*
  *1 John 2:16 (NKJV)*

# Chapter 8

The last thing Angelica wanted to do was have lunch with Daniel Cain. But she had seen the way he'd squirmed throughout the entire church service, had heard his groans, watched as he squeezed the bridge of his nose and shook his head, and she thought perhaps this would be an opportunity to discuss what had transpired—to open his eyes to the truth. But now as his Porsche pulled into a driveway long enough to be a football field and parked before a mansion, she regretted accepting his invitation.

She parked behind him and met him as he leapt from his car and slammed the door.

"Where are we?" she demanded.

He gestured toward the two-story villa towering before them. "My home."

"I thought we were going to lunch."

"We are. But I can't very well take a lady out looking like this." He gestured to the syrupy mess on his pants. "I'll only be a minute." Then, at what must have been a look of horror on her face, he reached for her hand. "Don't worry, Angel. No sinister intentions. Come in for a sec while I change." He gave her his most charming grin…complete with that irresistible dimple, and she found herself unwittingly agreeing.

The house was right out of the *Lifestyles of the Rich and Famous* magazine. Her entire apartment would fit in the entranceway alone. Everything was decorated to perfection, from the elaborately carved crown molding to the marble floors in which Angelica could see her reflection, to the original oil paintings, luxurious furniture, sparkling glass-top tables, and a flat-screen that took up an entire wall. And that was just the living area. An open kitchen stood off to the side, bigger than her bedroom, looking like it had never been used. And best of all, the entire back wall was one giant sliding glass door that opened to a lush backyard. A waterfall spilled from a man-made cliff into a pool that was surrounded with tropical plants and flowers. Over the back hedge, the beach extended to a glistening sea.

"So this is how the other half lives," she commented as he tossed his keys onto the counter and slid the glass doors open.

He flinched as if she'd insulted him. "I'll only be a minute. Make yourself at home." Then he was gone, the tap of his shoes echoing over the marble.

Drawing in a deep breath of gardenias and the sea, Angelica wandered out to the pool. With its black bottom, figure-eight shape, and cascading waterfall, it looked like a hidden pond on a tropical island, and she longed to dive in. Instead, she settled for kicking off her shoes, rolling up her jeans, and sitting at the edge with her feet in the water.

"What am I doing here, Father?" She sighed. If she were truthful, it was Thomas' threat that had forced her to see Daniel again, not God's prompting. Something for which she'd already repented. She'd been so angry at Thomas' arrogance, at his demand to leave Daniel alone...well, suffice it to say, it seemed she still had a bit of pride. Regardless, it was a good thing, right? Not the pride, but Daniel coming to her home church.

She kicked her feet through the warm water, hoping it would sooth her nerves. *Father, help me know what to say.*

"It's relaxing out here." Daniel's voice startled her and she turned to see him wearing camo Bermuda shorts and a white T-shirt that left none of his muscular physique to the imagination. The sun, high in the sky, shone from behind his head, blurring his features, and for a split-second, it was twelve years ago, and he was the boy she had given everything to—soul, heart, and body. Settling her breath, she snapped her gaze back to the pool as he sat down beside her.

Too close. So close she could smell his aftershave, feel the warmth of his body. What had they been talking about? Oh, yeah, his relaxing backyard. "Reminds me of what heaven will be like," she finally muttered.

He gave her a look, as if that were the oddest thing to say, before he cleared his throat. "Speaking of, I'm a little ticked at you for inviting me to an illegal gathering."

"It's not illegal in the eyes of God."

He raised his brows. "God says to obey the laws of the land. You could all be arrested as a terrorist group. Not to mention what would happen to my career if I'd been caught with you."

"I'm sorry. I should have told you." Though she knew he wouldn't have gone if she had. "I wanted you to see what...my church is like."

"You call that chaos 'church'?" He snorted and leaned back on his palms, lifting his face to the breeze. "Listen, Angel. You know I care about you. And because of that, I need to tell you that you've gotten yourself involved in a cult."

Scooting away, she glared at him. "How can you say that? Everything that happened there was biblical. Have you read the book of Acts lately?"

He gave a haughty snort. "You ask *me* that?"

Flattening her lips, she looked away. This was not going well. "I'm talking about the original book of Acts, not the watered-down version."

The crash of waves sounded in the distance as a colorful bird landed on a tree branch above them and began warbling a tune. When he didn't respond, she turned to him, lifting an eyebrow.

"All that hocus-pocus spirit stuff stopped with the apostles. Minds far greater than ours taught me that in seminary." His eyes grew serious. "And since I haven't seen anything to the contrary in the twenty years I've been a Christian, I'm sticking to that."

A breeze tore in from the sea, styling his hair in a dozen directions, and sweeping away her anger.

"I have a gift of prophecy," she said. "I see visions and have dreams, often about the future."

He chuckled, but stopped when she glared at him. "Sorry. I guess I'm one of those guys who has to see to believe."

"But you believe in Jesus and don't see Him."

"That's different."

"I don't see how." She flung her hand through the air. "There's an invisible realm all around us, filled with good and evil spirits battling over kingdoms, a place more real than this one. Who are we to limit what God can do through us?"

Tipping his head, he gave her a placating smile. "You certainly have changed, Angel. What a party girl you were back in the day. Remember how I used to tell you all the time to give your life to Jesus?"

She chuckled and swept her feet through the water. "And I would tell you to quit shoving your religious crap on me."

"Yeah. But in much more colorful language, if I recall."

She smiled sadly. Memories returned of how she had made fun of him for being a goodie-two-shoes and for believing in fables from thousands of years ago. But Daniel had never been put off, never gotten angry. He had only loved her all the more. Even after they'd slept together, he had not blamed her, though she'd thought it was perfectly natural. But as the weeks passed, she could tell he felt guilty, like he had betrayed his God. So, when he insisted they stop, she agreed and loved him all the more for his morals and convictions. He even promised to marry her.

Until he discovered it would ruin his future.

Yes, she had definitely changed, but so had he. But she wouldn't tell him that. She wanted him to see for himself how far he had drifted from the true God.

"But didn't you feel the presence of God—His Holy Spirit—today at Scottie's?" She knew he had. She'd sensed the battle going on within him. Even now, as she sought the Spirit, a pair of red eyes appeared, slithering around Daniel, firing hatred her way.

*Father, help him to see.*

"Nice home," Baliel said to Nazare as they stood on the other side of the pool, watching the couple.

"Indeed. But he is hardly ever here. In truth, even with all this luxury, he's lonely, and I fear the huge house only reminds him of that."

"Sad. When will humans learn that such trivial possessions never satisfy?"

Nazare shook his head. "After nearly seven thousand years, my guess is that only God can teach them that. And only when they receive His Spirit."

Baliel smiled and gestured toward Angelica and Daniel. "These two still have a connection. See the way their souls reach for each other."

"I'm sure you remember their past. Though immoral in their actions, they developed real love for one another."

"So rare among humans these days. She cried for over a year after he left her." Baliel remembered too well the agony she suffered, especially before she received the Father's comfort.

"Which is why she still fights the Father's will."

"Yes, but she's here." Baliel defended her. "And she's trying to lead him back to the Father. See how the light flows from her mouth and showers over him."

Nazare nodded. "Indeed. I pray she succeeds. I, too, have appealed to the Father for such. It is too much to bear watching his chains tighten day after day."

"But you must. And you must be strong. We are not to become overly entangled with them."

Nazare gripped the hilt of his sword. "Ah, the battle commences. Behold, the demons rise."

Baliel glanced toward Daniel where a horde of dark spirits began spinning around him, eyes flaring, claws extended. One was wrapping a thick chain around Daniel's head. "Aye, he's wavering. Something she said has made him question his beliefs."

"Be ready, my friend." Nazare's fingers itched to draw his sword.

"I am. But only when the Father commands." Baliel drew a golden dagger, excitement buzzing through him. "See? The light begins to pierce the darkness."

*Now the Spirit expressly says that in latter times some will depart from the faith, giving heed to deceiving spirits and doctrines of demons, speaking lies in hypocrisy, having their own conscience seared with a hot iron.*
*1 Timothy 4:1 (NKJV)*

# Chapter 9

Angelica waited for Daniel's answer, watching the battle raging behind his eyes. He *had* sensed the Spirit at church today. She knew it. How could anyone not have? His presence had been so strong, so sweet and powerful. Even the angels she'd seen about the place had been singing and dancing along with her friends. Now, if she could only get Daniel to admit it, maybe she could get an inroad into further discussion.

"You *did* feel the Holy Spirit," she finally said.

Daniel looked down and sighed. "Sorry, Angel. The only thing I felt was uncomfortable." Before she could answer and before he could see the frown on her face, he hopped up. "I'll get us something to drink. Iced tea?"

She nodded and watched the wind stir ripples over the water, feeling like she was banging her head against the flat stones that surrounded the pool. Strongholds. At least that's what the Bible called the fortresses of deception the enemy erected in human minds to block out the truth. But what to do?

He returned with two glasses and handed her one before he sat beside her again. The scent of his Aqua Velva drifted over her, and she smiled, wondering why he would wear such cheap cologne when he had so much money. He swiped a hand through his thick, gorgeous hair…oh, how she had always loved his hair. But it had been longer and sun-bleached when she knew him. A flaxen-haired surfer dude who loved God with all his heart.

The sun sizzled on her skin, and she leaned over to splash water on her arms and neck. "You used to love the Word of God, Daniel. How can you use that new version?"

"All they took out was the hateful stuff. The message of the gospel is still in there, and that's what matters, isn't it?" He sipped his tea.

"You mean hateful stuff like people need to *actually* repent, there's a real hell, and there will come a judgment day?"

Though her tone was snarky, he merely smiled. "That's all implied in the gospel message. No need to scare people. I mean that stuff about homosexuals, couples living together before marriage, alcoholics, drug addicts, prostitutes, even simple liars and gossips all going to hell—those scare tactics only keep people away and make them hate us." He raised a brow above eyes full of conviction and kindness. "And isn't it the role of the church to bring more people in? To be more inclusive and not exclusive? Didn't Jesus love everyone?"

Angelica could see why this guy won over so many people. Not only was he handsome and charming, but words flowed from his mouth like honey—sweet to the taste and easy on the ears. And if one didn't know better, they made perfect sense.

A green bird with bluish wings joined his friend on a palm branch and both began conversing in melodic tune. Angelica wondered what they were saying, or maybe they were just laughing at the two foolish humans below.

"Of course, Jesus loves everyone." Wind brushed a strand of hair in her face and she eased it behind her ear. "But once they receive Him as Lord of their lives, they aren't supposed to purposely continue doing things He says not to. We all screw up now and then, but we aren't supposed to intentionally continue to live in sin. God is very serious about this." She proceeded to quote from Corinthians, "Do you not know that the unrighteous will not inherit the kingdom of God? Do not be deceived. Neither fornicators, nor idolaters, nor adulterers, nor homosexuals, nor sodomites, nor thieves, nor covetous, nor drunkards, nor revilers, nor extortioners will inherit the kingdom of God."

He shuddered. "Wow. I can see why they took that one out. It flies in the face of the message of Christ's love and His free gift of salvation to all. It's all about grace, Angel. Not works. We can't earn our way to God. So why scare people away?"

"No, we can't earn God's grace, but once we receive it, it should change us. Our lives should clearly show that we are truly God's children. There's no such thing as a gospel that doesn't change you, Daniel." She pursed her lips, thinking. "Here's another verse they took out of your changed Bible, 'No one who is born of God will continue to sin, because God's seed remains in them; they cannot go on sinning, because they have been born of God.'"

He chuckled. "But that's the thing, Angel. This is why lay people like yourself shouldn't try to interpret Scripture." He set down his cup. "Have you committed a sin after you were born of God?"

"Of course. We all do."

"Then, obviously, that's not what John was referring to in this passage."

She repressed a growl. "That's not what I'm saying. He's talking about continual, purposeful sinning."

"Listen, why don't you leave the sermons to the experts?" He smiled and patted her hand. "Isn't it obvious from the number of people my church draws in that I'm doing something right? Millions across the world are hearing the gospel."

Those gorgeous blue eyes of his stared at her with such sincerity, she had a hard time being angry at his arrogance.

Setting down her tea, she gripped his hand. "But my concern is what gospel and what Jesus are you actually presenting?"

His face scrunched. "The same one from the Bible. Listen, I don't want to argue theology with you. But in hindsight, I'm glad you invited me to your church. It's given me an opportunity to warn you." He squeezed her hand. "Please, Angel, I beg you, break it off with these crazies before it's too late."

Angelica's stomach clenched in defeat. "You won't report us?"

"Not as long as you and Isaac are there. But surely you know that religious nutjobs like that are turning people away from God, not drawing them close."

She studied him, wondering how he'd become so deceived. Sorrow weighed her down when she saw the desperation lingering behind his gaze. He *was* searching for something, answers, truth, something to cling to. The problem was, he had no idea he was even looking.

He smiled. "I guess I promised you lunch, didn't I?"

"I'm not hungry." Picking up her tea, she sipped it. Sweet, just like she liked it. "It's fun catching up."

"Is it?" He raised a brow and chuckled. "Seems like we are just arguing."

Which is why she was going to change tactics. She glanced over her luxurious surroundings. "So, why haven't you married, Daniel? I'm sure women must be falling at your feet."

There came that grin again—boyish, devilish, and charming all mixed together. But then he grew serious and ran a finger down her hand. "Haven't found the right woman yet."

She pulled away, sorry when she made him frown.

He picked up his cup. "How about you?"

"Not many men want to take on a child. Besides, I'm too busy for dating."

"You never went to college like you wanted. English Lit. Wasn't that what you wanted to study. Become a writer?"

A breeze whipped around them, cooling the perspiration on her neck and bringing the scent of chlorine and the sea. "You remembered." She could hardly believe it. Especially when she barely remembered that old dream herself. "No time or money for college with a child to raise. Waitressing was the only thing that paid enough for us to live."

Daniel sighed. "That one mistake cost you a lot."

"Isaac is not a mistake!" She jumped to her feet.

"Of course not. I didn't mean…" He stood and touched her arm. "Forgive me, Angel. I didn't mean it like that. He seems like a wonderful boy."

"He is my *life*." She stepped away from him, settling her breath. "It's okay. I guess I'm just sensitive about him." And protective and fierce and worried all the time.

"I suppose if I had a kid, I'd feel the same way," he said, and she knew he meant it. He'd always wanted children. They used to talk about it for hours—their dreams of getting married and having enough kids to form a baseball team. Him pastoring a small church, her writing best-selling novels.

"It must be hard raising him alone."

"Terrifying." She admitted, hugging herself. And it wasn't getting any easier.

"Why don't we sit by the waterfall? There's a cushioned ledge in the shade." He led her to the cascading water where a seat had been carved into the side of the pool just above the waterline, complete with built-in cushions. Sitting, she stretched her legs in the shallow water while he darted off, returning in minutes with a bag of some sort of grain-free chia seed chips and more tea.

She laughed. "Don't you have any real potato chips?"

He looked horrified. "Do you want me to die of heart disease?"

"No, but I think it's okay to enjoy life now and then."

"Who says I don't enjoy these?" He sat beside her, grabbed a chip and took a bite. Yet the look on his face was anything but enjoyment. He offered her some. "How's your mom and all your siblings? Five of them, right? I'm sure they all pitched in to help with Isaac."

Stunned, once again, at the details he remembered about her life, she turned down the chips as sorrow overwhelmed her. "My mother disowned me when she discovered I was pregnant. I haven't heard from her or my sisters and brothers since."

Silence, except for the sound of crashing water, filled the air between them for a few moments before Daniel groaned. "Man, that's horrible. I'm so sorry. I remember her being super strict religious, but I had no idea…"

"Super strict is one way to put it. She kept us kids under a tight reign. So tight, I guess that's why I rebelled as a teenager." And, boy, had she rebelled. Though God had forgiven her, the regrets of those years were hard to live with. "The drugs, drinking, and partying were bad enough, but when I got pregnant, well, the stain on the family was more than Mom could bear. She'd already suffered agonizing humiliation when my dad left her for another woman."

"And she's never met her grandson? Even after you became a Christian?"

Angelica shook her head, desperate to change the subject, desperate not to resurrect the festering wounds in her heart. She'd forgiven her mother and siblings long ago and would rather just forget about them. "What about your parents? They must be so proud of you. I really liked your mom."

"She *was* incredible." His smile faded. "She died. Cancer. Eight years ago."

"Oh my, Daniel." Angelica took his hand in hers. "I'm so sorry."

He gripped her hand and rubbed it with his thumb, stirring feelings long since buried, but obviously not dead. "Thank you. She was my rock growing up. I don't know what I would have done without her."

"What about your dad?"

Daniel instantly stiffened, and his lips tightened. "Still a drunk, living down by the docks, I guess. Haven't seen him in a while."

"Don't you think he'd be proud of you?"

Daniel shrugged, not meeting her gaze. "I have no idea. Nothing I did was ever good enough for him. I'm sure you remember how furious he was when I entered seminary instead of going to engineering school."

She remembered. All too well. Daniel's father was a terrifying man. At least to a twenty-one-year-old girl. He never had a kind word to say, either to her or his son. "No father should call his son such names."

He tossed the bag of chips aside. "Nothing I hadn't heard before."

"But it doesn't lessen the hurt." Or the feeling of worthlessness it caused. Which was probably why Daniel worked so hard to make a success out of his life—to prove his value to the world and himself. "Surely by now he's heard of your success. He's got to be proud."

"I don't intend to find out." He continued caressing her fingers. "You're the only one who knows about him, Angel. I could always talk to you. Nobody ever listens to me like you do."

*Then why did you dump me?* She wanted to ask. But she knew the answer. Thomas had made it quite plain.

Uncomfortable with the direction of the conversation, Angelica pulled back her hand and stood. She should leave. She had come here to lead him closer to God, but the only thing she was accomplishing was rekindling old feelings that would only cause her pain.

"You aren't leaving yet, are you?" Daniel stood. The pleading look in his eyes transported her back in time to another day at another backyard pool. He was young, his hair longer, his eyes brighter. And his physique just as alluring. They'd been invited to a pool party at a friend's house. Everyone was drinking, and Angelica was wearing her skimpiest bikini. Other girls were there too, far prettier than she—girls from his seminary, smart girls who were going somewhere. And she remembered being so jealous. She was just a cocktail waitress with no future. But Daniel only had eyes for her. Not only that, but he had protected her when one of the guys who'd had too much to drink tried to hit on her.

He'd always made her feel like a princess.

Just like he was doing now... simply with his gaze.

"Yes," she said nervously. "I need to pick up Isaac. Thank you for the tea." Retrieving the glass, she hurried to find her shoes as Daniel's footsteps pounded after her. Why wouldn't the man leave her be? She swept up her shoes from the pavement and spun around to leave.

Bumping straight into Daniel.

The iced tea glass slipped from her grip and crashed to the pavement in a thousand glittering shards. Before she could react, Daniel hoisted her up in his arms, lost his balance...

And they both fell into the pool.

Water surrounded her. Her jeans turned to lead, and she struggled to the surface, gulping for air. Daniel popped up after her, looking like a drowned seal, staring at her in horror.

And all of a sudden, laughter bubbled up from her gut. Low and soft at first, but then a full-throated guffaw. Daniel joined in, and together, they continued chuckling as they swam to the edge and gripped the tile. They remained in the water, breathing hard, just inches from each other, smiling as if there hadn't been a twelve-year gap in their relationship.

He gently wiped water from her face. "I've missed you so much, Angel."

She knew she should hoist herself out of the pool and leave immediately. But something kept her in place, something kept her studying every feature of his face, the lines and angles she knew so well, the stubble on his jaw she used to love to touch, the warmth of his breath, the slant of his nose, and those eyes, so blue and mesmerizing. She couldn't breathe.

Before she knew it, his lips touched hers. And everything she remembered about this man exploded within her in a heated rush—every sensation, every fun time, every meal they shared, every deep conversation, every dream... and every intimate touch. She melted against him.

Only for a second.

Then she came to her senses.

Chest heaving, she backed away in horror. In one desperate motion, she hoisted herself from the water. "I can't see you anymore, Daniel. Please don't contact me again," she shouted as she turned and dashed from the house.

*Very truly I tell you, whoever believes in me will do the works I have been doing, and they will do even greater things than these, because I am going to the Father.*
*John 14:12 (NIV)*

# Chapter 10

Angelica set up her folding chair beneath a palm tree and watched Isaac dash to the water, surfboard in hand, kicking up sand as he went. Though the hot sun glared down over the beach turning sand into glittering crystals, dark clouds huddled on the horizon. Wind stirred up sandy whirlwinds and drove high waves to the shore. Perfect for surfing. Not so perfect for sharing God's love with the lost. Particularly if it rained.

But it was Saturday and people expected them to be here. Word had spread that some had been healed from diseases and delivered from addictions, and each week, the crowd grew. Commotion drew Angelica's gaze and she waved at Anna, Clay, and Robert as they made their way over the sand from the parking lot, and she wondered how much longer they would be able to push back the kingdom of darkness and open people's eyes to the truth. The GIFP was cracking down on true Christian gatherings, and reports were splattered over the news about home churches being invaded and everyone thrown behind bars. Hate groups, they called them. Terrorists.

That couldn't be farther from the truth. Oh, how the enemy loved to stir up lies.

Angelica shook her head and gazed at the water, searching for Isaac among the crashing waves.

There—mounting his board several yards out next to a man doing the same. Alarm stiffened her spine. Isaac made friends so easily. People of all ages loved him and were drawn to him instantly. Which only made her fears rise even more. He was so innocent, so young…vulnerable. How could she keep him untainted from the horrors of this world? If only she could keep him in a giant bubble of love, joy, and peace until Jesus came back for them.

At least she had ended things with Daniel—one less person who would influence her son negatively. *And* one less person who would rip out Angelica's heart and stomp it to dust. *Yet again.* Then why could she not stop thinking about his kiss? She had not felt such overwhelming sensations since the last time they had kissed all those years ago. And it infuriated her. Why was she so weak when it came to this man? She had prayed all morning during her walk along the beach, begging God to free her from the hold Daniel had over her, pleading with Him to keep Daniel away and not ask her to see him again. But she had received no answer.

And no peace.

"Morning, Angelica!" Anna dropped her towel and bag and planted hands at her waist, gazing over the sea. "Beautiful day."

Clay promptly dropped to the sand and began tuning his guitar, while Robert greeted Angelica with a huge smile, rubbing his hands together. "Let's do some warfare."

"Amen." Anna lovingly gazed at her husband, then grabbed Angelica's hand and pulled her to her feet.

But Angelica's gaze was still on Isaac surfing to shore.

"He'll be okay," Anna assured her. "Let's pray."

Clay joined them as they stood in a circle, bowed their heads, and prayed for angelic protection, God's Holy Spirit to be present, and many to be saved and healed.

When they separated, there was already a crowd forming around them—mothers with young children, a few teenagers, two elderly couples, and several young adults. All with looks of anticipation on their faces. As Clay led everyone in a song, Angelica kept her eyes on Isaac. He'd made it to shore and was talking with a man. An oddly *familiar* man. They both laughed, grabbed their boards, and plunged back into the water.

She knew that laugh. *Daniel.*

Fisting her hands, she repressed a growl as she watched the two of them paddle out and then sit atop their boards waiting for the next good wave. What did he think he was doing? She should march down there and demand he leave at once. She started to do just that when someone tugged on her hand, and she turned to see Anna gazing at her curiously. "You okay? We're about to start the lesson."

Which meant Angelica was up. Since they couldn't bring their Bibles, they each took turns memorizing Scripture. And this week Angelica had memorized John 1.

*Focus. Focus.* She closed her eyes for a second and prayed for God's help to put aside her anger and minister to these people. She would have to deal with Daniel later. She glanced once more in his direction and watched as he dropped into the wave, leapt atop his board, and carved the water, going down the line with incredible skill as the swell raced toward shore. Finally, it fizzled out and he plunged beneath the water. Beautifully done. Just like a pro. Just like the many times she had watched and cheered him on as he competed in the World Surf League. How proud she had been of him as she watched from shore, enduring the jealous glances from bikini-clad surf bunnies. But when Daniel reached the sand, he'd always grabbed his board and headed her way, his eyes only for her.

Shaking off the memories, she sat before the crowd, smiled at everyone, and began her recitation of one of the most beautiful passages in the Bible.

Daniel hadn't planned on surfing with Angel's son. He'd heard on the news that the swells were prime, so he'd grabbed his board at the last minute. Man, was he glad he did! The waves were perfect, and Isaac had exceptional skill for one so young. Daniel was enjoying himself immensely. In fact, he and Isaac had just shredded a wave when he spotted Angel's hard glare on him from the beach.

Now, as he approached her in the sand, Isaac by his side, she fired a look at him that would melt all of Antarctica.

She moved away from her cult—yes, he'd seen them—and led Isaac and Daniel to the other side of a palm. But it was Isaac who saved him from a scolding that would no doubt scorch his ears.

"Mom! Mom! Did you see us?" The boy grabbed a towel from the sand and started drying himself. "Daniel's teaching me to pump. Did you know he won the WSL Qualifying Series when he was younger? And did you see him drop into a bottom turn? It was so cool!"

Daniel gave Isaac a fist pump. "You got real talent, kid. In a few years with lots of practice, I bet you'll win more medals than me."

Isaac fisted him back. "Really? Did you hear that Mom?"

"Yes, I did." Finally, Angel smiled as she gazed at her son.

Daniel didn't blame her. He was a good kid. Smart, fun, and talented.

"Now, run along and help Anna and Robert."

"But Mom, Mr. Cain was going to teach me how to catch air."

"Maybe later. Go." Her voice was stern.

Frowning, the boy ambled away.

Thunder rumbled from the horizon, an omen of the chiding to come.

Angel's expression turned to spikes—sharp spikes. Even so, she was beautiful in her white Capris and pink blouse, her hair tossing around her in the wind and those lashes long enough to be brushes.

"What do you think you are doing?" Her tone brought him out of his trance.

Daniel swept his arm out from behind him. "Bringing your shoes back." He handed her the pink tennis shoes and offered her a sheepish smile, suddenly glad he'd thought to bring them along.

She snagged them from his grip and tossed them to the sand. "I told you, I don't want to see you again."

She was so adorable when she was angry. He had forgotten that. "Just because we kissed?"

She took a step back as if he had stabbed her. "I'm sorry that happened."

"I'm not."

A gust of rain-spiced wind danced through her hair as she offered him a pleading look. "Please, Daniel. Leave me alone. Leave my son alone."

Daniel's gaze found Isaac mingling with the cult. "He's a good kid. You've done well."

"I don't need your approval."

"Hey, just offering you a compliment."

The waves crashed behind her, mimicking her low growl. "Please go find another woman to harass."

"Ouch." Daniel flinched from the palpable pain in his heart, then tried to cover it by changing the subject. He gestured with his head toward the mob of people. "Why are you still doing this?"

She fisted hands at her waist. "We are telling people about Jesus. That's all."

*And performing your hocus-pocus.* A thought Daniel wanted to add, but that would only push her away. He watched the woman named Anna stop to pray over each of the gullible people, while the guy who looked like a reject from Hells Angels followed behind her. The young seventies-rock-star-lookalike was playing his guitar as Isaac sat beside him singing.

Stubborn as always, Angel would not likely heed any of his warnings until it was too late. In fact, she seemed intent on converting him to her dangerous ideas. And although he couldn't let that happen, perhaps he could use that fact to keep seeing her. Cheap shot, he knew. But what else could he do? He wasn't ready to let her go again. *If ever.* Other than a few one-night stands, which he regretted and repented of, he'd never had a relationship with another woman. No one he'd met could compare to Angel, no matter how beautiful or alluring or how they'd thrown themselves at him. Even now, with her green eyes hard as marbles and her lips tight, he wanted—no, he needed—to be with her.

"I have to get back." She turned to leave.

"Can I listen in for a while?"

"Are you sure you want to risk being spotted with a cult?" she snapped before stomping away.

Not really. But he stayed, nonetheless. He watched Angel join Anna and Robert as all three circled through the entire mob, which had grown to at least thirty people. They stopped before each one, listened to them, and then prayed. Not wanting to get too close, he could barely hear what they were saying over the crash of waves and chatter of beach-goers.

A cloud stole the heat of the sun as more thunder shook the horizon. One peek at the sea showed the waves had grown, and he itched to go back out. Anything rather than stand here watching these charlatans giving people false hope. Yet, he had to give the three of them credit. They appeared to really care. Angel took each person's hands in hers and bowed her head, he assumed to pray silently. After a few minutes, she'd either speak to them or tell Anna and Robert something, which led *them* to pray. Then she moved onto the next poor soul.

They were nearly at the last person when two men carrying another man between them came and lowered him to the sand before Anna and Robert. A wheelchair sat empty on the sidewalk.

The wind picked up and Daniel could only hear pieces of the conversation. "Can't walk…bone disease…doctors no help…"

Huffing, Daniel crossed his legs and leaned against the tree trunk. Yeah, right. Like these guys could do anything about that.

Anna motioned for Angel to join them, and all three laid their hands on the man's legs and prayed for several minutes.

Nothing happened. *Of course.*

Robert stood and extended his hand to the man. "Get up," he said.

*Come on, no way.* Daniel started toward them before they actually injured the poor guy.

The man hesitated, but then gripped Robert's hand and allowed him to gently pull him to his feet.

He stood, wobbly at first, but finally remained steady. His face lit like a beacon on a dark night. "I can walk!" he shouted. His two friends stared at him, blinking, mouths open. Then gripping his arms, they steadied him and began to laugh. Laugh and then shout for joy.

"Thank God, I can walk!" The man spun to tell the mob.

Daniel halted. No. Couldn't be. Obviously, the guy could already walk. This was just a cruel trick to get these people's money—naive, foolish people who continued singing and praising God so loud that Daniel looked across the beach, uncomfortable.

Yup, these people were good. *Real* good. He shifted his feet uncomfortably in the sand, waiting for the shouting to stop and the offering basket to be passed.

But as things settled down, no such basket appeared. Angel smiled as she approached him. "Did you see that?" Excitement tainted her voice.

"I'm not sure what I saw," he returned a bit too harshly.

Isaac came running over. "Can I go surfing with Daniel now, Mom? Pleeeeease!" He made no mention of the healing as though it was something that took place every day.

Daniel could use another dunk in the sea. If only to clear his head from this madness. He raised a brow her way. "How about it, Mom? I could sure use a surfing buddy."

As she shifted her gaze from Daniel to Isaac to the ocean, a glorious idea occurred to him. "And, by the way, how about you two join me at SeaWorld next Saturday? I have free tickets."

"SeaWorld! SeaWorld!! Can we, Mom?"

She shook her head and opened her mouth to utter what he was sure would be a "no" when he added, "It would give us a chance to talk about what happened here today. In public. Where you have nothing to fear."

He gave her his most pleading look and could see her defenses crumbling.

Finally, she released a sigh. "Very well. And yes, Isaac, you may go surfing."

*Victory!* With a playful punch to Isaac's arm, Daniel led him away, grinning at Angel over his shoulder.

As Angelica watched Daniel and her son stroll away, surfboards under their arms, fury pinched every nerve within her. *Drat!* SeaWorld! Of all the places. How dare he ask her in front of Isaac! She'd said no to her son so much lately, how could she deny him something he'd been begging her to do for years?

Anna slid beside her. "Now I see what has you so distracted today. The handsome pastor."

Handsome was an understatement. Especially with seawater glistening over the rounded muscles of his chest. Especially with that strong, stubble-peppered jaw and deep-set blue eyes.

"I'm sorry, Anna. I keep trying to stay away from him, but he keeps showing up wherever I am."

"Hmm. Seems the Lord has other plans."

"He keeps questioning what we are doing here. I feel like he's searching." She sighed and rubbed her temples. "I don't know. Maybe he's playing me."

"Why would he do that?"

"To rekindle something we once had. Feed his ego. Who knows?" She faced her friend and gave a half smile. "I imagine he's not used to women turning him down."

Anna laid a hand on her arm. "I know he hurt you once very badly. Listen carefully to the voice of the Spirit. He will lead you down the right path. Don't trust your feelings or anything else."

Angelica smiled. "I'm trying." But even now as she watched Isaac and Daniel paddle out, terror gnawed at her soul. Her son latched onto any adult male who gave him attention. It broke her heart to admit it, but he desperately needed a father, especially now that he was maturing. *Just not this man!* Not one who would lead him away from the true God.

Her prayer was interrupted by gasps from the crowd, and she turned to see two policemen strolling toward them. "Who's in charge here?" the short, beefy one shouted.

"No one's in charge, Officer." Robert halted his prayer with an elderly lady and stood. "How can we help you?"

Breath coming hard, Angelica gripped Anna's hand and approached.

"Move along, everyone. Move along." The taller officer waved his hand over the crowd, and instantly people stood and scattered across the beach.

"What's going on here?" the first policeman demanded.

Releasing Angelica's hand, Anna stepped forward. "We are singing and praying for people. That's all."

"Proselytizing?" the man barked.

"Just praying," Clay said, rising.

"Public prayer is forbidden. You know that."

"We aren't bothering anyone," Robert interjected. "We're just helping people."

"We've had complaints."

"From who?" Angelica asked.

"People who come to this beach to relax and not have to hear a bunch of Jesus crap."

"We don't spread any Jesus crap. We spread truth."

The man narrowed his eyes upon Anna. "What *is* truth?" He snorted. "Consider this a warning. If I hear any more complaints, or I come back here and find you at it again, I'll arrest the lot of you and toss you in jail."

*And he who does not take his cross and follow after Me is not worthy of Me. He who finds his life will lose it, and he who loses his life for My sake will find it.*
*Matthew 10:38-39 (NKJV)*

# Chapter 11

D aniel had not been able to wipe the smile from his face ever since he left Angel and Isaac at the beach. He had not only wormed his way into her son's graces, but back into hers as well. All by expressing an interest in her so-called religion. He grabbed the coffee from the attractive barista at the church coffee shop—who gave him a seductive smile—and spun around lest anyone accuse him of flirting. Unfortunately, he slammed into Rubio the music director. If not for the cap on his cup, he would have spilled his hot coffee on the poor man, who, by his angry expression, looked like someone already had done so.

"Dan, we need to talk."

*Grr. Why didn't the man address him as Pastor Daniel?* Pasting on a smile, Daniel nodded, though he'd rather eat bricks at the moment than deal with another one of the man's emotional tirades.

"It's the play," Rubio said, leading Daniel away from prying ears. "I just can't deal with the incompetence of these actors!" He wiped the back of his hand on his forehead as if he were going to pass out. "Amateurs. They are all such amateurs."

"Well, they *are* amateurs, Rubio. This isn't a Hollywood production." Daniel would laugh if the man weren't so serious. "Listen, just do your best." Daniel started to leave when Rubio grabbed his arm.

"It's not just that. How can I work with musicians who don't even show up to practice? The play is in two weeks, and we are nowhere near ready."

Daniel cleared his throat, seeking the best way to handle this. He'd been meaning to talk to Rubio about his managerial skills anyway. Now was the perfect time. "Maybe if you didn't scream so much at everyone and insult them, they'd work harder for you."

Rubio flinched and let out a gasp. "How can you say such a thing? I'm under tremendous pressure, and you give me imbeciles to work with." Tears flooded his eyes.

"Now, now, Rubio." Daniel laid a hand on his shoulder. "I put you in charge of this play because you're the best and most talented musician and director I know. You can do this. I have every confidence." Daniel sipped his coffee and glanced around, seeking an escape. "Try a little patience with these *amateurs*. It will work out, I assure you." He clapped a supportive hand on the man's back.

Rubio nodded and wiped a finger beneath his eye. "Very well."

Heading for the door before the man broke in sobs, Daniel spotted Marley sitting at a table in the corner, peering into an open Bible as if it were a letter from a long-lost love.

*Strange.* Daniel stopped. "Everything okay, Marley?"

He looked up and smiled. "Yes. Just reading."

"Did you see the crowd that came forward to join the church yesterday?"

Marley only smiled.

"At least fifty."

"God be praised," Marley said without conviction.

"Must have been some great sermon I delivered." Daniel half-kidded, expecting Marley's usual praise. His good friend and youth pastor normally couldn't wait to tell Daniel how good his message was or share his excitement over the number of people who came forward. But now that Daniel thought about it, he hadn't done that in quite a while.

"Yup," was all he said.

"You sure everything's all right?"

"Yes, thanks. Just doing a lot of thinking…and praying these days."

"Well, there's no harm in that." Daniel smiled. "See you later."

Out in the cafe garden area, he passed Isabel Garcia, a short, plump middle-aged woman who was in charge of missions.

She stopped before him. "Quite the offering we took in yesterday for missions! I can't tell you how much we need that money."

"Your talk on Sierra Leone did the trick. But remember, only half the money collected goes for missions."

Lines formed on her forehead.

"The other half needs to cover administrative costs," he added. Why didn't these people understand that it took money to run a church as big as FLCG?

"Of course I realized some would be taken out," she mumbled, clearly flustered. "But that's well over ten grand."

"But just think, ten grand will also go to Sierra Leone."

Frowning, she glanced over the patrons laughing and chatting over coffee. "Our missionaries have made such inroads with the people there. You wouldn't believe their miraculous stories. Perhaps I can share them with you sometime?"

Daniel looked at his watch. "I'd love that. Not today, but soon." He walked away, lifting his coffee in her direction. "Have a great afternoon."

He entered the maze of halls behind the sanctuary, hoping to make it to his office without further interruption. No such luck. Harold Jakes stood chatting with an admin up ahead.

Ducking into another hallway, Daniel took the long way to his office through the administrative wing.

Mrs. Clipton was hard at work at her desk, while several other workers flitted about or were on phones. It still amazed Daniel that he was the CEO of this well-oiled machine. He stood for a minute, watching, remembering the words of his father.

*You're gonna be a preacher?* From the look of disgust on his face, you would have thought Daniel had told him he was going to be a garbage collector. *One of those deluded charlatans who rob weak people of their money. Liars, the whole lot of them. And most of them don't got two coins to rub together. It's your mother filling your head with such nonsense. What a waste of a life.* With that, he had waved Daniel off, belched, and continued drinking his beer.

Part of Daniel wished his father could see him now. Part of him wished the man were six feet under.

He stopped before Mrs. Clipton's desk. "Got that spreadsheet ready yet?"

She glanced up, a nervous look on her face. "No, sir, not yet. I'm sorry, but my niece is in the hospital this week."

Daniel let out a frustrated sigh at her continual excuses. "I'm sorry to hear it. I hope she is well." He glanced at his Rolex yet again. "But I need those figures."

"She had a blood clot in her brain, but they believe they caught it in time. We are praying for her recovery."

"That's good news. I will pray too."

"Perhaps you could visit her? She's at Holy Cross. I know it would mean the world to her."

Daniel frowned. Did people realize how busy he was? He couldn't possibly visit every sick person in the church. "Of course. Check my schedule, will you? If you can't find time, I'll ask Pastor Thomas." He started away before she put more demands on him. "But I want those figures on my desk before I leave today," he said over his shoulder.

"Yes, sir."

Daniel sipped his coffee and turned down the last hallway before his office. A curse rose to his lips when he spotted Kimberly and Thomas talking in front of his door. Couldn't people leave him alone for a minute?

Thomas whispered something in Kimberly's ear, causing her to giggle and Daniel to shake his head. As soon as they spotted him, they separated and Kimberly hurried past him, giving him that alluring smile of hers.

"What's that all about?" Daniel entered his office and set down his coffee.

"Nothing. You know Kimberly."

"Yes, and I know you, too." Leaning back on his desk, he crossed arms over his chest.

"Never mind about that." Thomas shut the door, his tone growing serious. "I have some good news."

"Then why so glum?"

Thomas ran a hand through his sun-bleached hair. "The Chief of Staff called when you were out yesterday."

Daniel's brows rose. "The *President's* Chief of Staff?"

Thomas grinned. "One and the same. You're not only attending the annual National Prayer Breakfast, you've been invited to deliver the keynote." His eyes flashed.

"Really?" Daniel could hardly believe his ears.

"That gets you right in front of the most important people in the nation. We're on our way, buddy." He rubbed his hands together. "Straight to D.C."

Daniel stared down at the floor, stunned.

Thomas' jovial mood instantly soured. "But none of this will matter when you are arrested and thrown in jail."

Daniel looked up. "What are you talking about?"

"Attending a hate group meeting. What were you thinking?" Anger flared from his friend's dark eyes.

Daniel ground his teeth. "So, you're having me followed now?"

"Someone has to keep you in line."

"I don't need a watchdog." Daniel spat out, his anger rising.

"Apparently, you do."

"Don't follow me again."

Thomas released a long sigh. "I'm only looking out for your best interest. You know that."

Daniel studied him, saw the concern in his eyes. Yes, he did know that. "Listen, I didn't know what it was. Angel invited me to meet some of her friends."

"And if you had listened to me in the first place and stayed away from her, you wouldn't have been there at all! Do you know what would happen if you'd been arrested? Everything would be ruined! All of this." He waved his arm over the luxurious office. "The church, your position, your salary, your fancy home and car, and especially your chance at a power seat in Washington. All for what? Some cocktail waitress you had a fling with twelve years ago?"

Anger boiled in Daniel's gut. Nobody told the great Daniel Cain what he could and couldn't do. No matter their good intentions. Pushing from his desk, he circled to stand behind it. "I don't plan on going to her home church again."

"But you intend to see her?" Thomas approached, his face reddening. "She's trouble, Daniel. She nearly ruined you once and she'll do it again."

Daniel stared at him, too angry to respond.

"You owe me." Thomas pointed a finger at him. "You wouldn't be here, you wouldn't have all this, if not for *me*."

Daniel should have seen that one coming. Even if it was true, it was a cheap shot coming from a friend. But certainly one Thomas used often to get his way. With Daniel's background and grades, he would have never been accepted into seminary if not for Thomas' father, a deacon in the Lutheran church, who spoke up for him.

Daniel uttered a low growl. "How long are you going to hold that over me? You could always start your own church and make it to D.C. yourself."

Frowning, Thomas sank into a chair. "We had a deal. You have the charm and charisma and I have the brains and connections." He leaned forward on his knees. "So then listen to me. Stop seeing Smokes. We've come too far to throw it all away."

*For He shall give His angels charge over you, to keep you in all your ways. In their hands they shall bear you up, lest you dash your foot against a stone.*
*Psalm 91:11-12 (NKJV)*

# Chapter 12

Angelica could not shake the feeling of dread that had darkened her spirit ever since she'd crawled out of bed two hours ago. Not even reading her Bible and spending nearly an hour in prayer had lifted the foreboding. Maybe it was because today she would be forced to spend the day with Daniel at SeaWorld. And even worse, her son would. Though, in all honesty, Isaac seemed more excited than he had in a long time when she'd tucked him in last night. Which only increased her fears. She didn't want him getting attached to Daniel. It was one thing if God wanted her to help Daniel and quite another to involve her son. He was too vulnerable to be taken in by the charming Daniel Cain. More than a dozen times in the past week, she'd wanted to call Daniel and cancel, but each time, she'd hesitated...how could she disappoint her son?

Now, as she switched to the independent news station she normally watched and opened the fridge to see what they had for breakfast, she determined that after today, she would keep her son as far away from Daniel as possible.

Unfortunately, the fridge was nearly bare. Grabbing a half loaf of bread, she slammed the door shut as the news blared—something about a NASA warning issued for incoming asteroids.

"How can you listen to that crap?" Leigh ambled into the kitchen, rubbing her eyes, her bunny slippers scuffing across the floor.

"Good morning to you, too." Angelica smiled.

Grabbing a mug, Leigh poured herself some coffee. "Why don't you listen to the regular news?" She spooned honey into her cup and stirred, then leaned back against the counter and took a sip. "Aww. Nectar of the gods."

Angelica dropped the bread down on the counter and withdrew two slices as the newscaster droned on about earth entering a period of increased asteroid activity and a mysterious planet X. "I told you the mainstream news is all state propaganda. They're not telling us the truth. Only what they want us to know."

Leigh shrugged. "Maybe. But at least it doesn't scare the heck out of me."

Angelica popped the bread in the toaster. "So, you'd rather be lied to?"

"Yes. I prefer my head in the sand." She smiled and sipped more coffee.

The talking head continued, "In other news, the famine in the Midwest is growing increasingly worse. Farmland that used to be covered in lush grain is now dry and arid, and farmers are abandoning their land to move to the city." Pictures of desert-like landscape filled the screen.

"See? More bad news." Leigh poured herself more coffee.

"At least it explains why food is so expensive."

The news continued, "Threats to annihilate Israel are mounting from a new alliance of nations—Turkey, Iran, Libya, and Russia, among the most prominent. Yet despite the looming war, the Jewish people continue to build their third temple right beside the Al-Aqsa Mosque."

"Why should we care what's going on in Israel?" Leigh shuffled across the floor and sat at the dining room table. "We have enough problems here."

The toast popped and Angelica buttered it, slipped it in the oven on warm, and then put another two slices in the toaster...all the while praying silently for what to say next. "Do you know that God in the real Bible told us all of this would happen?"

Leigh rolled her eyes. "Yeah, right."

"I'm serious. I can show you. He told us asteroids would strike the earth in the book of Revelation. In Matthew, Jesus told us there would be wars, earthquakes, famines, and diseases, even signs in the sky, and a host of other events. And these nations threatening Israel?" Angelica gestured toward the TV screen. "They are all listed in Ezekiel thirty-eight."

"No, they aren't."

"I'll show you. If you'll let me?" Angelica gave her friend a questioning look.

"Okay," her roommate finally said, her lips slanting.

Dashing into her room, spirit soaring, Angelica brought out the Holy Scriptures, flipped them open to Ezekiel and read the passage to Leigh. Thankfully, Angelica had done her homework on the archaic names of the nations and could identify who they were today.

Leigh sat back in her chair, an unreadable expression on her face.

"And the temple they are building now, it was foretold in both Daniel and Matthew."

Leigh shook her head. "They musta added this stuff in afterward."

"The original Bible has not changed for thousands of years. Many scholars have proven that. But at the very least, you know it hasn't changed for the past ten years since I've had it, right?"

Something registered in Leigh's eyes then, a flicker of light, a spark of understanding, that made Angelica smile and add, "Who else can tell the future but God?"

*Oh, Lord, please help her see.*

Leigh was about to say something when Joel dashed into the room, stuffed elephant in hand. "Mommy!"

Leigh swept him up in her arms as Isaac ambled behind, yawning and shouting. "SeaWorld today!"

And that one little phrase managed to steal all the joy from Angelica.

Seven hours later, Angelica could not deny that Isaac was having the time of his life. When he had turned five, he had proudly announced that he wanted to be a marine biologist. Since then, not a year passed in which he hadn't begged her to take him to SeaWorld. But she never had the money. Not only was the park expensive, but it was a three-hour drive there and back, and Angelica's car was not in the best of shape. The last thing she needed was to be stranded on the interstate with a child and no money.

But in Daniel's limo, they had made the trip in under three hours. *And* in the lap of luxury. Which was another exciting adventure for Isaac as he examined every cool feature of the car and waved to passersby, pretending to be a movie star.

Yet, after four hours in the park, Angelica realized there was no way to see everything in just one day. So far they'd only seen two shows, the orca whale and dolphins, and five exhibits—the manatees, Turtle Trek, Shark Encounter, Stingray Lagoon, and the penguins. Now, as Daniel and Isaac stood in line to go on some roller coaster called the Manta, she couldn't help but notice how talkative Isaac was, how often he glanced up at Daniel and smiled, and how easily the two of them kidded back and forth.

They even looked like father and son as they moved past the attendant, same casual gait, same lift of their shoulders. Cringing, she gripped the railing and closed her eyes. *Father, I can't handle this. Please help me...give me wisdom.* Casting a smile at Daniel's bodyguard, she found a seat and waited for the ride to finish.

During lunch, when Isaac had been busy feeding ducks, Angelica had asked Daniel what his thoughts were on the healing he'd witnessed at the beach. She had hoped he would bring it up himself, but no such luck. At least he hadn't laughed at the absurdity, warned her, or shrugged off the incident as hocus-pocus. Instead, he appeared genuinely interested. He even asked her questions about the identity of the man who was healed and how they knew he had been truly crippled.

"I never saw him before," she had answered. "But why would he fake his paralysis? What purpose would the miracle serve anyone? There was no money exchanged, no one benefited but the man who can now walk."

He rubbed his jaw. "Well, actually it might bring more people to your Saturday meetings."

"Yes, but we don't charge money. We minister completely for free." She set down her lemonade. "Why fake something to draw others to come for healing if the entire thing is a sham? It doesn't make sense."

He had nodded then, confusion in his eyes, and gripped her hand. "Please be patient, Angel, I'm just not sure yet."

His hand felt so good, so familiar, all strength and warmth circling hers. And she remembered how this man had always made her feel safe. A tingle traveled from her belly outward, and she pulled her hand away. But when she lifted her gaze, she found him staring at her...just like he used to...as if, even after all these years, their souls were still connected.

Thank God, Isaac had darted up at that moment. "Mom, do ya got more bread? The ducks are hungry!"

His smile made both her and Daniel laugh.

The ride—and her reminiscing—came to a halt as she spotted the two of them heading her way, giving each other fist pumps.

"Mom, Mr. Cain said he'd buy me an ice cream sundae."

She gave Daniel a look of disapproval. "After the popcorn, hamburger, and churros? You'll never eat dinner."

"Aw, come on, *Mom*." Daniel gave her that charming grin of his. "It's not every day you go to SeaWorld."

She sighed. "Very well." And off they strolled through the crowd, the heat of the day suddenly increasing her desire for ice cream with each step they took.

"Lookie, Mr. Cain!" Isaac darted to a railing behind which several flamingos stood knee-deep in a pond. Daniel joined him, the two of them leaning over the railing discussing the oddity of pink birds who stood on one leg.

And standing there, seeing Daniel in his T-shirt and jeans, laughing and being his witty self, unwanted memories flooded Angelica, sweeping away the past twelve years as if they'd never happened. They were at Disney World, his one-year anniversary gift to her, standing in line for the Pirates of the Caribbean—her favorite ride—for the twentieth time that day. Even though it wasn't *his* favorite ride, he went on it over and over just for her. Even after she relieved him of any obligation.

"No. I want to be with you," he had said. "Besides, I love watching your expressions. You're like a little kid in there." He had rubbed his finger down her cheek like he usually did and kissed her.

Even now, Angelica couldn't help but smile at the memory. They'd had the time of their life, running around the park, going on every ride, watching every show, eating themselves sick with junk food. She had given her heart and soul to this man, who, as she glanced at him now, looked nearly the same today as he had then, only *better.* And her heart did an unexpected flip in her chest.

That he bonded so well with her son didn't help the sensation.

She shoved it down and stared at the bodyguard standing off to the side. Good. He would remind her that Daniel was *not* the same man. And that no matter how kind he was, he would only corrupt her son.

"Dinner of champions." Daniel announced as he set down his spoon, eliciting a giggle from Isaac, who had long since finished his sundae and was squirming in his seat.

Angel shook her head and pushed away her half-finished bowl. "What happened to your healthy diet?" She teased.

"I took your advice and decided to give myself a break. Though"—he patted his stomach—"I'll have to hit the gym extra hard tomorrow."

"Not that you need to." She smiled, her eyes admiring him, and Daniel warmed beneath the compliment. Suddenly, he felt like he was twenty-one again and in love for the first time. The *only* time, if he admitted it.

He could hardly take his eyes off her as she sat across from him with the sun setting behind her in swaths of red and gold, the wind fingering her blond hair, her sea-moss eyes surrounded by lashes as thick as a forest, and that cute little nose of hers. She looked angelic. Maybe she *was* an angel. For she made him feel something he hadn't felt in years. Alive.

What surprised Daniel even more was how much he liked Isaac. Sure, he'd always wanted kids, but if he were honest, most of the ones he'd met annoyed the heck out of him. Isaac was a joy to be around—fun, witty, interesting, and fascinated by everything around him. How lucky Angel was to have such a son.

How lucky Daniel was to spend the day with them, for he couldn't remember having this much fun in a long while. His

life for the past ten years had been all work and business—
gaining converts, planning programs, handling the business
of the church, counseling, speaking, writing…making his
way up the ecclesiastical ladder, as Thomas called it. Even
his spare time had been devoted to working out and eating
right. No time for fun when one was headed toward a seat of
power in D.C.

Isaac leapt from his chair and tugged on Angel's arm.
"Mom, can we go see the mantas?"

Easing hair behind her ear, she shielded her eyes and
glanced over her shoulder at the sun. "It's getting late, and
we have a long ride home."

"No worries, my driver will get us back in no time."
Leaning toward her, Daniel pointed at Isaac and whispered,
"He'll probably sleep in the car." A whiff of her scent drifted
over him, and he felt his body react. Ah, the memories it
invoked. Baby powder. That was it. She always smelled like
baby powder.

As if sensing his reaction, she moved away and faced her
son. "Okay, the manta rays and then we head home."

"Thanks, Mom!" Isaac tugged her to stand, and the three
of them started off, Isaac taking the lead.

"Thank you for being so kind to him," Angel said,
watching her son with a smile. "He's really enjoying
himself."

"I'm glad. Like I said, he's a good boy. Makes me wish I
started my own family." *Makes me wish I'd started one with
you.*

"I suppose you've been rather busy for that."

Busy, yes, but honestly, he hadn't found a woman worthy
of his time. Until now. But how could a man of his position
pursue a woman caught in an illegal cult? His church would
never accept her. Nor would anyone in D.C. In fact, if the
truth were known, she'd be arrested. Thomas was right. If
Daniel continued seeing her, he'd lose everything.

Yet, as she gazed up at him now with her innocent smile and admiring eyes, he almost thought it was worth it.

Almost.

Why couldn't he have it all? He was Daniel Cain. With his charm and skills of persuasion, he had brought thousands of converts into the church. Surely, he could convince one woman of the error of her ways, get her to leave that ridiculous home church, and break all ties with those fanatics.

Then, it would be no trouble at all to convince Thomas that Angelica Smoke would make Daniel the perfect wife.

Baliel, Nazare, and Zarene followed close to their charges, keeping their eyes focused and their swords at the ready. They'd received a warning from the Commander of Heaven's Armies that the enemy had planned an assault on those under their protection. They'd also felt it themselves— a malevolent darkness looming nearby. Hence, they had kept conversation limited as they maintained a vigilance over the three humans.

Nazare, however, had briefly expressed his joy at seeing Daniel bond with the boy—at their camaraderie and the easy way they conversed. Baliel and Zarene had agreed, albeit tentatively due to what they all knew were Daniel's ulterior motives.

"He uses Isaac to get to her," Zarene said, angry that his charge was being manipulated. "The boy needs a father, one who truly loves him."

"He has a Father," Baliel said sternly.

"Of course. But I speak of an earthy influence. You know how important good earthly fathers are to these humans. Without them, so many drift into darkness."

"Agreed. How fragile are these children of God," Nazare said as they followed the trio into the manta ray exhibit and watched Isaac study the rays with glee.

Zarene drew closer to the lad and smiled proudly. "He loves the Father's sea creatures."

"He is gifted for their care. Perhaps he will be put in charge of them in the next age," Baliel commented.

Zarene smiled.

Nazare huffed. "If only Daniel would respond to Angelica's leading."

"Be patient, my friend. The Father has a plan."

They continued on in silence as the three humans walked through the exhibit and enjoyed all the various displays, including a huge 360-degree aquarium that formed a circle in the center of the room.

"If they think this is wonderful, wait until they see heaven," Zarene said, hovering over Isaac.

Nazare chuckled. "Indeed."

Finally, the humans had seen enough and headed out into the crowd once again.

A chill shivered down Zarene's back, and he gripped the hilt of his sword and glanced around. Baliel and Nazare felt it too and did the same. The human guard was staring at a female dressed in tight shorts, oblivious to the danger, while their three charges strolled down the walkway, unaware.

Zarene scanned the crowd, ignoring the demons that surrounded so many of the people. He spotted an unusual darkness among the throng—moving slowly and stealthily, like a human made of tar. A man stood within its shadows, barely discernible through the black sludge. His narrowed gaze was upon their charges.

"That's the one," Nazare said.

"I'm on it." Baliel pulled his sword. "I'll hold him back. You two protect them."

Nazare and Zarene dashed away as Baliel approached the demon-infested man and sliced through the blackness.

Otherworldly screeches of agony filled the air as the demons drew their blades to counter his attack. *So many!* Baliel slashed this way and that, dipping in low, then spinning to meet another blade. Nazare appeared by his side, and the two charged at least a dozen specters coming at them from all directions.

Baliel thrust his blade through a particularly thick, oozing demon, hitting his mark. Shrieking, the beast crawled off to lick his wounds. Nazare attacked a pair of short, sharp-fanged specters, their eyes dripping blood, their mouths foaming. *Hatred and Murder.* He'd met them before. They growled, teeth sharp and jagged. He swung his sword low and met both their blades with an ear-piercing crack. They fought with such ferocity, Nazare was forced to retreat. He glanced at Baliel for help, but his friend fought against three other dark spirits.

Nazare charged them again, slashing and thrusting, yet they refused to release the human, who relentlessly continued forward. Reaching inside his shirt, he pulled out a pistol. Nazare heightened his attack, glancing over his shoulder at Zarene who protected the humans, blade drawn.

"There are too many of them!" Nazare shouted.

"Keep fighting, my friend." Baliel slashed another demon in half.

The man cocked his pistol.

"No!" Nazare shouted and started for Daniel as Zarene did his best to shield the three humans.

The *pop pop* of gunfire crackled the air.

*At that time many will turn away from the faith and will betray and hate each other, and many false prophets will appear and deceive many people. Because of the increase of wickedness, the love of most will grow cold, but the one who stands firm to the end will be saved.*
*Matthew 24:10-13 (NIV)*

# Chapter 13

A strange sensation came over Daniel. He couldn't explain it. A foreboding, an anxiousness that was completely foreign to him. Glancing casually behind them, he spotted his bodyguard smiling and laughing with a young woman. Great. Some protection he was.

Daniel scanned the crowd. Something caught his eye. A man—tall, thick-boned, a gauge hanging from one earlobe—staring straight at Daniel.

With a gun in his hand!

"Noooooo!" Diving for Angel and Isaac, he shoved them to the ground and covered them with his body as the eerie *pop pop* of a gun ricocheted through the throng.

Someone shouted, "Gun!" and hysteria ensued as people screamed and scattered in all directions, pushing and shoving and tripping over each other in an effort to escape. The man with the pistol was swallowed in the mob. Daniel's bodyguard stood frozen in place, gun drawn, staring at the chaos.

"What are you doing? Go after him!" Daniel shouted before turning to gather Angel and Isaac in a tight embrace. "Are you both all right?"

Angel was shaking. Isaac snapped wide eyes to Daniel.

"Yes, I think so." Her voice quavered as she frantically brushed hair from her son's face. "Are you hurt?"

Isaac shook his head. "What happened?" Though his lips trembled, the boy stood and helped his mom to her feet before falling into her embrace.

"Let's get out of here." Daniel glanced around, his one thought to get Angel and her son to safety. Who knew if there wasn't another shooter or if the first one wouldn't come back? And now his inept bodyguard was gone too. In fact, there wasn't a soul in sight. Music still eerily played over the intercoms, interrupted by a voice announcing that the sea lion show would begin in ten minutes...as if nothing at all had happened.

But something *had* happened. Someone had tried to kill him! Again.

Angel grabbed her purse and her son and gazed up at him in disbelief. "You saved our lives."

He shook his head and glanced in the direction his bodyguard had run.

"You covered us with your body," she insisted.

"Just a reflex."

"Not many people would risk themselves like that." She drew her son close, her eyes moistening.

Daniel smiled at the affection he saw there, suddenly glad he had played the hero. So unlike him. In all honesty, he'd always looked out first for number one. But in that split second, when he'd seen the gun, all he could think about was Angel and Isaac.

"Why did that man shoot at us?" Isaac clung to his mother as Daniel hurried them away.

"Dunno. Lots of crazies in the world." Daniel put a hand on Angel's back and glanced around just to make sure no more gunmen were about. The sooner they reached the limo, the better.

Unfortunately, they were stopped by park security and then by the police, and Daniel and Angel had to give their statements before they left. An hour later, as they were climbing into the back of the limo, Daniel's bodyguard ran up, shook his head as if to say he hadn't found the shooter, and sat up front, frowning at the angry scowl Daniel gave him. And for good reason. Daniel would fire him as soon as they returned.

The trip dragged on in silence as Angel embraced her son, calming him with whispers and kisses to his forehead. Finally, the boy drifted off to sleep, and Angel lovingly laid him down on the cushioned seat.

"I'm sorry things turned out this way," Daniel said, angry that their beautiful day had been ruined.

She gazed at her son. "Don't be. He had a great time."

"Until he almost got shot." Daniel grunted and ran a hand through his hair.

She faced him with concern. "Does that happen often? I assume whoever it was, was after you."

"No." His voice came out a little too loud, and he quickly lowered it, glancing at Isaac. "Only once before. Just some crazy at a crusade at FAU stadium. Guess being famous has its price." And he now wondered if that price would be losing the woman he loved. No mother in her right mind would put her child in danger by hanging out with a man who people wanted to kill.

"God took care of us." She smiled.

Hope ignited in his heart. "He did. And He will continue."

Her green eyes lit with excitement. "Did you see the angels too?"

"What angels?"

"Never mind." She hugged herself. "It's been a long day."

Daniel glanced at Isaac again. "He was as brave as any man. What a great kid. His father doesn't know what he's missing."

For some reason, that seemed to upset her as she glanced out the window, her eyes moistening.

*Stupid, stupid, Daniel.* "I'm sorry. I wasn't thinking. You must have loved him very much."

Still, she said nothing for several minutes until she shifted angry eyes his way. "It was a great day, Daniel, but you and I"—she pointed between them—"Whatever this is. It has got to stop."

That night, Angelica didn't dream of assassins or dolphins, as one would expect. No, her mind was full of strange scenes that made no sense. Random acts plucked from a play or a storybook, yet without rhyme or reason— Daniel and Isaac tossing a baseball back and forth, Angelica sitting in the grass, leaning her head on Daniel's shoulder, Isaac and Daniel doing cannonballs into Daniel's pool, the two of them fishing off a pier, Angel sitting in the front pew of Daniel's church, watching him preach. And finally, a mystical scene of the three of them, walking hand in hand through a field of the most beautiful flowers she'd ever seen. The sky was a deep azure blue with crimson streaks, and butterflies flitted about the flowers, their wings dipped in shimmering gold filigree.

Then they were at the beach and thick black clouds advanced on the horizon, growing larger and larger...rolling toward them. Pitchforks of silver lightning shot out from the darkness in all directions. A trumpet sounded. The ground shook. The sand shifted like water, a building crumbled to the earth in a cloud of dust, a mother wept over her dead child, and an otherworldly creature appeared—tall, scaly, powerful.

She woke with a start just before dawn. A muggy breeze stirred the curtains and cooled the sweat on her neck as she tossed off the covers and dropped to her knees.

"Father, what does this mean? Why am I with Daniel in these visions?" She breathed out a sigh. "And what is coming on this earth? Please, please help us." She leaned her head on her bed, arms stretched out, palms toward heaven, waiting to hear… "Father, I can't see Daniel again. It hurts too much." Tears slid down her cheek onto her sheet. "Please don't ask me to see him. It isn't good for Isaac. Please."

The gentle lap of waves rippled over her ears, joining the first chorus of birds as they welcomed a new day from their Creator. She felt His presence before she heard Him speak within her.

*I love you, daughter. All is well.*

"I love you, too. But things don't seem well. What is coming on this earth?"

*Never fear, for I am with you. Time is short, precious one. You must warn him. I have chosen you.*

She pressed her forehead into the soft mattress and sobbed. "Why me? He doesn't even listen to me."

But he *had* risked himself to save her and Isaac. She still couldn't believe it. Yes, the old Daniel she knew might have done that. But this one? She wished he had seen the angels protecting them—three of them, armed with swords and shields, her angel and Isaac's among them. Powerful beings. Protective.

She leaned her head in her hands, staring at the damp circle of tears on her sheets. Maybe deep inside the narcissistic preacher there was still some of the man she'd once loved. Which only made her want to stay away from him all the more.

Not to mention she wouldn't put Isaac in danger. She couldn't.

"Surely, you don't want me to risk my son?"

But no answer came. There was none needed as a vision of Jesus on the cross blazed across her mind. God had risked His own Son—had piled the sins of the world on Him and watched Him suffer and die. For *her*...for *Isaac*.

Rising, she sat on the bed and batted tears from her face.

A breeze tossed a curl across her cheek and swept it behind her, as if God Himself were easing her hair aside. His comfort surrounded her, such love...such overwhelming love blanketed over her, filling her soul, body, and spirit, until she felt her heart would burst. Oh, if only the lost could feel this love, they'd give up everything to possess it. Finally, her tears of pain turned to joy, and she spent the next hour praising God and reading His Word. Nothing was impossible for her. She knew that now. As long as God was with her.

That night, the Mermaid Den was its usual hovel of havoc. As she traversed the many tables delivering drinks, she *felt*, rather than saw, a multitude of dark spirits that had entered with the patrons—Suicide, Alcoholism, Pornography, Lust, Greed, Insomnia, Addiction, Hopelessness, and Rejection, to name the worst of the bunch. On occasion, she could see them glaring at her with malicious eyes and evil intent. But she didn't fear them. Instead, she kept in constant prayer and offered as much joy and hope as she could to each person she spoke with. A few responded with curious glances and smiles, and after ensuring Sal was nowhere around, she would simply tell them there was a God who loved them more than they could ever know, and He wanted to help them.

Some within earshot laughed at her. Others cursed. But at least she got the truth out there. After all, Father said time was short, and she didn't intend to waste a second of it.

"One Margarita no salt, a White Russian, Mexican Coffee, Gin and Tonic, a Long Island Iced Tea, and a

Cosmo," she spouted off the list of orders to Greg, standing behind the bar.

Without looking up, he sped off to work and returned quickly with the first drink. Reaching over the bar she touched his arm. "Everything okay?"

He finally looked up at her with eyes that seemed vacant and lost. "Yeah." He flashed a fake smile and attempted to tug away from her.

She held fast. "I mean it. Something's up."

"Just don't feel well. Tired of all this, I guess."

"I don't pay you two to chat!" Sal's angry voice blared above the music, sending Greg speeding off.

"Give him a break, Sal." Angelica set the drink on her tray. "He's not feeling well."

"Really?" Sal sat on the stool and gave her his usual skin-crawling glance-over. "He looks fine to me. And so do you, I might add."

Ignoring him, she started loading up the drinks Greg was delivering, praying the man would stop undressing her with his eyes.

"Oh my God!" an elderly man sitting at the bar pointed at the flat-screen hanging over the rows of alcohol. "Turn that up!"

Greg picked up the remote as some of the patrons drew closer. A raging fire took up most of the screen. People ran back and forth, looking terrified, bewildered, shocked, and unsure of what was happening.

"The Chicago O'Hare airport has been attacked!" the newscaster said. "Multiple explosions have been reported throughout the airport. There was at least one suicide bomber, according to an eyewitness."

Angelica's heart nearly imploded as scenes of injured people passed across the screen, including some screaming for their lost loved ones. Closing her eyes, she began praying for the injured, for law enforcement, and for the emergency medical teams.

"Hey, where's my drink?" a drunken man yelled from one of her tables.

"Get to work, Angelica." Sal ordered, staring at the screen with a scowl. "It's horrible, but these things happen every couple of months. Nothing we can do."

In fact, after hearing the initial report, most of the people went back to their tables and their drinks, continuing to party as if hundreds of people, maybe even thousands, had not just died.

*Because of the increase of wickedness, the love of most will grow cold.* Angelica remembered a verse from Matthew. "Father, forgive them," she whispered as she delivered her tray of drinks.

During the next few hours, Angelica did her best to do her job while keeping an ear to the TV for additional information. Of course, no one knew very much at this point. They were still searching for survivors and trying to get statements out of traumatized witnesses. Sal was right about one thing. These attacks were coming so frequently across the world that people were becoming immune to them. Another day, another terrorist attack, and another hundred or so people cast into eternity.

Between drink deliveries, she tried to talk with Greg, but he seemed to retreat even further into a shell after the bad news. Instead, she merely told him she was praying for him, which at least gained her a smile. She hoped he would join her in the break room as he had before, but instead, she spent her half hour alone, rubbing her feet and eating a tuna fish sandwich. And of course, praying. Returning to the floor, she nearly bumped into Melody as the woman hurried to the bar, empty tray in hand.

"Hey, Mels, haven't had a chance to say hi tonight."

"Yeah, it's been crazy busy." She blew a black curl from her forehead and hurried along.

"How's Jackson doing?" Angelica followed her to the bar to get a tray.

Halting, Melody stared at her as if she'd asked if her son were from outer space. "You remembered he was sick?"

"Of course. I've been praying for him."

Melody smiled. "He's good. No more fever or throwing up. Back to school today, actually."

"I'm glad to hear it."

Slamming down her tray on the bar, Melody handed Greg her drink order, giving Angelica a moment to study the single mother, asking the Father if there was anything else she could pray about, or anything she could say to lead the woman closer to Him. But something wasn't right. Angelica felt it in her spirit, a sense of dismay, sorrow, and loss. But from what? She sought God's spirit within her and instantly, the vision appeared—as it usually did, in the form of a small TV screen hanging in the air. As Angelica watched the scenes unfold, her heart turned to stone, and it took everything within her to keep her emotions from her face. Finally, the vision disappeared, and she drew a deep breath and faced Melody.

"You normally drive down East Broward to get home, right?"

Melody placed drinks on her tray. "Yeah, why?"

"Don't go that way tonight."

"What are you talking about?" Sighing, she picked up her tray as Greg wiped down the counter, listening.

"Something bad is going to happen. Just don't go that way. Promise me, 'kay?"

Melody shook her head and laughed. "Okay, Twilight Zone. But just for you." She winked and headed out. Greg shook his head and walked away.

"That's me, Lord. Making friends and influencing people." With a sigh, Angelica headed to a table of thirsty-looking college kids, wondering if she was doing any good at all.

By the end of the night, she wanted to crawl in a hole for a year. She'd been insulted, lusted after, propositioned, had made zero headway with Greg, laughed at by Melody, and been hit on by Sal. Twice. All for a lousy one hundred NWOs in tips. At this rate, she wouldn't be able to buy food for next week.

Hiking her purse on her shoulder, she exited the back door into the balmy Florida air and headed for her car. *Father, I know You'll provide for my needs as You promised.* One good thing Sal did was keep the parking lot well-lit so she wouldn't be surprised by criminals lurking around. Except…there was a man standing against her car. Stopping, she kept her distance and studied him. Despite looking familiar, he didn't appear threatening. Nor was he Daniel. His hair was too light and his body too thin.

"Can I help you?" she said from where she stood, ready to bolt back into the club if need be.

"It's me, Smokes." He pushed from the car.

"Thomas?" No one else ever called her Smokes. She slowly approached him, noting his fancy suit and Italian shoes. "You know you can get robbed out here looking like that."

He snorted, his eyes shifting to the club. "Really done well for yourself, Smokes."

"What do you want?"

"Apparently, you didn't get my last warning."

"I got it." She waited, fingering the mace in her purse. "The problem is I don't take orders from you."

"You did the last time."

She sighed and stormed toward her car. "Yes. I stayed away just like you said. Just like *he* wanted. And you were right. He became someone important."

"Then why are you intent on ruining him? Especially now that he's successful."

She frowned. If she wasn't a Christian, she'd slap his face. "You know I never cared about that stuff."

"Fame? Money? A comfortable house? Who wouldn't want all that?"

"Are you done?"

"Stay away from him." His tone sent a shiver down her back.

"As I told you before, that's what I'm trying to do. He is the one who keeps coming after me."

"You could have said no to SeaWorld."

Yes, she could have. *Should* have. But she hated this man's arrogance. Twelve years ago, he was nothing but a scared boy with big dreams who lived in Daniel's shadow. Now, just because he wore an expensive suit and probably had a mansion like Daniel's, he thought he could tell her what to do. But he was just the same scared little boy. She lifted her chin. "I answer to a higher authority than you."

He laughed and gave her a spiteful look. "In your pathetic little world, there is no higher authority."

She clicked her lock and opened her car door. "Good night, Thomas."

"This is your last warning," he said.

"Or what?"

"Well, let's just say, it would sure be a tragedy to leave your son an orphan." Grinning, he turned and sauntered away, whistling as if he owned the world.

Terror robbed Angelica of every last ounce of her breath.

*But before all these things, they will lay their hands on you and persecute you, delivering you up to the synagogues and prisons. You will be brought before kings and rulers for My name's sake.*
Luke 21:12 (NKJV)

# Chapter 14

The next week passed in a haze of mundane activities—and terror, if Angelica admitted it. Thomas had threatened her life...hadn't he? She still couldn't believe she'd heard him correctly. He was definitely no saint, but she had a hard time believing he'd stoop to murder. He was probably just trying to scare her away from Daniel. It was working. Now, more than ever, she never wanted to see him again.

Surely God would find someone else to help Daniel—someone who posed no threat to Thomas. Wouldn't that be for the best? Maybe even Thomas could be helped as well. Yet when she had made her case before God, heaven remained silent. Or maybe she just didn't want to hear the answer. Regardless, she would not risk her son's life—for anything or anyone. Isaac was everything to her, her reason for getting up in the morning, for wanting to survive each day. The thought of leaving him alone to face this crazy world terrified her more than him dying. At least in death, he would be with the Lord.

Daniel, of course, had not honored her last request to leave her and Isaac alone. He had called, texted, sent cards and flowers, but so far, she had managed to successfully avoid him in person.

"Father, if you want me to see Daniel again, You're going to have to set it up. There's too many reasons not to see him and none I can think of to continue." She stared into her empty fridge, continuing to pray silently that the illustrious preacher would give up on her soon and move onto his next conquest.

The lock clicked, the door flew open, and in barreled Isaac, Joel, and finally Leigh, looking gorgeous despite her baggy sweats and chaotic hair. Plopping down her purse on the table, she brushed past Angelica and glanced into the fridge.

"No soda." She slammed it shut and faced Angelica, her black hair falling in waves around her face.

"Thanks for picking up Isaac," Angelica said, then scanned the room for her son. "Hey, mister." She raised her brows and held out her arms.

"Aww, Mom." He dashed to her and gave her a hug as Joel grabbed the remote and flipped on the TV.

"How was school?"

"Fine," he gave his usual answer. Easing out of his backpack, he dropped it on the table. "Can I watch TV before I do my homework?"

"Sure. But only a half hour."

Angelica faced Leigh. "Sorry about the soda. I know it's your favorite after a hard day at work."

Leigh attempted a smile and glanced at her son with the same look Angelica imagined she so often glanced at Isaac—extreme love *and* extreme concern.

"You look tired," Angelica said.

"I am. We're out of food."

"I know. I'll make a run to the store. Do you have any money? I have thirty notes, but that won't be enough."

"I'll see what I can scrounge up." Leigh dropped in a chair at the table and sighed. "Everything is getting so expensive."

Angelica nodded. "I remember the days when the fridge and cupboards were full, and we had to force ourselves to stop eating everything we wanted."

Leigh began sifting through her purse for coins. "I suppose this is one of your prophecies?"

"Actually, yes... food shortages, famine. It's all prophesied in the Bible for the last days."

"Does this God of yours ever give any good news?" Leigh dropped a handful of coins on the table and went fishing for more.

"He does. That's His specialty." Angelica leaned against the kitchen counter. "The word 'gospel' means good news. All this trouble we are seeing leads up to the best news of all. Jesus will return to set the world right. There will be no more pain or sickness or sorrow. No more hunger and empty fridges. And no more death."

"Hmm. Sounds wonderful. If it's true."

Angelica smiled. At least Leigh's tone was not angry or defiant as it usually was when discussing God.

Leigh added more coins to her pile. "Well, at least we don't have to stand in those long food lines out in the Florida heat for a bag of flour and some canned veggies."

"True. God has been good to us."

Strange noises coming from the TV raised her mother hackles, and she glanced in that direction to see two naked people in bed together on the screen. Darting into the living room, she leapt in front of the TV and switched the station. "That's enough for today."

"But we just started watching." Little Joel protested, no doubt oblivious to what he just witnessed.

Isaac's red face and wide eyes, on the other hand, indicated that he knew exactly what he had seen. She would have to discuss this with him later.

Angelica put her hands on her hips. "Go do your homework. Both of you."

Rising, Isaac scowled.

"I don't have any homework," Joel announced proudly, his innocent eyes staring up at her.

"Come here and draw Mommy a picture." Leigh grabbed paper and crayons from the shelf and placed them on the table while Isaac begrudgingly grabbed his backpack and trudged off.

Something fell from it onto the floor, and Angelica headed over to pick it up. "I wish you'd agree to cancel the cable."

"Yeah, you're probably right. I can't believe what they're putting on during the day."

Surprised at her roommate's response, Angelica halted and faced her.

"Not that there's anything wrong with sex," Leigh added. "It's perfectly natural, and they're gonna find out about it sooner or later." She lifted Joel into a seat and handed him a crayon.

"What's sex, Mommy?" he asked.

"Never mind that. Draw me something pretty."

Angelica gave her an incriminating look. "I'm sure you agree that your son is a tad bit too young to be exposed to it."

She shrugged. "Yeah, I guess."

"Jesus has finally arrived." A mocking voice from the TV announced, drawing both their gazes and a chuckle from Leigh.

Angelica cringed at the picture of a bearded man in a white robe wandering through the streets of London.

"Seems your God has come back just in time," Leigh teased.

"False messiahs were also foretold." Angelica headed for the TV set.

"An 8.2 earthquake has struck Morocco," the newscaster continued.

Grabbing the remote, she flipped off the TV. Enough bad news for one day. Making her way back to the kitchen, she leaned over to pick up the item Isaac had dropped.

And couldn't believe her eyes.

*Condoms.* "Isaac!" Her shout brought him dashing from his room.

"Where did you get these?"

A red tide rose up his neck and swamped his face. "They're handing them out at school, Mom. I didn't want them. Honest."

Angelica closed her eyes. "Okay. It's okay. Come here." Taking him in her arms, she kissed him on the forehead. "I love you."

"Love you back, Mom." And off he ran.

Leigh gave her a sideways look. "Kids his age are having sex these days."

"At ten? Is that even possible?" Angelica groaned as she opened the cupboard beneath the sink and tossed the condoms in the garbage. "Doesn't make it right."

Grabbing her cell, she called the school principal. The woman was impossible. No matter how ardently Angelica protested, she wouldn't budge. "Besides," she said. "It's a state mandate to hand out condoms to every child ten and up. You religious types want to avoid unwanted abortions, don't you?"

Angelica had informed her that no abortion was unwanted. It was a choice to murder a child, plain and simple. To which the woman said she had to go and hung up.

Leigh handed her twenty-nine notes and a handful of coins, one brow arched. "Didn't go well?"

Angelica took the money. "No, but I really didn't expect it to." Still, she had to try. Another thing she needed to talk to Isaac about—the sex talk. At moments like these, she longed for a father for him, one who could speak of such things from a godly man's perspective. Who was she kidding? *Every* moment since Isaac's birth, she had longed for a father for him, someone to help raise this precious boy. From the first time she looked at his sweet face, she'd been terrified to do it alone, unsure of herself, of her ability to be a good parent, to lead him down the right path.

Dropping the notes in her purse, she was about to leave when a knock sounded on the door. Her heart froze, praying it wasn't Daniel.

But it was Melody who entered when Leigh opened the door, a young boy in her arms and another about Joel's age clinging to her leg. Angelica hardly recognized her in her jeans and T-shirt with no makeup.

"Melody, what a surprise. What are you doing here?"

"I guess we've been on different shifts at work, but I couldn't wait another minute to thank you." She glanced at Leigh.

Angelica made introductions. "Thank me for what?"

"You saved my life."

The little boy sat at the table beside Joel and watched him draw.

Angelica smiled at the child in Melody's arms. "This must be Jackson."

"Yes. He's so much better." Melody kissed her son then stared at Angelica as if she were a ghost. "How did you know?"

"Know what?"

"That there was going to be a huge sinkhole on East Broward that night."

Leigh glanced up from helping Joel draw.

"Oh, that." Angelica smiled. "I was so glad to hear you avoided it. God revealed it to me that night at the Den."

"God?"

Angelica pulled out a chair for the lady who suddenly seemed wobbly on her feet. "Yes, who else?"

"I almost went that way," she mumbled. "But at the last minute, I thought about your warning."

"Wait a minute." Leigh pointed a red crayon at the lady. "You're trying to tell me that Angelica told you not to drive down East Broward before that sinkhole happened?"

Melody nodded. "Several hours before."

"Which proves there's a God." Angelica placed her hand on Melody's arm. "And that He cares about you."

Both the women gaped at her as she silently thanked God for the chance to bring Him glory.

That euphoria continued the next day at the beach with Anna, Robert, and Clay as they ministered to the crowd. She half expected Daniel to show up again, but for her son's sake, she was glad he didn't. Though, if she admitted it, a small part of her heart felt the pinch at the thought that he had probably moved on. What made it more difficult was that every day Isaac asked when they were going to see Daniel again. The look of expectation in her son's eyes nearly killed her, and she had tried to let him down gently by saying that Daniel was important and a very busy man.

Now, as she glanced at her son, dripping wet and board in hand, heading her way from the water, she smiled. Hopefully, he would soon forget all about the famous pastor.

Clay strummed his guitar as a crowd of people gathered close. Today, it was Robert's turn to recite Scripture, and he had chosen Isaiah 53, a messianic prophecy. Isaac joined them and dropped to the sand as the people listened with rapt attention to the words that described Jesus' suffering with precise accuracy—over 500 years before He was even born.

"He was oppressed and afflicted, yet he did not open his mouth; he was led like a lamb to the slaughter, and as a sheep before its shearers is silent, so he did not open his mouth," Robert continued.

An older woman began to cry.

"After he has suffered, he will see the light of life and be satisfied. By his knowledge my righteous servant will justify many, and he will bear their iniquities."

Robert finished the passage with his own testimony. Though Angelica had heard it a dozen times, she never grew tired of the story of how God had pulled him from drug addiction and gang violence, forgiven him of every sin, and given him new life and purpose.

"Not only that," Robert added, his eyes aglow. "But when my time here on earth is done, I will live forever with my Father in a beautiful place without evil, sorrow, or pain. And all you have to do to receive this free gift from God is repent of your sins, accept the sacrifice of Jesus, confess Him with your mouth, and follow Him the rest of your days. This life has only two doors that lead to eternity. Choose the right door."

What a gift this man had for evangelism. If Angelica wasn't already saved, she would go forward with the five people who now answered Robert's call to receive Jesus. As it was, she, along with Anna, Clay, and some of the others present, offered praise to God for the lives saved.

At the edge of the crowd, her angel appeared, along with others she didn't know. All of them were dancing and singing, leaping like little children and kicking up sand. What a glorious sight!

Until two police officers walked right through them and they disappeared.

"Break it up! Break it up!" one of them shouted. "What's going on here?"

One of the new converts dashed up to them, tears streaming down her cheeks. "I'm saved! I've met God!"

The man humphed and glanced at his partner, who was already pulling out his handcuffs and calling for backup.

"Get out of here!" The officer waved at the crowd and most of them scampered away. The few who didn't remained at a distance.

"We told you the next time we found you proselytizing on this beach, we'd arrest you."

"That you did, Officer." Robert turned around and flung his hands behind his back.

The other policeman hauled Clay to his feet, a bit too harshly, as other officers advanced toward them from the parking lot.

Angelica couldn't breathe. She drew Isaac close, her first thought to run away with him, but one of the policemen grabbed her arm and swung her around so fast, pain etched across her shoulders.

Cold steel encircled her wrists, and the handcuffs clicked shut.

*And you will be hated by all for My name's sake. But he who endures to the end will be saved.*
   Matthew 10:22 (NKJV)

# Chapter 15

Daniel pressed the BACK key on his keyboard and erased the sentence he'd just written. Garbage, pure garbage. An unintended growl rose in his throat. He'd been working on this speech for hours and only had two paragraphs written. And they weren't even good paragraphs.

It was all Angel's fault. Why couldn't he stop thinking about her? He could have his pick of women, yet here he was pining over a cocktail waitress like a lovesick college boy.

Ridiculous! The woman had made it plain she wanted nothing to do with him. Especially after he'd put her and Isaac in danger.

But he missed her. Terribly. He felt like he was twenty-two all over again standing in the rain at the coffee shop off Sunrise. For hours. And she'd never shown. Why was he putting himself through this again?

A knock on the door brought him relief from his thoughts, and he was glad to see his good friend Marley enter the room. Or was he? The poor man looked conflicted. And Daniel definitely didn't need any more conflict today.

Marley approached Daniel's desk, a thick book in hand.

"What's up, buddy?" Daniel's attempt to be cheerful had no effect on the man's contemplative look.

"I think we're doing this all wrong."

"Doing what wrong?"

"Everything. I've been studying the Bible."

Daniel chuckled, still hoping to lighten the man's mood. "Course you have, you're a pastor."

"No, I mean *really* studying it, asking the Holy Spirit to instruct me."

Daniel stared at him, fearing the worst, fearing he was becoming one of those illegal fanatics. "What are you talking about?"

"I'm talking about compromising with the world, about defying what God says"—he held up his Bible—"for the sake of political and cultural correctness."

Rising, Daniel circled his desk, his eyes on the Bible in his friend's hand, his suspicions rising. "Is that—"

"Yes." Marley nodded, his jaw stiff. "An old one. I've had it for a while."

Daniel squeezed the bridge of his nose and growled. "Do you know what could happen to us if someone found that in this church? I can't believe you!"

"I'm sorry, Daniel. Really." Marley sank into a chair and leaned forward on his knees. "I'll take it home today." He shook his head and stared at the carpet. "I've just...I've just not been feeling right about things...in my spirit, you know?" He looked up at Daniel.

No, Daniel didn't. At least not in his spirit. His heart was another matter. "Everything is fine with the church. I assure you. In fact, never better. We are doing good work here."

"Are we?"

Daniel closed his eyes, seeking his dwindling patience. "You gotta pull it together, man. Do you hear me? I can't have my youth pastor going all wacko on me."

"I know, Daniel. It's just that...well, we're supposed to make disciples, not fill pews. We're supposed to teach them to follow Jesus, to obey the Word of God, and from what I'm reading, God says that any form of immorality is a sin and an abomination to Him."

Daniel pointed at him. "That's exactly why they took out those verses. They scare people. None of us can be perfect, right? Even our good deeds are like filthy rags to God. I'm sure you read that verse as well. So, why fret about it? Accept the free gift of salvation and forgiveness of sins and then love everyone. Isn't that the real message of the Bible?"

"Yes, of course," Marley said, but his tone lacked conviction.

"Let's focus on God's love, goodness, and grace as we've been doing, not on His judgment and rejection. That stuff only turns people off. It's exclusive and not inclusive, and God is an inclusive God." Daniel offered his friend his most reassuring smile.

Frowning, Marley pushed to his feet and headed for the door. Before he reached it, he spun around. "You know, I think we're close to the end, Daniel."

"What end?"

"The end of this age. You know, when Jesus comes back."

"Yeah." Daniel waved him off. "People have been saying that for hundreds of years."

"But this time is different. We should be warning people, telling them to repent and get ready."

The phrase *get ready* reminded Daniel of Angel's first warning to him, but he shrugged it off. "Listen, Marley." He used his boss tone. "Take that Bible and get rid of it. That's an order." He'd had enough of this religious craziness. Not only was it bad for his church, but even allowing Marley to speak about it could land them both in jail.

After Marley left, Daniel sank back into his comfy chair and stared once again at the computer monitor, feeling a headache rise.

"Good. I hope you're working on your speech for the prayer breakfast."

Daniel looked up to see Thomas' head poking in the open door.

"I'm trying." Daniel sat back in his chair and waved his friend inside.

"I won't stay long. I'm just checking on your progress. It needs to be proofed a couple of times before we leave for D.C. You know that's in a month, don't you?"

"No need to remind me." Daniel stared at the picture of his mother on his desk, wishing she hadn't died all those years ago. Her strong faith was such an inspiration to Daniel, and she always knew the right thing to say, the right advice to give—the right way to comfort him after his father had belittled and berated him into dust. Sort of like he felt now. After Angelica's rejection and now this pressure to write the speech of his life, to be great and charismatic when inside he felt like the loser his dad always told him he was.

Thomas patted the hair at his temples. "Then I also don't need to remind you how important this exposure is. If you nail this, everyone in D.C. will know your name."

Daniel rose and walked to the side bar for coffee. "Want some?"

"No, I'm good."

"Then what is it?" Daniel asked as he turned around. "Something's on your mind."

Thomas fingered a crystal dove paperweight on Daniel's desk. "It's just that for the past week you've been moping around here like you just found out you have cancer or something."

Daniel sipped his coffee, regretting that his friend had noticed. "I'll be fine."

"It's Smokes, isn't it?"

Daniel hesitated, wondering how his friend knew. "I miss her. But she's made it clear she doesn't want to see me again."

Thomas' smile was a little too victorious. "Good thing. Since you won't listen to me and stay away from her yourself."

"Then you must be very happy."

"I can't say I'm not, Daniel. Especially with what she's gotten herself into now."

"What are you talking about?"

"You haven't heard?" Thomas snorted. "She and her gang of Jesus freaks were arrested yesterday and thrown in jail."

Baliel and Zarene stood side by side against the cold steel bars, along with five of their companions. All of them watched their charges huddling together at the far end of the large cage that housed at least fifty people—most of whom were drunks, drug addicts, and prostitutes. A few thieves were added to the mix and a man accused of molesting his nine-year-old niece. Baliel noted that the man's heart was completely dark, his conscience seared by repeated sins, which now forbade him to feel pity, remorse, or even regret for his vile actions.

"There is no hope for him, is there?" Zarene asked.

"Nay. He has chosen his path."

"So sad, these humans."

"Aye. But let us focus on our charges." Baliel couldn't help but smile as he gazed at Angelica. How proud he was of her for obeying the Father rather than man, for risking her life and safety to do His will. And especially for risking the safety of her son.

"She worries overmuch about Isaac." Zarene gestured to the way she drew the lad close to her on the bench.

"It is her weakness. One she must overcome soon."

Zarene gazed up at Baliel, who stood at least two feet above him. "He is a good boy. I have been blessed to watch over him since his birth."

Baliel only nodded.

The two of them stood in silence for a moment watching Robert, Anna, Clay, Angelica, and Isaac form a circle, grip each other's hands and begin to pray.

Some of the prisoners mocked them and spit on them, uttering all manner of foul curses. Yet the group persisted in their petitions to the Father. Beams of light surrounded them, shooting up into heaven as each word they uttered became perfumed incense floating before the throne.

The other angels smiled and nodded at Baliel. "They are doing well," Hikith, Robert's watcher, said.

"Indeed," Baliel answered.

Zarene tugged on Baliel's robe. "Remember when Paul and Silas were singing hymns in prison and the Father sent an earthquake to shake off their chains and open the door?"

"I do, indeed," Baliel said. "I was there, watching over Silas."

"You were? I only heard about it." Zarene looked up at Baliel with admiration. "How blessed you were to guard such a man."

"We are blessed now, my friend, to be assigned to such holy end-times warriors."

Nodding, Zarene's gaze sped back to Isaac, excitement in his voice. "I wish the Father would do something like that again."

"He has other plans this time. Watch and be patient."

Not one of Zarene's best qualities. "There is much at work here." Baliel studied Angelica, noting the sweat on her forehead and the way she leaned against Robert for support. "Much evil has been unleashed on Angelica, many dark assignments from the enemy, for she has been given an important task from the Father, one which could lead to thousands gaining entrance into heaven."

"Thousands?" Zarene said. "Then I must remain ever vigilant over Isaac."

"Agreed. Behold, his mother now." Baliel pointed at Angelica and Zarene finally noticed that she faltered.

"She is ill," he said.

"Aye. She has Gecka."

"The plague that has killed so many humans? Where did she get it? How did she get it? Why did the Father allow such a thing?"

Baliel said nothing.

"Tell me this will not end in her death."

"I do not know."

Something was terribly wrong. Angelica had known it for a while. She'd started feeling unusually warm just an hour after they'd been tossed into the cell. Then came the chills, the stomach upset, and finally the itchy rash that blossomed in pink dots on her stomach. She had prayed against it for hours, but she had only gotten worse. The enemy kept whispering in her ear that she had the plague and would die and leave her son alone in prison. And no matter how hard she tried to ignore him, her fears rose until they nearly strangled her.

She was not afraid to die, but leaving Isaac...especially in prison! How would he get out? Who would take care of him, protect him, keep him from being deceived and ending up in hell? Of course, she knew God would. At least she knew that in her head. But her heart was in a state of panic.

Within minutes of arriving, they'd all been booked, fingerprinted, and had their mug shots taken. They were criminals now. Criminals for Christ. Though this meager suffering could hardly be compared to the thousands of saints being butchered by the Islamic State or worked to death in labor camps in North Korea, it was terrifying enough for her. Yet after twenty-four hours in this cell, crowded with the dirtiest, smelliest people she'd ever seen, there was still no sign of being released or even of speaking to a judge or having a fair trial. Nothing. They hadn't even been allowed a phone call, and Angelica wondered when that right had been stripped away...like so many others.

Now, she was sick. And getting worse by the minute. And though she had tried to keep Isaac from getting too close to her, the poor, terrified boy had not stopped clinging to her since they'd been arrested. If only they'd allow her to call Leigh, she could arrange for her to pick him up and take him home. He was just an innocent boy! But her constant pleas to the jailers fell on deaf ears.

Finally, when the others in her group noticed her illness, Robert had suggested they form a circle and pray for her. The act only seemed to upset Isaac and cause a truckload of foul curses to be shot at them from the other prisoners. She had wanted to cover her son's ears, but instead just embraced him and sat down.

Anna held her hand, while Robert reassured her God had a plan, but her mind was growing hazy as if she were living in a nightmare. If only that were true.

Somewhere in the distance, she heard someone vomiting and another prisoner banging on the cell door, yelling for a guard. Minutes passed, or was it hours? Angelica's brain sizzled, and she clung to Isaac like a lifeline. The jangle of the cell door filled her ears, followed by approaching footsteps and a harsh voice.

"Alright, you religious kooks, you're free to go." The officer motioned in their direction. Angelica felt Anna's arm wrap around her and help her to her feet. The five of them shuffled out of the cell to the sounds of cursing and complaints from the rest of the prisoners. They marched through a maze of cells, then up a set of stairs, finally ending up in some kind of office, where they were each instructed to sign release papers.

"Why are you releasing us?" Robert asked.

"Some fool paid your bail," the man behind the desk answered. "But you'll have to come back for your court date next month."

"Praise God!" Anna signed the paper. The rest of them did the same and just like that, they were free. Or were they? To Angelica everything seemed like a dream. The world hazed around her in a surreal vision as if she were watching a movie in 3-D—there, but not there. And why was it so hot, so horribly hot? She looked around for her angel but saw nothing as they exited the police station, nothing but blue skies and puffy white clouds...

And Daniel leaning back against his limo.

*Now a great sign appeared in heaven: a woman clothed with the sun, with the moon under her feet, and on her head a garland of twelve stars. Then being with child, she cried out in labor and in pain to give birth.*
Revelation 12:1-2 (NKJV)

# Chapter 16

Daniel tried to deny the leap of his heart when Angel walked through the front doors of the police station. Man, but it was good to see her. And Isaac, too, who much to Daniel's surprise, broke away from his mother and came dashing toward him. Before Daniel could react, the boy plowed into him and gave him the biggest hug he'd had in a long while.

Swallowing his emotion, Daniel tousled Isaac's hair. "Hey, little jailbird."

The boy gazed up at him. "I knew you'd come save us!"

"You did?"

"Just had a feeling." Isaac looked over his shoulder. "But you gotta help Mom."

Daniel looked up as Anna and Angel stumbled toward him, the rest of her friends following behind.

He'd been all ready to unleash his "I told you so" speech when he noticed Angel's pale face, the sweat on her brow, and how much trouble she was having walking.

"What's wrong?" he questioned Robert, who followed close beside his wife.

"I'd stay back if I were you, Dan. We think it's Gecka. Can't be sure though."

"I don't care what it is. She needs a doctor." Daniel motioned for his driver to open the door and then took Angel from Anna and helped her climb inside.

"Thanks, preacher," Clay said. "Was it you who paid our bail?"

After settling Angel, Daniel motioned for Isaac to crawl in beside her. "Yup." He faced Angel's friends. "But I won't do it again if you continue this nonsense."

Robert slapped him on the back. "You're a good man, Dan. I don't know how to thank you."

"No need." He wouldn't tell them that he actually considered just springing Angel and Isaac and leaving the rest of them in jail—as a lesson. "Do you need a ride?"

Clay whistled. "In this thing? How can we resist?"

"Yes, if you don't mind." Anna's shoulders slumped. "It's been a long night."

The cult members climbed into the limo with oohs and ahhs and comments about the luxurious seats and carpet that made Daniel's face grow hot with embarrassment. He longed to set them all straight about their illegal activities and false religion while he had their undivided attention, but he was more worried about Angel at the moment. One touch to her forehead revealed a fever that was out of control.

"We should take her to the nearest hospital," Robert said after they dropped off Clay.

Anna shook her head. "They won't do much. She has state health insurance and no money. They'll just put her in quarantine, is my guess."

"Don't worry. I'll take care of her," Daniel offered, anxious to be rid of them and do just that. "I'll call my personal doctor."

"You would do that?" Anna smiled.

"Of course."

"Told you he was a good guy," Robert said as they pulled up in front of his house, and he opened the door and got out.

Anna scooted to the edge of the seat and hesitated. "Maybe we should stay with her." She glanced at Angel then up at her husband.

"She's in good hands." Robert helped her up. "Besides, we can pray for her right here."

No sooner did the limo drive off than Daniel called his doctor and demanded he meet them at Daniel's home.

"What's wrong with my mom?" Isaac's voice trembled.

Daniel squeezed his hand. "Don't worry. We're going to find out. I'm getting the best doctor in Fort Lauderdale to take care of her."

But he couldn't help the fear rising within him. If it was Gecka, there may be nothing he or anyone else could do.

Angelica stood on her favorite beach, staring out upon the calm sea. She loved this time of day when the sun barely peeked over the horizon, reaching golden fingers over crystalline blue waters, kissing them to life. There was such purity to the morning and such magnificence to the sea, that the combination never failed to remind her of her Creator.

The ground shook. Sand shifted over her bare feet. The morning turned to noon and a crowd instantly appeared on the beach—families picnicking, women tanning, teenagers flirting, and children building sand castles.

The waves withdrew from shore as if something frightened them. Back…back…back, they sped toward the horizon, leaving behind foamy arcs upon wet sand, flopping fish, and a treasure trove of shells.

Searing heat from the sun fired down upon Angelica. Shielding her eyes, she watched as children and adults alike scrambled with glee to collect shells and fish and venture out into the soggy seabed.

A blue mountain appeared in the distance, spanning the horizon. No, not a mountain. A wave. A wall of water rose from the deep like an otherworldly dragon rising from its lair. Higher and higher it grew until it blacked out the sunlight.

Angelica dashed toward the people collecting shells. "Tsunami! Run!" She pointed at the wave, but no one was listening. "Run everyone! We have to get out of here!" She grabbed a little girl and began to drag her toward the parking lot, but her mother picked her up and gave Angelica a spiteful look.

"It's coming. You have to leave!" Angelica shouted again, waving her hands and trying to get everyone's attention.

But no one listened. They continued eating, tanning, collecting shells, and playing in the sand as if they weren't about to be swept away.

The wave now tumbled toward them—a giant Leviathan of angry, foamy water.

Dropping to her knees, Angelica bowed her head and prayed.

The water struck.

She heard herself scream.

"It's okay, Angel. Just a dream. It's okay. You're safe."

That voice…strong, deep, reassuring. *Daniel.*

Where was she? Why was it so hot?

"The tsunami," she managed to mumble.

"She's hallucinating…" an unfamiliar voice said. "Part of the fever."

Her last thought was of Isaac before everything went black once again.

"It's definitely Gecka," Doctor Milson said through his face mask as he packed his instruments back in his bag. "I'm sorry." He faced Daniel, but the words refused to register.

Numb, Daniel dropped to the chair beside the bed.

Doctor Milson glanced at Angel with a look of defeat in his eyes.

*Gecka.* The name finally landed in Daniel's unwilling mind. "What can we do?"

"Nothing. It's such a recent virus, we don't have a cure. It ravaged South America last year, killing nearly a quarter of the population, and now there's been several cases in the U.S."

Sure, Daniel had heard of it. But this was something that struck other people, people he didn't know who lived in faraway places. Not his friends...

Not the woman he loved.

Daniel slowly rose. "There's gotta be something we can do."

"Keep her comfortable. Try to get her to eat something." The doctor checked the bag of fluids attached to Angel through an IV, then glanced at the masked nurse sitting beside the bed. No sooner had Daniel called Doctor Wilson and described Angel's symptoms, then he had called the hospital and arranged for a full-time nurse. She had arrived before the doctor and immediately applied cold compresses and an IV. Which had only increased Daniel's fears.

Fears that were now realized as a morbid cloud of doom descended on him.

"Call me if there's any change," Doc Wilson said to the nurse before he headed for the door. "I'll check on her tomorrow." Halting, he faced Daniel. "I wish you'd wear that face mask I gave you. We don't know how it is transmitted."

"I'll be fine, Doc." Daniel barely remembered walking the man to the front door. Or even returning to sit at Angel's bedside. What was he going to tell Isaac? He glanced at his watch. Two hours before he had to pick him up from school.

Angel moaned and tossed her head back and forth, and the nurse adjusted the cold compresses on her forehead and neck. She looked so pale, so weak. Her lashes fluttered against her cheeks, and he desperately longed to see those jade green eyes of hers again.

Feeling helpless, Daniel went to his room and closed the door. After pacing for several minutes, he did something he rarely had time for anymore. He prayed. *Hard.*

A gentle wave of warm water caressed Angelica's bare feet before bubbling back to the sea. Taking a deep breath of damp, salty air, she spread her arms wide and gazed up at billions of stars shining across the night sky—diamonds on black velvet. She couldn't remember ever seeing so many of them, sparkling so bright.

Some of the stars formed the shape of a woman lying on her back. A branch was in her hand, and she wore a crown of stars. The sun sat upon her shoulder and the moon shone at her feet. But something was terribly wrong. Screaming in agony, she gripped her belly as if she were in labor. A red dragon, fierce and terrifying, spanned the heavens before her, mouth gaping, teeth dripping with blood.

Angelica wanted to scream a warning to the woman, but instead she could only stare as the play was being acted out in the dark expanse above her. The woman gave birth to a child. The dragon snapped its jaws. But a mighty hand reached down and snatched the child, carrying it out of harm's way.

The dragon roared so loud, the ground shook beneath Angelica. He swept his tail across the skies and a thousand flaming meteors fell to the earth.

Fire, fire, everywhere! Flames devoured everything in sight, red-hot fingers reaching for the sky. Heat seared her skin. Angelica was in the middle of a large city. Which one, she could not tell. Buildings collapsed around her. People darted this way and that, screaming and wailing. A loud boom in the distance stopped everyone to stare. A mushroom cloud the size of a mountain rose above the glowing horizon.

The blast hit.

Angelica gasped for air. Sea air filled her lungs. And, oddly, the scent of lavender. She tried to lift her hand, but it felt like lead. Someone was pounding her brain with a sledgehammer. *Stop it!* She tried to speak but nothing came out.

"I love you, Mom," she heard Isaac say, but his voice sounded so sad. Desperate, she tried to respond, but she couldn't move, couldn't even open her eyes.

"She's going to be okay," Daniel said.

Someone kissed her on the cheek. She smelled Aqua Velva.

Minutes passed, maybe hours or even days, she didn't know. A familiar voice awakened her. Robert. It had to be Robert. And there was Anna's voice too. And Scottie's. Was she at church? Had she fallen asleep? How embarrassing.

Hands touched her. Someone spoke in a foreign language. The name of Jesus filled the air. What a sweet, sweet name!

Was she dead? If so, where was the light? Wasn't there supposed to be a light and her angel to lead her to heaven?

What would happen to Isaac? Terror squeezed her heart.

She tried to move, but everything collapsed into darkness again.

The sweet sound of birds singing dangled joy before Angelica's ears as a breeze caressed her face. She moved her hand. Silk sheets met her touch. *Silk?* Whoever had been jackhammering her head had stopped. Her skin no longer felt like a frying pan, and her lungs no longer rumbled with fluid.

She must be in heaven.

Isaac's laughter floated on the wind. Had they died together?

Prying her eyes open, the blurry vision before her slowly cleared to reveal a mahogany four-poster bed, matching carved dresser, gold-gilded mirror, dressing table, and Tiffany lamps. Definitely *not* the hospital. Or her apartment. Which left heaven still on the table.

But then she heard Daniel's voice, and knew that could not be the case. *Drat.*

It took several tries for her to rise to a sitting position. The room spun, and she leaned back on the bed for what seemed an eternity. Finally able to swing her legs over the side, she noticed the IV in her hand and cringed. Definitely not heaven. She hated IVs! Closing her eyes, she grabbed the tube and tore it from her arm then tossed it aside. Good heavens, how sick had she been? And more importantly, where was she?

But, of course, it had to be Daniel's house. She didn't know anyone else who lived in such luxury. But how she got here and *why* was another question. The last thing she remembered was being in jail, worried to death for Isaac.

No, she remembered other things. Strange visions and dreams. And voices, some familiar, some not—worried voices, then voices of praise. Ah yes, she *had* woken up before, briefly, but everything had been a blur. Someone had helped her to sit and given her ice chips, then later she remembered warm broth sliding down her throat.

Fear returned to taunt her. Pressing a hand to her stomach, she glanced down at a large T-shirt that fell to her knees.

Daniel's no doubt. Who had dressed her? Or rather, who had *undressed* her? Mortified, she attempted to stand, but her legs gave out and sent her dropping back down to the bed. "Father, I need your strength," she whispered a prayer, and after two more tries, she managed to stumble out of the room and make her way—very slowly and clinging to the banister—down a spiraling staircase. The sound of laughter and water splashing lured her through the kitchen and living room.

She rounded a corner and halted at the sight. Isaac stood atop Daniel's shoulders in the pool. They both laughed as Daniel grabbed his legs and flung him into the air. Her son formed a perfect cannonball in the deep end. If not for the smile on his face when he surfaced, she would have rushed forward and chastised Daniel for performing such a dangerous stunt.

The two began splashing each other, then dove beneath the water to wrestle. When both their heads surfaced, Daniel challenged Isaac to a cannonball contest, and off they went to the deep end of the pool.

Only then did she remember her vision of the two of them playing in Daniel's pool. Heaven help her, it had come true! Did that mean the rest of her visions would also come to pass? Her legs wobbled, and she leaned against the wall and watched, unable to take her eyes off the casual, fun way the two of them played. No man she'd ever met—including those at her church—had ever taken such an interest in Isaac. Or bonded with him so well and so quickly. Though Angelica had prayed over and over for a father for her son, God had not yet answered her prayer.

But now as she watched the two of them together, tears burned behind her eyes. *Not this man. Anyone but him.*

"Angel!" Gripping the edge of the pool, Daniel hoisted himself from the water and jumped to his feet—a Greek god rising from the sea and looking just as solid as one of those ancient statues. He shook water from his hair, ran a hand through it, and headed her way.

Yup. She was definitely feeling better.

"Mom!" Isaac was fast behind him, and she knelt, arms open to receive her slippery fish. He barreled into her, drenching her shirt and embracing her so hard she couldn't breathe.

"Careful, buddy." Daniel loomed above them. "Your mother's still weak."

Weak and embarrassed, now that her T-shirt was wet, Angelica released her son and allowed Daniel to help her up, but then quickly wrapped her arms across her chest.

Daniel walked to the patio and returned with a towel. Ever the gentleman.

"Come, sit. You shouldn't be up yet." He gently ushered her to one of the patio chairs as Isaac grabbed her hand to assist.

"I'm all right," Angelica said, taking a seat. "Just a little lightheaded is all."

"Get your mom some water, buddy, will you?" Daniel asked Isaac, sending the boy dashing to the kitchen.

*Buddy?* When did that start? And more importantly, how long had she been sick? What about her job? She had so many questions she didn't know where to start. Finally, she simply asked. "What happened?"

"You died, Mom." Isaac returned with a glass of water, his eyes sparkling. "You died and Jesus brought you back to life."

*But you, brethren, are not in darkness, so that this Day should overtake you as a thief. You are all sons of light and sons of the day. We are not of the night nor of darkness. Therefore let us not sleep, as others do, but let us watch and be sober.*
*1 Thessalonians 5:4-6 (NKJV)*

# Chapter 17

Daniel watched as Angel wrapped the towel around her shoulders and covered her chest. She worried her lip, and the tiniest of lines formed between her brows at the news that she had died. Certainly not the reaction he expected—no hysterics or terror, shock or dismay. Tangled spikes of golden hair surrounded her gaunt face, shadows rimmed her eyes, and she looked thin and frail. But at the moment, she was more alluring than he'd thought possible. She caught him staring at her and blushed, endearing her to him even more.

"I don't remember dying," she said with a smile.

"Well, you didn't really stop breathing, Mom." Isaac plopped in a chair beside her. "But the doc said you wouldn't make it through the night."

Angel's eyebrows rose. "Really?"

"Yeah, you had Gecka."

She snapped her surprised gaze to Daniel and he nodded.

Isaac continued, "Yeah, Mr. Cain—I mean Daniel—hired the best doctor in all of Florida."

"He did, did he?" She smiled, and his heart swelled at the look of admiration in her eyes.

"Isaac was so worried about you," Daniel said. "He refused to leave your bedside. I kept dragging him away, worried he'd get sick too, but he would have none of it. Stubborn like his mom."

This gained him a smile.

"But then Robert, Anna, and Scottie came," Isaac announced proudly.

Angel gasped and glanced at Daniel. "You called the cult?"

"More like they called me. But hey, I was desperate."

She rubbed her forehead and closed her eyes for a second. "I remember hearing their voices."

Isaac grabbed her hand and squeezed it. "They prayed over you, Mom. Then Scottie said you were healed and they left."

Daniel remembered the moment well. He had laughed at the man, at all of them, as he escorted them out. He had thought them fools. Angel was still feverish and having trouble breathing. She'd not been healed at all.

But then…

Less than an hour later, she began to improve. Slowly at first, but within four hours, her fever was gone, the rash disappeared, and she was breathing again. Daniel had called Doc Wilson, who came over and immediately pronounced her completely recovered, much to their amazement. Even the nurse was astounded. Which reminded Daniel, he should call her and tell her there was no need to come by this afternoon.

"I've never seen anyone recover so quickly. Or at *all* from Gecka," the doctor had said.

Daniel couldn't believe it either. Sure, he believed in God, but this sort of thing just didn't happen. There had to be another explanation. Perhaps it hadn't been Gecka at all, but just the flu.

"So." She raised a brow in his direction. "You believe in supernatural healing now?"

Daniel frowned. "I don't know what I believe." He shifted his gaze to Isaac. "Except that you, young man, have some homework to do."

Isaac moaned. "Do I have to? Mom just got up."

"Yup, and she's going back to bed, too. She needs her rest."

Rising, Isaac slogged back into the living room, groaning along the way, where Daniel saw him sit on the floor by the coffee table and open a book.

Angel sipped her water. "I should get home."

"I should get you back to bed," Daniel said. Angel's face turned a deep shade of maroon, and he shifted in his seat, adding, "I mean... *you* should get back to bed."

She lowered those incredibly long lashes of hers. "I can't believe you brought me here...cared for me."

"Why wouldn't I?"

"You could have caught this Gecka. I hear there's no cure." She reached for his hand across the table. "Why would you do such a thing?"

Happily, he threaded his fingers with hers. He wanted to say because he loved her, because he realized now that he had never stopped loving her. "I'm a pastor. I help people."

Pulling her hand back, she cocked her head and studied him in that cute way of hers, and he knew she wasn't buying it. A breeze tossed her hair about her face as the sound of crashing waves serenaded them from the beach.

"Oh, my goodness, my job! How long have I been sick?" She started to get up, but he gently nudged her down.

"Four days. And I already called your boss and told him what happened."

She breathed out a sigh, rubbing her temples. "Leigh must be worried sick."

"Took care of that too. She sends her love and tells you to get well soon."

She studied him as if he were some strange anomaly.

"I should get you something to eat. You need your strength back." He rose, but she waved him back down.

"I'm not hungry." She glanced over her shoulder at Isaac. "*You've* been driving him back and forth to school and helping him with his homework too?"

He shrugged. "I've actually enjoyed it." He smiled toward the living room where the boy was hard at work. "He's so smart and fun to be with. And after you were out of danger, he and I have been enjoying the pool and the beach. He's actually good at ping pong too."

She smiled. "Yes, he is. What about your church, your work?"

"Thomas is handling things."

She instantly frowned and shifted in her seat. "I really should go home. Get out of your hair."

"I like you in my hair," he said, causing her to stare at him again in wonder. He leaned toward her. "Angel, you've got to stop preaching on the beach. Promise me you will."

She looked away and sipped her water, sunlight rippling off the glass. "Whatever God wills."

"Do you think He wills you and Isaac to spend the rest of your lives in prison?" He sat back with a huff. "Some believers have already been arrested and sent to FEMA camps around the country. For doing exactly what you and your friends are doing, preaching and praying publicly, meeting illegally, and using the banned Bible. For Pete's sake, I understand your passion to do what you think is right, but this borders on insanity."

He watched her swallow hard and saw the struggle behind her eyes. Maybe he was finally getting somewhere. If he could just convince her to give up these things, not only would she and Isaac be safe, but Daniel could pursue a relationship with her as he so desperately wanted to do.

"They're really stepping up their crusade against fanatics," he continued. "Christian books are banned, blogs are being shut down. We have to work within the system and at least be grateful we can still preach the gospel."

Instead of answering, she merely stared at the wind dancing among the palm fronds.

He took that as a sign to continue. "We can save more people, do more good, if we abide by the rules, don't rock the boat, and present the gospel in the allowed form in sanctioned churches."

He knew he'd crossed the line when she faced him, her jaw tight and her eyes hard as the patio stones beneath their feet. "Really? Is that what Jesus did? Seems to me he rocked quite a few boats when He was here. And I don't remember Him serving up a watered-down, politically-acceptable message either."

"Why are you so stubborn?" he shot back.

"Why are you so dense?"

He smiled. He couldn't help it. He'd missed their banter. No woman could match him wit for wit like Angel could.

"I insult you and you smile," she said with a grin of her own.

"Only for you, Angel."

She looked down. "We really should go. You've done quite enough, and I can regain my strength just as well in my own home."

He had so hoped she'd stay another couple of days. "I'll take you home on one condition."

She looked at him with suspicion.

"When you're well, you let me take you and Isaac for a picnic."

"You would keep me a hostage in your home just for a picnic?"

He smiled. "Try me."

It was the perfect day for a picnic. Certainly not Florida's typical hot, muggy fall weather. A cool breeze blew in from the sea while occasional clouds drifted over the sun, shielding them from its heat. The sound of children's laughter eased over Angelica from a playground not far away. In the distance, two Little League teams were playing an exciting game from the sound of the cheers from their parents, while joggers and mothers pushing strollers circled the path that framed one of Pompano Beach's favorite parks. A dog barked and she glanced at a man tossing a Frisbee to his pet.

How odd that life went on as if the world weren't falling apart, as if war drums weren't beating in the Middle East and China, as if food was plenty and disease wasn't rampant, and the earth wasn't shaking and spewing forth ash in a spoiled fit of anticipation for the next age.

As if people who followed Jesus weren't being tossed in prison.

But isn't that what the Bible said? In the days before Noah's flood, people were eating and drinking, marrying and giving in marriage, up to the day he entered the ark. Jesus said it would be the same way before His return. She fingered a blade of grass, glancing at the empty plates and cups from their lunch. Daniel had packed a gourmet lunch—well, if you called kale-and-raisin salad, tofu burgers and quinoa French fries "gourmet." Despite the odd taste, she had devoured every speck. Just a week past her near-death experience, she was still regaining her strength. And continually thanking God for healing her. Apparently the Almighty still had work for her to do on earth. Part of that work, she believed, involved warning others of His soon return.

Angelica sat beneath a tree on the cool grass watching Daniel and her son toss a baseball back and forth—watching her son laugh and joke with a man who had once torn her heart into shreds. And it occurred to her that she'd seen this exact scene before in a vision a few weeks ago—the second one that had come true. The thought made her shiver.

A distant sound reverberated in the sky, almost like thunder, but it wasn't. No, it was one of those trumpet-like sounds again, low and deep and so strange that nearly everyone at the park stopped for a second to listen and look up. But then it was gone as quickly as it had come and people went back to their activities as if nothing had happened.

"What is that, Father?" Angelica murmured, but no answer came.

Daniel called Isaac over and showed him the proper way to hold a baseball mitt, something Angelica could never do. They separated again and Daniel tossed the baseball harder this time. Isaac caught it *smack* in his mitt, and a huge grin lit up his face.

She could not deny her burst of joy at the sight. If the way to a man's heart was his stomach, the way to a woman's heart was through her children.

A group of boys came up and spoke with Isaac, sending him darting her way to ask if he could play baseball with them. Daniel came and sat beside her as she examined the boys and the proximity of the field, unsure...fear tightening her heart yet again.

"Ah, let him go," Daniel said. "We are only yards away."

She frowned at him, wanting to tell him to butt out, but instead, she gave her permission and watched her son speed away.

"He's got a good eye," Daniel remarked.

"I guess I should sign him up for Little League. He never expressed any interest until now."

"He's good at surfing too. Athletic kid and smart as a whip."

Her anger quickly dissipated, and she glanced at him coyly. "If you're trying to win my heart, you're doing a good job."

Leaning back on his palms, he smiled, charming her with that dimple of his.

She had meant her words to be teasing, but the look on his face unsettled her, sending her traitorous heart into a rapid beat.

She quickly changed the subject. "I remember dreams I had while I was sick. They were so vivid. I was on the beach and a tsunami was rumbling toward us, but no one was paying attention. Then, there was a pregnant woman in the stars at night, delivering a child." She had since looked up any reference to a woman in labor in the Bible and discovered that Revelation 12 described the exact thing she had seen. But why had God shown it to her? She would have to check star charts to see if this configuration ever happened, or if it was still in the future.

Chewing on a piece of grass, Daniel stared off into the distance.

"Then a dragon tried to eat her child, but God snatched him away." A pigeon landed nearby and crept toward them, eyeing the crumbs on their paper plates. "Then a bunch of meteors crashed to the earth, setting everything on fire. And worst of all, a nuclear blast. It was all so horrible."

"Just dreams," he finally said. "From your feverish brain. You got up to 105, you know."

"No, I think they mean something. Warnings, maybe. I've been getting many visions like that lately. I just don't know what to do with them." What scared her the most was if the ones she had about Daniel were coming true, what about these more horrific ones?

He sighed and looked at her as if she'd lost her mind. "I'd keep them to myself if I were you. Things like that just scare people and get them all riled up."

A breeze brought the scent of fresh grass, sunshine, and Aqua Velva to her nose, and Angelica glanced at her son swinging a bat. *Smack!* He struck the ball, sending it flying high.

"Maybe people ought to be a little scared," she said. "Maybe we Christians should be warning them."

The pigeon continued inching toward them.

"About what?" Rubbing the stubble on his jaw, he lowered onto his elbows.

"The end of days. Jesus' return."

Daniel tossed the piece of grass to the ground. "Oh, come on, people have been predicting His return for centuries. We aren't supposed to know when He will come. Not the day or the hour, right? He comes like a thief."

Angelica smiled. "So, you *do* remember the passages they removed."

His blue eyes sparkled. "Yeah. I guess I used to be interested in that stuff."

"Then you should know that Jesus is only coming like a thief for those who aren't looking for Him. That's what the Apostle Paul said in 1 Thessalonians 5."

"What does it matter?" He shrugged. "He'll come when he comes."

Angelica glanced to make sure Isaac was okay. "It matters a great deal. Do you know that for every prophecy in the Bible about Jesus' first coming, there are five about His second? Most of the people missed Him the first time He came, and He chastised them for not knowing the time of His visitation. How much more will we be chastised for not knowing the time of His second?"

The pigeon tentatively pecked at the crumbs on the plate, shook his head in a sputter, and flew away.

Angelica couldn't help but laugh.

Frowning, Daniel picked up the empty paper plates and shoved them in a plastic bag. "Still, we aren't supposed to know the day or the hour."

"Day and hour, yes. But what about year, season, month, or week? It says nothing about that."

He tied the sack and put it aside, giving her a placating look. "Even so. Let's say you're right. All that does is scare people or get them to stop living their lives and just sit and wait."

"Not true believers. It actually inspires us to get out there and warn people, save people, and get our own lives in order—to pursue good, holy lives that will please Him." Angelica watched her son leap to catch a ball on first base.

"We should be doing that anyway."

"True. But do most of us?"

He squeezed the bridge of his nose. "Let's not fight about it, Angel. See? End times' stuff always causes arguments. It's frightening and divisive. Best to leave it alone."

He might be right about that. She'd overheard many an argument from believers who got quite heated about their interpretations on end-times prophecies. Ridiculous. "I still think it matters that we keep watch and be ready. There's a passage that says Jesus is coming for those who are longing for His appearance. And…" Sensing his growing frustration, she slammed her mouth shut, deciding to change the topic. "I'm not sure I thanked you properly…for taking me and Isaac into your home and hiring that doctor and nurse—wait, there was probably more than one, if I remember—and well, for everything you did."

The right side of his lips quirked upward, forming that dimple again. "My pleasure." He scooted closer, and before she could stop him, he wrapped an arm around her and drew her close. Too close, but she didn't want to stop him. It felt good. In all honesty, she had missed the strength and warmth of a man's touch. Especially Daniel's.

Pressing her head against his shoulder, she relaxed as he rubbed her arm.

A chorus of sounds eased over her like a summer breeze—birds singing, the wind dancing through leaves, people laughing, kids playing, the distant lap of waves... all so soothing...

Just like Daniel's warm breath drifting over her face, reminding her of days gone by. And for a moment, just a moment, Angelica allowed herself to enjoy it all.

He shifted and before she knew it, his lips were on hers, warm, soft, hungry. She lost control and allowed him the kiss—not only allowed it, but she returned it with equal fervor. Such a sweet kiss, gentle, loving...not demanding, urgent, or lustful. She breathed him in, her heart pounding, her body warming as his arms pressed her against his chest.

A memory taunted her of a time long ago, in a city park much like this one. They'd been walking, holding hands, sharing, laughing...and it had started to rain. Not just rain—it poured in drops as large as baseballs. But instead of dashing to his car, Daniel took her in his arms and began to dance down the path as if they were a prince and princess at a ball. What sort of man does that? Only Daniel. They laughed and smiled and swirled until they were both completely drenched.

And then, with water running down both their faces, he had kissed her.

With the same intensity and love he was doing now.

*NO!* She pushed away and stared at him in horror.

Lowering his gaze, he expelled a deep sigh. "Why do you keep resisting me? I've missed you so much, Angel, and I can tell you've missed me too." He took her hand in his. "Please, why can't we pick up where we left off?"

*Where they left off?* Where they had left off was her standing alone at their favorite restaurant, clutching a trampled, bleeding heart—a heart that bled out for over a year afterward. And she had no plans to give him the chance to do that again. Besides, it wasn't just her heart she'd be risking now. It was Isaac's, too.

Pulling back her hand, she moved away. "Won't your association with a 'cult follower' destroy your career?"

He rubbed his chin and gazed at her like a little boy who'd been caught with his hand in the cookie jar. "I guess I hoped to persuade you to abandon your cult." He grew serious. "At the very least, your experience in jail should help you see how dangerous they are." He glanced toward the baseball field. "How bad they are for Isaac."

Clever. Using her fear for Isaac. "What if I asked you to give up your church and attend mine?"

"That's different. I'm the pastor. It's my livelihood. You can't ask me to give up my job."

"You can find another one."

He snapped a hard gaze her way. "I won't be a nobody again."

"You were never a nobody, Daniel." A warm breeze swept her hair aside, and her gaze found Isaac once again. "Besides, you're not preaching the right stuff, anyway."

"Really? Like what?" He laughed. "Wait. Don't answer that. Here's an idea. We're putting on a play this Sunday—big production—and I'm giving a small sermon. How about you come? Then afterward, you can tell me exactly what I'm doing wrong."

*The angel of the Lord encamps all around those who fear Him, and delivers them.*
  *Psalm 34:7 (NKJV)*

# Chapter 18

At Sal's "Come in," Angelica slipped through the door into the dingy office. The smell of vodka and cheap men's cologne stung her nose as her eyes avoided the pinup calendar on the wall behind her boss's desk.

Laying down his pen, he sat back in his chair and examined her as a fox would a rabbit. She half expected him to start drooling from that evil smile that curved his lips. "How can I help you, Angelica?"

She drew a deep breath. She might as well just spit it out. "I need an advance on next week's pay, Sal. Being sick for a week really set me back, and I have rent to pay and other bills that are due now." She bit her lip, silently praying he would grant her wish. *Without* any strings.

She spotted the thrill of power in his eyes, the glow of authority he held in his tiny little world. Pushing his bony frame from the chair, he slunk around his desk, then leaned back on the top, not two feet from where she stood.

His frown was as fake as the gold watch around his wrist. "I don't know. Things are tight this month. Business hasn't been good. You know fall is our slow season."

"I know, Sal. I'm just asking." Begging was more like it, since the pleading look she gave him nearly made her sick.

He cocked his head and spread two fingers down each side of his mustache. "You know, Angelica, all your money troubles could come to an end just like that." He snapped his fingers.

She pursed her lips and resisted the urge to take a step back. "And I've told you more than once, that's not possible."

He snorted. "Of course it's possible. You just keep turning me down."

He stood and attempted to stretch his frame taller than his five-foot-seven height, then slid a finger down her jaw. "I want to take care of you, Angelica. And your son. You would never have to work again or worry about money."

Nausea gurgled in her belly, but she held her ground. "My answer is still no. I'm sorry, Sal."

With a growl, he stormed back behind his desk. "Then my answer is no, too."

"You would deny me an advance just because I won't sleep with you?"

He sank back into his chair. "No. Because we don't have the funds," he snipped back. "Now, get back to work!" He waved her away.

Back on the floor, tray of drinks in hand, Angelica stifled her anger and did her best to forgive Sal. Not an easy accomplishment, and certainly not something she felt in her heart. Instead, she silently prayed for him, for her finances, for God to provide her with a better job, and finally for the lost customers she served.

So many of them were lost...so many seeking answers in alcohol, drugs, and sex. She prayed over each one. One particular man was in the process of ordering his fourth drink. He sat alone, staring at the mermaids swimming in the tank and fingering a wedding ring he'd taken off his finger. Angelica took a moment to ask God for insight, anything that would help her reach him. Shadows slithered around him, stroking him, laughing, spinning a web of darkness over his heart.

She shook the vision away. "Maybe I can bring you a coffee instead?"

"Why would you care whether I get wasted or not?" he mumbled without looking up.

Hesitating, she waited for insight from above. There it came—knowledge she couldn't possibly know filled her mind. "Because you normally don't drink, and you hoped the alcohol would numb the pain in your heart from your wife leaving you for another man. But you're discovering that it is only making it worse." She ignored the stunned look on his face and continued, "There are whispers in your ears telling you to drink yourself into oblivion, to end it all, and I'm here to tell you that those are the voices of your enemy."

His glazed eyes stared at her as if she were from another planet.

"I know you think all is lost," she continued. "But there *is* hope. There is a God who loves you, who will never leave you, and who wants to help you. You can reach Him through His Son, Jesus, who died so you can be set free."

The shock in his hazy eyes faded, replaced by tears, and he dropped his gaze to the table. The shadows shrieked and retreated.

"Angelica!" She heard Sal yell for her, and she turned to leave when the man grabbed her wrist.

"I'll have that coffee, Miss."

Smiling, she nodded, no longer caring what Sal was going to chew her out about.

"You spent too much time with that customer when there are others waiting for their drinks!" He slammed a shot of vodka down his throat.

"It won't happen again." She smiled, a genuine smile that had nothing to do with him and everything to do with what had just happened. But when she headed back toward the man with his coffee, he was gone.

*Drat.* Had she reached him or had he merely gone to another bar where he wouldn't be harassed? Fighting her discouragement, she prayed for the man as she went about her duties.

In the break room, Angelica reached in her purse and handed a small book to Melody, who had just started her shift and was changing into her high heels.

"What's this?"

"A Bible."

Melody swallowed and flipped it open with more reverence than Angelica would have expected. "A real one?"

Angelica nodded. "Keep it at your home. Read it. Start in the Gospel of John. If you have any questions, please don't hesitate to ask me."

"Thanks." Her moist eyes shifted between Angelica's. "I'm scared to have it, but I want to know about this God of yours and why He cared to save me." She slipped the Bible in her purse, then grabbed a comb and ran it through her curly black hair. "Honestly, if He cares, why is my life nothing but a disaster? I mean"—she pointed the comb at Angelica— "two horrible marriages, this pathetic job, and raising two kids on my own with no help. What kind of God does that?"

"God didn't do that, Mels. You made those decisions yourself. Plus, we live in enemy territory."

Melody began combing again. "What are you talking about?"

"Just read…you'll see."

Greg walked in, saw them both, and went to the vending machine. Putting the comb away, Melody eased into her shoes and slammed her locker.

Before Greg slipped in his coins, he spun to face them. "Heard about the sinkhole," he said eyeing them both.

Melody nodded. "I would have died if I'd gone that way."

He took a step toward Angelica. "How did you know?"

Angelic lowered to sit and rest her feet before her break ended. "God told me."

"I've got to get out there. Talk to you later." Melody sped out the door.

Angelica looked up at Greg. "You don't believe me."

He turned around and inserted his coins, punching in the right numbers for a Snickers bar. "Doesn't matter."

"It does matter. What's wrong? You haven't been yourself lately."

"Nothing." Grabbing his candy bar, he started for the door then stopped to face her. "Thank you for always being so nice to me, Angelica."

It sounded like a goodbye.

"Of course. I'm here for you anytime. I mean that." She reached out for him, but he smiled and sped away.

The rest of the night passed without incident. Finally, Angelica traded her high heels for walking shoes and headed out into the muggy Florida night. Or morning, she should say, for it was well past 2:00 a.m. Despite her aching feet and heavy eyelids, she smiled and gave thanks to God for small successes—namely Melody's acceptance of the Bible, Greg noticing the miracle, and the man who had stopped drinking and left. She prayed for each one as she made her way across the parking lot. It had been crowded when she arrived, and she'd had to park far away from the door.

A low guttural sound blasted across the sky. The same sound she'd heard just recently at the park and on other occasions. Halting, she stared into the black sky splattered with stars and wondered, not only at the sound, but at how magnificent the universe was, how vast, how glorious.

So enamored with the beauty of God's creation, she didn't hear the car motor rev up or the tires squeal as a large vehicle headed straight for her.

Baliel stood guard beside Angelica as she gazed up at the wonders of God. This precious human never failed to amaze him. Her life was not an easy one. She was a single mother with a demeaning and tough job that left her with an aching body, exhaustion, empty cupboards, and an old junk-heap for a car. Yet she had lured so many people into the light this night—more than she realized. And here she was, after a difficult nine hours, not knowing how she would pay rent, staring up at the sky in worship.

Baliel could well understand such unreserved awe, for he had seen the Creator, had stood before His throne and witnessed His brilliant glory—the four living creatures, the rainbow, the lightning and thunder, the Seraphim with their six wings, and the crystal river of living water pouring from beneath His feet. Hosts upon hosts of angels sang in worship to Him, simply because they could do naught else in His presence.

But this woman had never seen the Father, had never witnessed His glory.

And still she worshiped as if she stood before His throne. Amazing.

A whisper of warning captured his thoughts—a word from above. It had not escaped his notice that the forces of darkness had grown stronger around Angelica of late. Though they were always present, always seeking a way into the fortress of light that surrounded her, this was different. More demons had been summoned, stronger demons, deadly. They'd already tried to kill her twice, once with a bullet, once with a plague. He harbored no doubt they'd try again. Gripping the hilt of his sword, he scanned the surroundings, spotting the horde at a distance, spitting and hissing at him, their hatred evident in their malicious yellow eyes.

But they had made their choice. As had he. And he would never allow them to hurt his charge.

An engine roared. A dark blue sedan appeared out of nowhere, heading straight for Angelica. He shouted at her in the spirit to move, but she was so intent in her worship, she didn't hear him. Though he longed to appear to her, speak to her in a human voice, he didn't have permission. He couldn't touch her. He couldn't shove her out of the way. What to do?

The car sped toward her. Two demons sat on the roof, their wicked laughter grating over him. More shadows filled the car, spinning around the driver.

Angelica finally glanced toward them. But there was not enough time for her to get out of the way. So Baliel did the only thing he could. Sword drawn, he stood between her and the speeding vehicle.

In the split second before the car hit, Angelica lifted up a prayer for Isaac. She knew she was going to die, and she didn't want her son to be left alone. "Please take care of him, Father."

The words barely left her mouth before the car struck.

*Wait.* She didn't feel anything. She didn't fly through the air and land on the hood. She wasn't violently hurled to the side. She wasn't being run over by tires, her internal organs crushed beyond repair.

Instead, the car went…right…through…her.

The hood passed through first. Nothing but a blue streak. Then she saw the interior—the bucket seats, stick shift, the driver, then the backseat—littered with empty fast food wrappers—and finally the trunk.

Then nothing but black asphalt.

Was she dead? Still standing in the same spot, she glanced after the car and saw it speeding away, tires squealing on the pavement.

Her legs buckled, the sky spun, and she dropped to the ground, breathing hard. What just happened? *Am I losing my mind?* She tried to slow her thundering heart. A flash of light brought her gaze up to see her angel. He was tall, so tall, all shimmering metal and light. Sheathing his sword, he smiled and pointed toward her car. And then he was gone.

Struggling to rise, she gathered her purse and finally managed with trembling fingers to unlock her car and climb in. Slamming the door, she locked it and sat. Just sat, trying to catch her breath. *And* her reason. Several minutes passed before she started the engine and headed home. Why would someone try to run her down? Maybe it was just some random person crazed on drugs and alcohol. Or one of her customers who didn't take too kindly to her mention of Jesus. Either way, Thomas' threat rose to haunt her.

But no, the man was *not* that evil.

"Father, you saved me! You sent my angel to protect me." She gripped the wheel, tears flowing down her cheeks, still having a hard time believing a car had passed through her without giving her a scratch. But she knew it had. Somehow God had given her angel the power to twist the laws of physics in order to save her.

Two days later, Angelica had convinced herself that the car incident was a random act perpetrated by a lunatic. Perhaps even a terrorist. They'd been known to run over people, except they usually attacked crowds with big trucks, not a single woman in the middle of the night. But hey, she lived in a crazy, upside-down world.

She thanked God over and over for saving her, especially as she now gazed at Isaac, still asleep in his bed. She always let him sleep in on Sunday, but it was well past his normal time to get up. The poor kid worked hard at his studies and then put in extra time with her going over everything he learned so she could do her best to reverse the indoctrination. Plus, he did chores and helped Leigh with Joel. Angelica was tough on him. But she wanted him to grow up able to handle living in this difficult world.

If they ended up being here much longer.

Which reminded her of the conversation she had about Jesus' second coming with Daniel. Which then reminded her that tonight was the play at his church she'd promised to attend. She should cancel. She wanted to cancel. After the way his kiss affected her, the fleshly part of her desperately wanted to see him again. Which, of course, meant she *must* never see him again.

She brushed a lock of brown hair from her son's face and resisted the urge to kiss his forehead. Instead, she wandered into the kitchen, smiled at Leigh who sat sleepily at the table, a cup of coffee in hand, and then flipped on her independent news—on low since Joel was watching cartoons in the living room.

She had barely grabbed a mug when she heard, "A 9.2 earthquake struck the Cascadia fault line this morning at 3:42 a.m." The announcer's voice was tight with fear.

"No." Leigh's jaw dropped as she rose and entered the kitchen to watch. Angelica turned up the volume. She always expected stories like this, but it was still a shock to see them happen, to witness the scenes of horror that were now flashing across the screen. Complete and utter devastation. Cities reduced to nothing but rubble, fires everywhere, the landscape forever changed.

The newscasters had no idea how many lives were lost. Rescue crews flown in were having a hard time landing due to aftershocks. And tsunami warnings were issued along the

Washington coast all the way down to the Bay Area in California.

"How horrible." Leigh leaned against the counter as Angelica just stood there, too numb to move.

"To make matters worse," the newscaster added, "Yellowstone Caldera is acting up again, this time spewing sulfur and fire into the air. All tourists have been evacuated from the park."

Leigh shut off the TV. "Sorry, I can't watch anymore." She turned fearful eyes to Angelica. "What is going on?"

Angelica poured herself some coffee, saying a quick prayer for the people on the West Coast. "It's the end of the age."

"I just don't know." Leigh glanced at her son and then hugged herself. "Why would God cause all this destruction and death? I thought you said He was good and loving."

"God isn't doing this. This is all part of the fallen world we live in. When man fell in the garden, the earth was affected too. Now, it is groaning and churning in anticipation for the return of the King." Angelica set her mug aside, her stomach uneasy, her eyes filling with tears. "Those poor people." She would spend a few hours today fasting and praying for them.

Leigh flipped hair over her shoulder and sighed. "I've been reading about the last days."

Angelica glanced up. "You have?"

"The passages you marked in the Bible you gave me. All of it, everything is coming true. Even this one-world government. That's the GIFP isn't it?"

"That's the start of it, yes. Along with the one-world religion that's already sweeping the world—the false church. But a man will rise up as supreme ruler over those currently in power. The Bible calls him the Son of Perdition, the beast, or the Antichrist."

Leigh shook her head. "Oh, come on, the Antichrist?"

"I can show you the scriptures. He'll be a thousand times worse than Hitler, and the world will adore him."

Leigh's brow wrinkled, her eyes full of fear. "I want to believe, I do. But I just don't know."

Oh, how Angelica wanted to seize the moment and force Leigh to give her life to Jesus before it was too late, but that's not how the Holy Spirit worked. He was a gentleman. The great thing was, Leigh was seeking. And those who truly sought would find.

A loud knock on the door startled them both, and Leigh crept to peek out the peephole. She glanced at Angelica. "It's a big guy dressed in a suit," she whispered, then turned and shouted through the door. "Who is it?"

"Bodyguard for Miss Smoke."

Leigh raised a brow and grinned. "For you, I guess."

Chain still on the door, Angelica opened it a crack to see a man the size of a football linebacker, dressed in a suit and tie.

"Can I help you?"

"Ma'am, just wanted you to know I'm out here and will be driving you to Fort Lauderdale Church of Grace at 3:00."

Angelica wanted to laugh. "Really? And just who might you be?"

"He's the bodyguard Daniel sent, Mom," Isaac's sleep-gravelly voice announced, and she turned to see him approaching in his X-Men pj's, rubbing his eyes.

"What?" No way. This was *not* happening. She faced the beast. "Mr...."

"Just call me Tank, ma'am."

*Of course.* She smiled. "Mr. Tank, I don't need a bodyguard, so you may leave."

"Can't do that, ma'am."

"It's very easy. Just turn around and go back where you came from."

"Only take orders from Mr. Cain, ma'am."

"Stop calling me ma'am!"

She finally got a reaction out of him as one brow dared to rise. Still, he stared straight ahead at her door, and she realized it would take a stick of dynamite to move him. Maybe two.

She closed the door and faced her son. "What is this about?"

"After you almost got run over—" Isaac began but was interrupted by a yawn as he opened the cupboard and grabbed a box of cereal.

"How do you know about that?"

"I heard you telling Leigh."

Angelica growled and exchanged a glance with her roommate. "Okay. But what does that have to do with Daniel?"

Isaac poured the rest of the cereal into a bowl, filling it only halfway, then set the empty box on the counter. "Well, I sorta told him about it."

"When?"

"When I talked to him on the phone."

This was getting worse and worse. "Why are you talking to him on the phone?"

"He called and asked me to go fishing."

"He did what—" She bit back her anger and drew a deep breath.

He opened the fridge and pulled out the watery milk Angelica had made from powder concentrate. "No real milk?"

"Sorry." Her heart broke as she watched him pour the fake milk on his cereal, but there was nothing to be done about it. "So...?"

Grabbing a spoon, Isaac sat at the table beside Leigh. "So he sent a bodyguard to protect you. Isn't it cool?"

She stared at Leigh who was suppressing a laugh. Not cool at all! How dare he intrude on her life without her permission? This was going too far, and she would put a stop to it tonight. She would go to the play as promised and then tell Daniel to back off—permanently.

*For the time will come when they will not endure sound doctrine; but wanting to have their ears tickled, they will accumulate for themselves teachers in accordance to their own desires, and will turn away their ears from the truth and will turn aside to myths.*
2 Timothy 4:3-4 (NASB)

# Chapter 19

Angelica ascended the rows of stairs leading to the main sanctuary of the Fort Lauderdale Church of Grace. She couldn't help but smile, remembering the last time she stood on these very steps. She was in her cocktail waitress uniform coming to give Daniel the message she'd heard from God. Nearly two months had passed, but it seemed like a lifetime ago. Now, as she pressed into the mob entering through the massive wooden doors, she wondered for the thousandth time why she was here.

Oh yes, to tell Daniel off.

She had left Isaac home with Leigh. Though he had begged to go, the last thing she wanted was for him to be exposed to any more indoctrination than he was already getting at school.

She glanced behind her to see Tank, towering over her like a bulldog on steroids. She hadn't allowed him to drive her, but he'd followed close behind in his black Suburban. He was good, she'd give him that. She'd tried to lose him twice in traffic—just for fun, of course—but she couldn't shake him. Not even when she parked and made a dash for the church. The man also didn't have a sense of humor, for she could tell he hadn't found her antics the least bit amusing. She wanted to tell him that she had far better protection than he could offer—an angel whom God had assigned to watch over her. But she knew that wouldn't make a difference.

Moving toward a side wall, she halted in the foyer, still unsure whether she should continue into the main sanctuary. An uneasy feeling shimmied over her, agitating her spirit. The crowd continued to pour in through the doors, chattering and laughing as if thousands upon thousands of people hadn't just died on the West Coast. Maybe they would mention the tragedy in the service and set aside some time to pray as a group. Like her home church was doing right now. Scottie had called an emergency prayer meeting tonight, and she longed to be among friends, lifting up the injured and those still trapped beneath the rubble and praying against further shock waves and the tsunami that was predicted to hit shore within the hour.

If she left now, she could make it to Scottie's in time.

But she had promised Daniel.

Gathering her nerve, she continued watching the throng pour through the foyer into the main auditorium like ants into an ant hole—families with small children, singles, the elderly. Some of the young ladies wore clothing that revealed far too much. And they were getting what they deserved—or maybe what they wanted—lots of leering glances from men. Two men strode by, hand in hand. Averting her gaze, she spotted a painting of Christ walking on the water, reaching down for Peter who had begun to sink in the storm. Appropriate for the events of the day, she supposed. On either side of him, hung portraits of Daniel and Thomas, strategically placed as if they were apostles themselves.

*Forgive me, Lord. I'm judging and I don't mean to be. Some of these people belong to You.* She could see their lights, like spires reaching from within their spirits for the sky. Others walked in darkness. Still others were bound in chains.

No one paid her any mind.

Until she entered into the main sanctuary and an usher dashed up to her.

"You must be Miss Smoke."

She stared at him curiously.

"This way, please." He smiled and led her down the main aisle. It was all she could do to keep from tripping as she took in the grandeur of the room. Hockey stadiums were smaller than this. And much less elaborate. Row upon row of red-cushioned, wooden pews extended from the stage to the back doors then up onto two balconies. Lush carpeting covered the floor. A velvet purple curtain crossed the stage, and above it was a screen as big as any she'd seen.

The usher led her to the front row and gestured to a seat on the aisle.

"I couldn't possibly sit here." She was too conspicuous. Felt too uncomfortable. Why was everyone staring at her all of a sudden? Whispers flew about her and people pointed, and she quickly lowered in her seat to hide.

Across the aisle, a young man winked at her, while behind him, a man, or was it a woman—she couldn't tell—glared her way. Heart slamming against her ribs, she faced forward. She would kill Daniel for this.

The play was spectacular. There was a full orchestra hidden beneath the stage and the acting was superb. Once the lights dimmed and Angelica no longer felt all eyes upon her, she enjoyed it. Though honestly, the spiritual message was weak. If there even was one. The story was more like a fairy tale than anything—with trees, animals, and plants taking center stage, dying off in a world gone bad, but then saved at the end by some vague creator.

After the actors and directors took a bow, Thomas moved to stand at the podium. If looks could kill, his glance in her direction would have incinerated her. She squirmed in her seat, longing to flee, but then he pasted on a smile and gave brief announcements, thanking those who put on the play, then congratulating a threesome—one man and two women—who'd just been married the day before. Angelica squirmed yet again. Finally, he instructed the ushers to take the offering and the velvet bags were passed.

No mention of the earthquake. In fact, no prayers at all.

Daniel came on stage. She knew the minute he had, not only because she could feel his eyes upon her, but because a reverential hush fell over the auditorium. She glanced up to his smile and a look in his eyes that said no one else mattered in the world but her. She remembered that look so well, too well. Fear rose in her heart once again, and she wanted to look away, to tell herself it didn't matter. But she couldn't take her eyes off him.

The man was handsome, commanding, and beyond charming. She could see why people followed him, listened to his every word. She had seen him give sermons on TV, but this was different. The electricity in the room surprised her. The rapt attention of the audience. And her mind drifted back to a time when he was in his first year of seminary. They had just met a month before, and Daniel and Thomas and a few other friends were preaching on the beach. Crowds of young people swarmed around him, listening to his uncultured and somewhat simple presentation of the gospel. Several gave their lives to Jesus, though she hadn't really cared about such things back then. She just loved watching him.

As she was doing now. But this time was vastly different. Now, his words were refined, well chosen, and executed for a specific purpose—to entertain, tickle the ears, and keep people coming back. He was funny, witty, and he gave them hope. What a gift he had. Too bad he was wasting it.

Backstage, Daniel flew down the steps, ignoring calls from his associates, a shout from Rubio, and even the congratulations cast his way. He had one thought in mind. Get to the privacy of his office where he'd instructed Mr. Roberts, a.k.a. Tank, to bring Angel. When he'd seen her sitting in the front row, staring up at him, his heart had nearly burst with joy. She'd come! And she looked stunning in a modest blue form-fitting dress, a simple gold chain around her neck, and her hair pinned up in an elegant bun.

The best part was the way she looked at him during his brief sermon…just like she had when they were younger and he preached to whoever would listen—like she adored him, admired him, and never wanted to leave his side. Why had he ever allowed her to walk out of his life?

He felt alive again for the first time in a long while, and he resisted the urge to whistle as he turned the last corner to his office. Once inside, he slipped into the bathroom, slicked back his hair and checked himself in the mirror before he posed casually against his desk, anxious to hear her praise for the wonderful production, her apology for insinuating that his church wasn't preaching the real gospel, and maybe even— dare he hope—her willingness to consider leaving her church to attend his.

A knock preceded Tank ushering her inside. Then after giving Daniel a nod, the bodyguard left and closed the door. Daniel had instructed him to not allow anyone else inside. He wanted tonight to be special. He wanted to talk with her like they used to and then take her out to dinner. A stunned expression claimed her features as she glanced over his office. "Wow," was all she said.

He took that as his cue. Gathering the dozen roses and gardenias on his desk, he held them out to her, awaiting her delighted expression.

Instead, she folded arms across her chest, cocked her pretty head and said, "You can't buy me, Daniel."

A sledgehammer to his heart would have felt less painful. He forced a mask of nonchalance. "Not trying to." Setting down the flowers, he approached her, swallowing his pride and hoping to start again. "Please, have a seat." He gestured toward his couch.

She didn't move. "You have no right to assign a bodyguard to me without my permission." Her eyes were green ice.

This wasn't going well. Turning, he began fingering paper clips on his desk. "Tank? He's harmless. Besides, you should have told me about that car nearly running you down."

"Why is it any of your business? And why are you calling my son?"

Turning, he leaned back against his desk and gripped the edge. "In case you haven't noticed, Angel, I care about you. This is a dangerous world, and I don't want to see you harmed."

She sighed and glanced around the room. "I appreciate that, Daniel, I do. But it is still my life, and you can't just intrude in it whenever you want." She fingered her necklace and gave him an angry glare. "I realize you are the big cheesemo here, but you hold no power over me."

*Ouch.* Daniel took a minute to recover, watching his dreams for the night shatter into a million pieces. When he found his voice, all he could say was, "I don't want to lose you."

His admission seemed to weaken her defenses as she sank onto the couch. "Listen, I know we had a thing once. I know we kissed at the park, but that doesn't mean anything."

"It meant something to me," he said, wondering how many more punches he could take.

Frowning, she looked down. "Call off your bulldog, please."

He pushed from his desk, collecting what was left of his pride. "You got it."

"And please don't speak to Isaac without my permission."

He stepped toward her, frustration rising. "Hey, he called me after the car incident. He's worried about you."

Her eyes narrowed. "Why would he call you?"

"I asked him to if he needed anything. Sorry." He raised his hands in surrender. "I had no right. You know me—I can be a bit pushy."

"You think?" Finally, he got a smile out of her.

Tentatively, he sat on the stool across from her. "Am I forgiven?"

She eyed him and shook her head. "Sure, I guess."

"Then, let me make it up to you and take you to dinner."

*Know ye not that the unrighteous shall not inherit the kingdom of God? Be not deceived: neither fornicators, nor idolaters, nor adulterers, nor effeminate, nor abusers of themselves with mankind, nor thieves, nor covetous, nor drunkards, nor revilers, nor extortioners, shall inherit the kingdom of God.*
  1 Corinthians 6:9-10 (KJV)

# Chapter 20

What was it about Daniel Cain that broke down all her defenses? Even when she was angry with him! The last thing Angelica intended was to have dinner with the man. Yet here she was, walking along the beach as the sun set over the everglades, her stomach full of fresh crab legs and hush puppies, and her heart leaning far too much toward this man. Of course, Daniel had ordered the Caesar salad—the only healthy item at the little crab stand he had taken her to. Or, rather *she* had taken him to, turning down his invitation to one of the best restaurants in town.

"It's the simple things in life that are the best," she'd said as they sat at a small table in front of the shack to eat.

He'd asked her then about the play. Had she enjoyed it? What were her thoughts?

Avoiding an argument, she told him how magnificent the church was, how beautiful and large and ornate and well decorated. And his office…better than the Oval Office.

At this, he laughed.

Yet now, as they walked side by side, shoes in hand, their bare feet sinking into the moist sand, he grew pensive and asked her what she really thought about the play *and* his sermon.

"The play was exceptional, Daniel. Professional and entertaining. And you've always been a great speaker."

"But…"

"But nothing." She stared at a sandpiper picking up a French fry from the sand.

"I know you too well. There's more."

They wove between a group of kids building a sand castle as Angelica chose her words. "It was all fluff, good will, hope, happiness. That's all great and nice, but people need to hear the entire truth. They need to hear how to be saved, truly saved, and that the Christian life is not easy. It's one of sacrifice and sometimes suffering and denying self." She sighed and looked up at him. "You didn't even mention Jesus."

He growled and dug fingers in the back of his neck. "Of course, I mention Him. Just not in every sermon."

"But this was an outreach, wasn't it?"

He kicked the incoming seawater, shooting foam into the air.

"I'm sorry, Daniel. You asked, and I can't lie to you."

"No, I value your honesty. Or I thought I did." He gave a sad chuckle. "But I'm glad for it. I could always count on you to tell me the truth."

She hated that she had disappointed him, but flatteries served no one. A wave crashed toward them, and he took her arm and drew her out of its path, giving her an idea. Perhaps if she skirted the issue and just got him to talk, he'd see the truth for himself. "Why don't you tell me about your church? What is it like being such an important pastor? What are your days like? The people you work with."

Her questions prompted him to begin what turned out to be a nearly hour-long conversation in which he described his many responsibilities and all the employees he had to manage. Especially the difficult ones—Thomas, always on his case, his admin, a Mrs. Clipton, who couldn't seem to get anything right, Rubio the music director who was never happy, along with a host of other employees and several members who constantly complained about everything from the temperature in the church to the topic of sermons.

"Big donors, you know, so I have to listen to them." He grunted as they reached a lighthouse perched on a wall of rocks and turned around.

"Sounds like you're the CEO of a huge corporation."

"It's exactly like that. Lots of work and responsibility."

"But not much time for God or doing real discipling."

"There are others for that."

Warm salty air blasted them, pulling her hair from her pins. "But you used to want to do that. Remember? You had such a love for the lost." She stared at him, shielding her eyes from the setting sun, and longed to reach the old Daniel still lingering deep inside.

He raked back his hair, sending it in a dozen directions, and gave her a sideways glance. "That was a long time ago. I had to grow up and face the real world."

"I still see that zeal in you, Daniel." She'd seen sparks of it at church when he'd taken the pulpit, sparks of it here and there when he spoke about God. Only sparks. But it gave her hope they could be fanned into flames.

Across the beach, people were packing up coolers and umbrellas, shaking out towels as the setting sun spun a golden ribbon over the western horizon. They walked on in silence, the wavelets tickling her feet and depositing tiny shells in the sand. She had no idea what to say next, but she had sensed Daniel's frustration as he spoke about his church, and maybe even a little sadness. "But you don't seem very happy," she finally said.

"Listen, Angel." His tone turned defensive. "If I want to be successful and make a living, I have to make compromises."

"Is it that important to be successful in the eyes of the world?"

"Of course. Only then do people listen to you. How else can I reach as many as possible with the love of God?"

She gazed at him as he walked along, eyes downcast, footsteps measured, jaw knotted. And despite his fame and prestige, he was suddenly the same insecure young man she'd known, determined to make a name for himself, to battle the insults and degradation his drunken father had beat into him as a child. Was he still fighting that same battle? He had everything, and his name was known all over the globe. But maybe it wasn't enough to satisfy his ravenous need to be *somebody*.

"You've more than proven yourself Daniel. To the world *and* to your father."

"He has nothing to do with it." His angry tone defied his statement.

"Okay. Okay. Sorry."

"I'm sorry." Halting, he faced her as a wavelet swept over their feet. "I guess I just wanted to impress you. Show you how far I've come, prove to you I *am* doing some good."

"You don't need to prove anything to me. You never have. Or to God. Just follow Him and quit playing footsies with the world."

He chuckled. "I'm not sure what that means."

She cocked a brow. "Like marrying two men."

His smile faded. "Hey, it's the law. And excluding them only turns them off from God." He started walking again. "I never figured you to be a hater."

A seagull screeched overhead. "I don't hate homosexuals. Or anyone for that matter. In fact, aren't you hating them more by your approval?"

Snorting, he shook his head as if she'd gone crazy.

"Think of it this way. You see a person running toward a cliff. They aren't paying attention and don't see that in just a couple more steps, they will plunge to their death. What do you do? Do you scream and tell them they are going the wrong way, try to leap in their path and stop them at the risk of them getting mad at you or calling you a bigot or hater? Wouldn't that be the loving thing to do? Or do you just smile and wave as they run right off the cliff?"

He was silent for a long time. Music started blaring from a nearby bar as the wind picked up, bringing the scent of suntan oil and beer. "Okay. I sorta see your point. But the state forbids me to leap in their path. And besides, don't you think God will give them a break? After all, they can't help it, and those old scriptures about it being an abomination are just plain archaic. You can't apply them to our culture today."

"What about the entire first chapter of Romans? It spells out quite clearly God's views on homosexuality and on all who deny Him. And in 1 John it says that a person who knows God does not keep sinning on purpose."

"We all keep sinning. That's why we need Jesus."

Another sandpiper darted in front of them, chased by an incoming wave, as Angelica drew a breath to calm herself. "I can't answer for God, Daniel. All I know is what His Word says. God doesn't change based on our culture. He loves everyone and wants each person to join Him in Heaven, and of course we do that by trusting in Jesus. But the Bible is clear in so many passages that we must also obey Him and continue to do His will. Like this one from 1 John 2, 'Whoever says, I know Him, but does not keep His commandments is a liar, and the truth is not in him.' Or this one in Matthew 7, 'Not everyone who says to Me, Lord, Lord, shall enter the kingdom of heaven, but he who does the will of My Father in heaven.' Shouldn't we be telling people the truth? Doing everything in our power to save them? Especially those who are trapped in habitual sin."

He was silent for a moment, giving her hope she had reached him, but then he laughed.

"What's so funny?"

"You. You wanted nothing to do with God twelve years ago."

She returned his smile. "I guess we've both changed."

"Not all that much." Much to her surprise, he slipped his hand in hers. "You know I love talking with you, Angel. You always challenge me."

"Is that a good thing?"

"It is." He squeezed her hand. "Tell me you're enjoying our time together as much as I am."

She was. In many ways, he was the same Daniel she'd always known—her knight in shining armor from years ago—witty, charming, caring, intelligent, good with people, and the way he looked at her...like he was looking at her now… brought back such sensations, she feared she'd lose all control and fall into his arms. It was as if she were twenty-one again, so enamored with him, she would have married him on the spot if he'd only asked.

Memories filled her thoughts of the first time they'd met. In the Seashore Lounge, her first job as a cocktail waitress. He and his buddies from seminary had come in for a drink. Only Daniel wasn't drinking. She remembered thinking how odd that was for such a young guy. Especially when his friends were getting more and more rowdy with each drink. And more and more fresh with her, including some not-too-pure comments they'd flung her way. If she'd known at the time they were churchgoing people, she'd have given them a piece of her mind. But as it was, she was used to being disrespected. Part of the job, her coworker had told her.

Daniel, however, had been nothing but polite. Though she had caught his eyes on her more than once, his gaze was not one of lust, but more of admiration. Or interest.

"What are you thinking?" he finally said, bringing her back to the present.

She shouldn't tell him. It would only stroke his ego. "Remember when we first met?"

"I will never forget it." He smiled and squeezed her hand. "You were so cute in that outfit they made you wear."

"Is that all you can think of?" She chuckled. "Remember getting tossed from the place?"

"Oh yeah, that." He shrugged. "Well, I couldn't very well let that guy put his hands on you like that. Not after you told him no. Twice."

"But you didn't have to slug him."

"Worked though, didn't it?" His dimple appeared.

She smiled, picturing the drunken pervert toppling backward after Daniel's punch, tipping the table over and sending all the drinks crashing to the floor. It was the table next to Daniel's, and she hadn't even known he was watching.

"You rescued me. No one had ever done that for me before."

"Earned me your phone number." He brushed hair from her face and then ran his thumb over her lips. "I should have never let you go. You've always been my Angel." He leaned toward her and stole a kiss.

But if she admitted it, he didn't steal it at all.

*Woe to you, scribes and Pharisees, hypocrites! For you are like whitewashed tombs which indeed appear beautiful outwardly, but inside are full of dead men's bones and all uncleanness.*
*Matthew 23:27 (NKJV)*

# Chapter 21

With the sensation of Angel's sweet kiss still thrumming through his body, Daniel slept sounder than he had in years. When he rose in the morning, he felt as if a burden had been lifted and he wasn't sure why. After making himself a fruit smoothie, he was still smiling when he walked through the doors of FLCG and made his way to his office. Man, but he had missed Angel. He'd forgotten how wonderful it was to just talk with her. She had a special way of listening, a rare gift among people today who were constantly trying to interject their opinions and advice. But not Angel. She just listened to him for hours. And more than that, she cared. He could tell by the questions she asked and the tone of her voice. She understood him, the stress he was under, the responsibility. If only she could see the bigger picture and understand why he had to compromise on some issues to affect more people for good.

All in time. She would see. And her kiss meant that there was hope for them to start up where they'd left off.

Turning a corner, he spotted Thomas' door ajar and halted, peering inside. He'd love to hear his thoughts on the play last night. The sounds of grunting and groaning met his ears, and he took a step inside and scanned the room. In the far corner Thomas was lying on top of a woman on a couch.

"What is going on?" Daniel shouted before he had time to think.

The woman screeched, while Thomas leapt from her and spun around, his shirt untucked and pants unzipped.

Kimberly Monroe sat up, clawing at her blouse in an attempt to cover herself.

Upon seeing Daniel, Thomas' shoulders lowered and he grinned. "Nothing much now," he said with a sarcastic slur.

"Oh, my." Kimberly searched for her shoes, slipped them on and stood, doing her best to straighten her skirt and button her shirt.

"Could you knock next time?" Thomas said, making himself decent.

"I didn't think I had to. What on earth are you two doing?" Disgust soured in his mouth.

Clearly flustered, Kimberly cast Thomas a look of alarm and passed by Daniel on her way out the door, uttering a quick. "Sorry."

Thomas watched her leave then dropped into a chair. "Has it been so long that you don't recognize it?"

Anger heated Daniel's blood. "What are my associate pastor and youth pastor doing having sex!?"

"Well, we actually didn't get that far."

"You think this is funny?" Daniel shouted, his grand morning ruined. "This is unacceptable!"

"Come on, man, relax. Everybody does it." Thomas put on his shoes.

"Not at my church."

Thomas snorted. "You'd be surprised."

"What does that mean?"

Rising, Thomas slicked back his hair. Rebellion sparked in his eyes, and Daniel longed to wipe that smirk off his face. "Good grief, I realize they took out the passages about fornication from the Bible"—Daniel huffed—"But two of my pastors boinking each other? Right in your office where anyone could see!"

"You have some right to talk, Daniel. Hanging out with that prostitute."

Fisting his hand, he took a step toward Thomas, then stopped. It would do no good for the senior and associate pastor to get into a fistfight. "You know very well she's no prostitute."

"She's a cocktail waitress with no education and a son out of wedlock. What does that look like?"

"I don't care what it looks like. I only care what I saw happening in here. And it won't happen again. Do you hear me?"

When Thomas didn't answer, Daniel stormed out and went to his own office, seeking his coffee pot, praying Mrs. Clipton had made a fresh batch.

She had. God bless her.

He heard Thomas' footsteps pounding the carpet behind him. "You'd better care because the entire church is talking about the little tart you invited to our play. Sitting her up front on display for all to see. What were you thinking?"

Daniel poured himself a cup, trying to control his anger. "I was thinking how nice it was that I could invite a friend to the play, that's all."

"But she's a woman, and an attractive one, and the way you were ogling her from the pulpit… you don't think people noticed?"

"I wasn't oglin—"

"Now the entire church thinks you're dating a cocktail waitress."

Daniel sat behind his desk and set down his coffee. "So what?"

"So what?" Thomas leaned his knuckles on Daniel's desk. "They are up in arms! Harold Jakes and his cohort

Brinkenburg are already calling a board meeting to discuss it."

"Discuss what? I invited a friend to the play. She happened to be a woman."

"You're going to ruin everything." Thomas pushed from the desk and walked away. "You know that, don't you?" He spun to face Daniel. "This Washington gig and any chance of getting elected, the New World Religion Conference. Everything. Including this church."

"Don't be ridiculous." Daniel knew Thomas had a flair for the dramatic, but this was too much. "For dating an old girlfriend? Listen, I almost got her convinced to leave these religious fanatics she's involved with. I can tell she's weakening. Just think what a great human interest story that would make." He waved a headline in the air. "Famous pastor rescues woman and her son from dangerous cult and then they fall in love." He smiled. "Everyone loves a story of redemption and romance."

"Please don't tell me you're in love with her."

Daniel made no reply.

Thomas growled. "If you can turn her, I suppose we could spin it into something people might accept. But that's a big *if*. I just don't get you. Why take the risk?" He took up a pace. "I know it sounds archaic, and you'd think with our permissive culture, people would move past it, but they don't. Not in religious circles. Not if you want to be a world spiritual leader. You have to be perfect, holy, without a past. And you can't date a woman with a past either. Sure, you might be able to convince the board and keep your position here, though you'd definitely lose members. But as soon as D.C. or the World Religions Conference hears about it, you can kiss any future beyond this church goodbye."

Daniel stared at the picture of his mother on his desk and longed for her advice. Everything was permissible in today's world. You could even marry your dog if you wanted. But

Thomas was right. Spiritual advisors and leaders were still held to a higher standard.

"How did you turn your little incident with Kimberly back on me?"

"I'll stop things with Kimberly if that'll make you feel better. Besides, she came on to me. But man, you gotta pull it together. We've come too far to lose it all now." Thomas halted and stared at Daniel. "And for what? A woman who dumped you and broke your heart. She almost ruined you once and she's gonna do it again." A look of disgust came over his features. "Unless you really *do* want to end up a failure…just like your dad."

Arithem released a sigh of frustration as he watched his charge, Thomas, try to convince Daniel to stay away from Angelica.

"I'm sorry," he said to Nazare standing beside him in Daniel's office.

"No need to apologize," Nazare said. "You cannot control him. Your job is to protect him, not influence him one way or the other."

"I know."

"The Father gave them free will, just as He gave us. Remember how Lucifer and a third of the angels chose to rebel against the Father long ago? They made their choice and were thrown out of heaven, permanently separating them from the source of all goodness, love, and light. Now they consist solely of evil and wickedness. They are no longer angels—but demons. But we chose to remain His servants, to obey His every command. When God made humans, He gave them the same choice to obey or disobey Him, starting with

Adam and Eve. We can only watch as they make their own decisions, just as we made ours."

Arithem shifted uncomfortably. "Very true. But I feel responsible in some way. See all the demons that have him in their grip?" He gestured to at least twenty foul spirits inhabiting Thomas.

"Yes. He follows their evil suggestions, which allows them to stay. We can't override his choices."

Arithem crossed arms over his chest. "It is hard to stand by and not be able to intervene. I wish the Father had assigned me an easier charge."

"He must have thought you were well equipped." Nazare watched as Daniel defended Angelica, feeling hope rise, but then it plummeted when he insisted on dragging her away from the truth. "He's so close." Nazare spoke with more emotion than he intended. "The darkness weakens in him. He must keep seeing Angelica. She is the only one speaking life to him."

"At least there is hope for yours. Thomas continues to slip further away from the light."

"Be patient, my friend. The Father would not have assigned you to him if he had hardened his heart beyond the point of salvation."

Arithem nodded.

"We must speak to Campana. Perhaps he can urge Marley to influence these two. Marley is walking in more light each day."

"Good idea."

Nazare glanced at his friend, noting the urgency in his eyes. "Don't get too involved. We are only to watch and protect."

"I don't know how you do it."

"Not well. For, in truth, I fear for Daniel every day. I have known him since he was born. I have seen him love the

Father with all his heart, and oh, how I long for those days again."

"How foolish these humans are. So many choose the path that leads to despair, rejection, and sorrow."

"They buy the enemy's lies, the deception he has placed over the entire world—that fame, power, and money will lead to happiness, that those things give value and importance to one's life."

"If they only knew how valuable they already are."

A warm breeze, ripe with the scents of the sea and suntan lotion caressed Angelica's face, and she opened her eyes. While Daniel and Isaac fished off the pier, she'd taken this rare opportunity alone to pray. There were so many requests, so many people in her life who needed to know God's love. And then there were the Cascadia earthquake victims. News had been filled with horrific stories of death, destruction, looting, crime, and so many homeless in need of basic necessities. Her church, though tiny, had taken a collection of goods and money to send to a church in that area for distribution. That and her prayers were all she could do.

Yet, despite the tragedies of the world, and much to her shame, her thoughts continually drifted to Daniel and the kiss they'd shared. She sighed, chastising herself for being so weak. Daniel had a way of stirring feelings within her that were not just physical, but that reached deep into her soul. It was one of the reasons she had fallen for him, and one of the reasons she must stay away from him.

Which, of course, begged the question why she was here with him now, allowing him to interact with her son. Her gaze found Isaac's small frame standing beside Daniel's large one on the edge of the pier, fishing poles over the railing, lines in the water. Another one of her visions coming to pass. The fishing trip had been planned over the phone days before Angelica had stormed into Daniel's office. Isaac had always wanted to fish, but Angelica had no idea how, nor the money for the equipment. How could she turn down an offer for both when her son was bursting with excitement?

*What am I doing, Lord?* Isaac needed a strong man of God to influence him in the right direction, not a compromising power-hungry pastor.

Hot, fiery rays showered down on her from above, and she grabbed her sunscreen and lathered more on her arms and legs. As a Florida native, she always had a tan, but she was prone to burn if she got too much sun.

"Hey, Angelica!" The cheerful voice caused her to shield her eyes and look up to see Anna approaching in a T-shirt, shorts, and flip flops.

"Anna! What a surprise."

The lady plopped down beside her. "I thought I saw you over here. Robert and I came for an early morning swim." She gestured to her husband sitting in a beach chair several yards away, book in hand, then drew a deep breath. "Kinda miss the beach since we stopped doing our Saturday thing."

"I miss our Saturday thing."

"Yeah, me, too. But we seem to be doing pretty good at Scottie's."

Children laughing brought Angelica's gaze to a group of kids in a sand fight. "True. There have been so many new people lately. Several who used to listen to us here on the beach."

Anna squeezed Angelica's arm, her eyes sparkling. "God is doing amazing things."

Angelica nodded. "How many got healed last week?"

"At least four. And two saved. And then Robert cast that demon out of that new guy, Rich." She smiled at Angelica. "Plus your prophetic word."

Angelica glanced at Isaac, then cupped a handful of sand, allowing it to sift through her fingers. "I just say what the Lord gives me."

"But it brings such encouragement. Especially when we hear the Lord telling us to hold on, to persevere in the face of such mounting evil." Removing her shoes, Anna dug her toes in the sand. "The Holy Spirit is being poured out everywhere. Scottie told me yesterday that he's been in touch with over forty home churches in Fort Lauderdale alone."

"Forty…" Angelica whistled. "I had no idea."

"And some of them are in touch with churches throughout the nation and the world. Things are happening Angelica. Miracles, healings, so many people coming into the kingdom. Exciting times."

"Such good news. I hope he shares that with us on Saturday."

"I'm sure he will."

Angelica watched a pelican dive bomb the water. Moments later, it surfaced, a fish in its mouth.

"Where's Isaac?" Anna asked.

She followed Angelica's point, squinted her eyes, and then smiled. "Is that the famous preacher?"

When Angelica didn't respond, she added, "Thought you were going to stay away from him."

She laughed. "Yeah, that didn't work out so well."

"And that's a bad thing because…?"

Angelica sighed and stared at the foam-capped waves crashing on the sand. "Too many reasons to list."

Daniel and Isaac drew in their lines and began packing their stuff.

"He broke your heart once…I know that."

*Broke, devoured, and spit out.* Anna had been the only person Angelica had told. Not even Leigh knew the whole story. "It's not so much that. He's part of the apostate church."

"Who better to influence him than you?"

"But he won't listen. He's too stubborn. Believe me, I've tried. He still thinks we are a bunch of kooks."

Daniel and Isaac reached the edge of the pier and started across the sand.

"You love him, don't you?"

"No." But her heart betrayed her as she watched him approach, his confident gate, wind in his hair, and the way he chatted with her son. "Yes, I guess. Maybe I never stopped."

Anna laid her hand on Angelica's. "Be careful. The man is obviously pursuing you, but since he's not following the Lord right now, you must seek God's guidance. Pray for him, be an example, but guard your heart. God may use you to bring him back into the light, but follow Him and not your emotions."

Angelica kicked the sand. "Easier said than done. But why me? I'm just a cocktail waitress, a single mother who can barely provide for her son."

"Because the man obviously loves you."

Angelica blinked. "What?"

"He bailed you out of jail and then risked getting Gecka to take care of you. I don't know many men who would do that."

"He likes playing the hero." Angelica dared to glance at him, his muscular physique admired by several women whose eyes followed him as he strolled by. "Besides, he could have any woman he wants."

Anna raised a brow. "Odd, then, that he chooses to hang out with you."

"More frustrating than odd." Angelica smiled. "Besides, I'm worried for Isaac. Daniel's not a good influence on him."

"Hmm. Perhaps." Anna stared out over the glistening sea as a gust of wind blew her brown hair behind her. Daniel and Isaac were just yards away when she faced Angelica again, a knowing smile on her lips. "By the way, when are you going to tell him that Isaac is his son?"

*The coming of the lawless one is according to the working of Satan, with all power, signs, and lying wonders, and with all unrighteous deception among those who perish, because they did not receive the love of the truth, that they might be saved. And for this reason God will send them strong delusion, that they should believe the lie.*
*2 Thessalonians 2:9-11 (NKJV)*

# Chapter 22

Angelica opened her mouth to reply to Anna's shocking question, but something had lodged in her throat—a clump of terror and shock. She glanced up to see Daniel and Isaac, laughing and talking, coming closer and closer.

"Mom, I caught a fish!" she heard her son shout.

But all she could do was stare at Anna.

Smiling, the lady squeezed her arm and struggled to rise. "Mr. Cain, good to see you again. And Isaac, look at that fish!"

Daniel greeted Anna while Isaac smiled proudly.

Thankfully, Angelica found her breath before she passed out.

The strong smell of fish bit her nose as the slimy gray creature filled her vision.

"Mom, you okay?" Isaac's face appeared behind it.

She forced air into her lungs, and excitement into her voice. "Did you catch this?"

He beamed. "Yup."

She glanced at Daniel who looked as proud as her son, and then her gaze sped back to Isaac. "That's awesome! Guess we're having fish for dinner."

"Cool. I can feed the family too!"

"That will be a huge help." She gave her son a hug. And she meant it. Any extra food would truly be a blessing. Except now she had to learn how to cook fish.

"He's a natural, of course." Daniel set down his pole. "Picks up everything so easily."

"Well, I'll leave you all to it. Robert looks lonely." Anna winked at Angelica, grabbed her shoes, and strode away.

Daniel glanced after her and rubbed the back of his neck. "For a minute, I thought the old gang was back causing trouble."

"Isaac!" A boy around Isaac's age called from shore.

After glancing his way, Isaac snapped pleading eyes toward Angelica. "Mom, can I go surf?"

Shielding her eyes, she checked the boy again to make sure she recognized him. "Sure. Just be careful."

After dropping his fish in the bucket, Isaac set down his pole, grabbed his board, and took off like the wind.

Plopping on the sand beside her towel, Daniel stretched out his legs as if he intended to stay. He smelled of fish, the sea, and Daniel, and she was having trouble concentrating.

Anna's declaration had sent such a streak of terror through her, she didn't think she would recover. She kept the identity of Isaac's father a well-guarded secret. But if Anna could figure it out, others could as well. And that must never happen.

For Isaac's sake.

Either Daniel would completely reject him to save his career—as he had already proven he was more than capable of doing—which would devastate Isaac and scar him for life, or Daniel would embrace him, sue her for partial custody, and sweep her son into the delusional apostasy he propagated from the pulpit.

And she'd go to her grave before she allowed either of those to happen.

Daniel could tell something was up with Angel. She'd been acting weird ever since he and Isaac had brought her the fish they'd caught. For one thing, she wouldn't look him in the eyes. For another, she kept staring at Isaac surfing as if she wanted to scoop him up and run away.

From what? Him?

He'd done nothing but help the boy. And not for any reason other than simply because he enjoyed his company. Daniel had always longed for a wife and children, but his career had taken precedence. Yet these moments with Isaac made him wish he could have fit in a family somehow. He would think Angel would be thrilled to have a godly man take Isaac under his wing. Yet most of the time, she seemed anything but thrilled.

"Thanks for letting me teach him to fish," he finally said.

"Are you kidding? He's been begging me for years." She drew her knees up to her chest. "I just can't wrap my mind— or my fingers—around worms and hooks and well...the stench." She gave a little laugh.

"Ah, I bet you could handle it. You're a pretty tough mom."

Her smile was sad. "There are just some things I can't do. Sports, fishing, and surfing, and I have a feeling one of these days, when he is taller than me, he will stop listening to what I have to say."

"Really?" Daniel shook his head. "I doubt it. You're raising him right. He respects and loves you, and that counts for something."

She finally looked at him. Curiously at first, but then something flashed in her eyes that resembled thankfulness. "I hope you're right."

Daniel longed to slip his hand into hers, to start back up where they'd left off on the beach two nights ago. But something had changed. He could sense it. A distance she was putting between them. Or maybe it was him. He was having trouble shaking the argument he'd had with Thomas. If anything, it had made him realize something he'd been trying to deny.

He loved Angel.

And he wanted her back. Even after she had walked out on him all those years ago. Back then, he'd been willing to give up everything for her. But what he didn't know—what had been nagging him ever since she'd walked back into his life—was if it came to it, was he willing to do the same thing now? This time around, he had much more to lose. And he was no longer a kid with foolish dreams.

A breeze stirred her hair over her bare shoulder, her tan skin sparkling like glitter in the sun. A whiff of baby powder tickled his nose, making him smile. Always baby powder, sweet and innocent just like her. Thomas had called her a whore. Daniel should have slugged him for that, for nothing could be farther from the truth. She wore the most modest swimsuit on the beach. And on top of that she wore shorts. If not for her loose past and her present involvement in a cult, he'd get on bended knee right there and ask for her hand.

At least one of those impediments he had a chance of destroying.

"I'm glad to see you and your church have stopped beach evangelism," he said to break the silence between them.

She released a long sigh and drew a handful of sand. "*I'm not. We were really helping people.*"

"Maybe, but you can't help anyone in prison."

"Really? This coming from a preacher?" She gave him a look of reprimand that must send Isaac dashing for his bedroom. "Does the story of Paul and Silas in prison ring a bell? The jailer who got saved along with his entire household?"

Shame heated Daniel. How did this woman know more about the Bible than he did? "I can't seem to make any headway with you."

She tilted her head. "Then why bother trying?"

Daniel laughed. "Ever my sassy Angel."

Finally, he got a genuine smile that even reached her eyes with a sparkle. She gazed at him for a moment as if she wanted to say something, but then glanced back out to sea.

Isaac waved at them from the shallows where he'd just rode a wave to shore with two of his friends.

Angel waved back and so did Daniel as a cloud obscured the sun and a breeze whipped over them.

"Must be tough being a single parent these days."

Planting her hands behind her on the towel, she leaned back, her eyes still on Isaac. "I won't deny it. He's growing up way too fast, and they are teaching him horrible things in school. Plus, money is always tight."

"Listen, Angel, I want to help." He truly did, but for all his eloquence, he suddenly could not find the words to proceed. "I want...well I want us to be more than friends. I'm begging you to stop going to that home church. If you get arrested again, I may not be able to help you."

She slid hair behind her ear and looked at him with those jade green eyes of hers, full of more strength than he ever remembered. "If God wills that, I will endure it."

"For what? Why are you so stubborn?" Daniel dug his foot into the sand.

"Why is it so important to you? We can still be friends, right? Oh, I get it." She flattened her lips. "You're afraid if I get arrested, it will affect your career."

"No, that's not it. Well, maybe part of it. But honestly, I'm more worried about you." That piece of honest truth shocked him. "Besides, when you kissed me the other night, I could tell you still have feelings for me." He slid his hand in hers.

Instead of facing him with that alluring smile of hers and admitting she did, she withdrew her hand and shouted for Isaac to come. Then leaping to her feet, she grabbed her towel, showering him with sand.

"You're leaving?" Heart plunging into the deep, Daniel rose and brushed sand from his chest and arms.

She folded her towel and plucked her bag from the sand. "I'm sorry, Daniel. That kiss was a mistake. I am never going to leave my church. I'm never going to abandon the truth. And if you can't accept that, we can never be friends."

Three days passed, and Angelica had not heard from Daniel. Apparently, her last brush-off had finally penetrated his thick skull. Good. One less thing to worry about for Isaac's sake. And hers. She should be thrilled, right? Then why did it feel like someone had poked her heart with a hot skewer?

Never mind. She had other problems to deal with, more important problems—her son's upbringing and protection, putting food on the table and a roof over his head, and sharing the love of God in a world that hated Him. Which brought her thoughts to Greg. He hadn't been at work the past two nights, and when she'd asked Sal, he told her Greg had called in sick. Of course Sal also called Greg a few colorful names and threatened to fire the man if he didn't show up soon. But it wasn't like Greg to miss work, at least not for more than a day, and Angelica couldn't shake the nagging feeling that something was wrong.

Pepper spray in hand, she dragged her sore feet up the stairs to her apartment, longing for nothing more than to sink into her mattress and sleep forever. But it would be light in four hours and it was her turn to take the kids to school. Afterward, she hoped to catch a few more hours of much-needed sleep before she had to pick them up and run several errands. Thankfully, she had the next two days off to recuperate—both her body *and* her wounded soul.

Inserting the key, she opened the bottom lock, then the top, and finally entered her beloved home. Darkness created dragons out of the furniture, but a beam of moonlight—bright and silvery—speared the shadows through the window. Light and dark. The endless battle between good and evil, between the truth and lies, between God and Satan. But no, not endless. The way things were looking, this war in the spirit realm would soon come to an end. The light would win and this present darkness would disappear. Forever.

Oh, how she longed for that day! Reminding her that, above all else, she needed to spend time with her Father.

Dropping her things on the table, she plodded toward her room, undressed, tossed her nightshirt on, and dropped into bed. Before a minute passed, her mind drifted into unconsciousness.

But her spirit didn't.

Scenes invaded, flashing through her mind—a man, handsome with penetrating eyes, speaking behind a podium to a crowd of people so large they would fill a city. Behind him, strange alien-like creatures glared over the throng with elongated heads and slitted eyes. Whenever he spoke, the crowds cheered with such exuberance they had to be quieted so he could continue. Then the scene switched to a war-torn field, desolate, smoking—twisted pieces of metal and human remains scattered about in a bloody stew. Massive tanks rolled over bones, crushing them to pieces. Drones buzzed overhead, searching for survivors.

Then Greg appeared, lying on a carpet in the middle of a room. Alone and in the dark. He held something in his hand. A container of some sort. His eyes were open, staring into the distance, empty and forlorn. A host of dark shadows slithered about him, tugging on his hand and whispering in his ear.

Angelica sat up with a start, her breath coming fast. Swinging her legs over the side of the bed, she grabbed her cell, found Greg's number, and called.

A man's groggy voice answered. "What?"

"Greg."

"Yup."

"It's Angelica."

Moaning sounded. "Do you know what time it is?"

She glanced at the clock. 5:00 a.m. "Are you okay?" she asked, the vision of him still stark in her mind.

"Yeah. What's up?"

How could she tell him what she saw? "Sal said you were sick. Just checking on you."

"At five in the morning?" Anger laced his tone.

"Yeah. Sorry. Just worried."

"I'm fine. Just a cold…" But he didn't sound like he had a cold. He paused for a moment, and she sensed he wanted to say something. "Thanks Angelica. You've always been a good friend."

"Listen, let me come by tonight. I'll bring you some chicken soup."

"No. I'm good. I'll be back at work soon. Gotta go. "

The line went dead before she could answer.

Setting down her phone, Angelica rubbed her eyes. He sounded okay, like himself, maybe a little down, but he'd been depressed lately. Yet, there was something—something she couldn't put her finger on.

"What are you trying to tell me, Father? Should I go to him?" And what about those other horrible visions? Instead of going back to sleep, she turned on a lamp, grabbed her Bible and spent the next hour taking in the holy words, allowing them to soak into her depleted soul.

At first light, she tossed on shorts and a T-shirt, grabbed her pepper spray, and crossed the street. No one was at the beach this early except a few homeless people the police hadn't scattered, and it gave her a chance to talk with God as she paced up and down the shore.

The sun peeked over the horizon, shoving back the darkness and painting ribbons of gold and orange across the sky. The glorious sight reminded her that God was pure light and pure love *and* in control. And that all she needed to do was lay her worries, fears, and problems before Him and they would dissipate like fog before the sun. How could she do anything but worship Him, her Creator, her Father, the One who would never leave her? So, she did just that, along with offering her prayers for those in need. An hour later, so saturated with God's Spirit, she longed to stay on the beach, talking to Him forever, but instead dragged herself back home.

After breakfast, Leigh went off to work. Angelica dropped the kids off at school and ran some errands, trying her best to keep that heavenly euphoria. But the world had a way of bringing her down. Especially when the food lines at the GIFP centers seemed to have doubled in a week's time, not to mention the zombie apocalypse of homeless wandering the streets.

She switched on the radio, trying to find some music to cheer her up when a news report blared that China had fired a missile at a Japanese ship, sinking it and killing all on board. The two nations had just declared war. At the news, the stock market plummeted—nearly tanked, and North Korea threatened to use their nuclear weapons on anyone who challenged them. In the midst of all that, NASA declared with great excitement that they had found intelligent extraterrestrial life and would soon make a worldwide announcement.

Angelica could hear people chattering excitedly about the news of alien life as she stopped at various stores to pick up necessities. She wasn't so sure that was a good thing. Aliens? Had God created life on other planets? If so, how did they factor into His plan for earth? And why was this information coming to light now? It seemed too convenient when the world was in chaos and people looked for a savior—eager to follow anyone who would rescue them and solve all their problems. Which reminded her of the powerful, charismatic man she'd seen in her dream and the strange creatures behind him.

How ripe this world was for such a leader.

Despite the frightening news, Angelica's thoughts remained occupied by two men—Daniel and Greg. She quickly shoved thoughts of Daniel aside, along with the pain they caused, and focused her prayers on Greg. But every time she prayed for him, a sinking fear gnawed at her soul.

Finally, toward the end of the day as Isaac was doing his homework and Joel was playing on Leigh's tablet, Angelica took a moment to stare out the window onto the beach and ask God what He wanted her to do.

*Go to him.* The voice came from inside—strong, commanding, yet full of love. The voice of her Father.

So, after Leigh came home, Angelica drove to Greg's tiny apartment on the west side of town. Whether he liked it or not, she was going to make sure he was all right. Even if she made a fool of herself.

Her knock on the door brought no sound from the other side. She knocked again. And again. And then shouted his name. Still nothing.

Fear rising, she grabbed her cell and tried calling him. No answer.

She peered through the window, but the drapes were drawn. Neighbors stared at her strangely, most refusing to answer her questions. One elderly lady said she hadn't seen him in days.

Finally, Angelica tried the door. Unlocked. Whispering her thanks to God, she opened it and crept inside. It took her eyes a moment to adjust to the darkness. A sour smell pinched her nose. A form lay on the carpet in the center of the room. Her heart lurched. Groping for a light switch, she found one and turned it on.

Greg lay on the floor, an empty bottle of pills in his hand.

*And these signs will follow those who believe: In My name they will cast out demons; they will speak with new tongues;*
Mark 16:17 (NKJV)

# Chapter 23

"Oh, no! Oh no, Father!" Angelica dropped to her knees beside Greg and laid two fingers on his neck. Barely a pulse, low and sporadic. Her own pulse was racing as she leaned her ear to his mouth. *Still breathing.* Thank God. Hands trembling, she punched 9-1-1 on her phone while grabbing the empty pill bottle. The words blurred in her vision as the phone rang and rang and rang. Finally, an answering machine picked up, informing her all lines were busy and her call would be answered in the order in which it was received and—

She hung up and called Scottie.

No answer. Where would he be? She jiggled Greg. No movement. No sound, not even a moan. Rushing to find the bathroom, she grabbed a washcloth and saturated it with water then laid it on Greg's forehead. Stupid thing to do, she supposed, but she needed time to think.

She dialed Robert and Anna. No answer. She shoved Greg. "Wake up! Wake up, Greg, Please!" A sob stuck in her throat. *Father, please help!*

Ring...ring...ring... *Pick up, Robert!*

His voicemail answered. Pacing, she waited for the beep then shouted into her cell. "Robert, I need you! Come to Greg's house. I think he's committed suicide. I don't know what to do. Please help!" She gave him the address and hung up. Then punched in 9-1-1 again.

Setting it on speaker, she laid the phone on the floor and shook Greg again, then wiped his face with the wet cloth.

Each unanswered ring sent a stronger wave of alarm through her.

Finally, a voice came through the speaker. "9-1-1, what is your emergency?"

"It's my friend Greg. I...I just found him in his apartment. I think he took a bunch of pills. He's unconscious."

"Okay, ma'am. Does he have a pulse?"

"Yes, faint."

"What pills, ma'am? Can you read the label?"

Grabbing the container, Angelica moved to hold it under the lamp.

"Xanax," she said. "And there's an empty bottle of bourbon here too. Please send an ambulance."

"One is already on the way, ma'am. Keep calm. They should be there in half an hour."

"Half an hour? Are you kidding me? He could die!"

"Sorry, ma'am. We've got lots of emergencies tonight. They'll be there as soon as they can."

Stunned, Angelica could only stare at the phone.

"Listen, ma'am, try to get him up. He needs to remain conscious. Get him up and walking. That will help." The phone went dead.

"Walking?" Angelica glanced back at Greg. No way she could lift him, let alone walk him around. "Father, what do I do?"

Pesha stood at Greg's feet, jaw tight, sword drawn, staring at his ward. Baliel stood by his side, having only recently arrived with Angelica.

"I failed him," Pesha said as he stared at the host of demons—at least twenty—filling Greg's body and the dozen or so hovering about his head, gloating in their victory.

"You did all you could," Baliel said. "He wanted this. It was his choice."

"He didn't want it. He fought it. But there are so many of them. And their lies erected a wall of deception around him so thick, the Father's voice couldn't get through."

One of the demons faced Pesha. As tall as the ceiling, his body was thin, emaciated, yet dark and shifting, like a column of black smoke. No, not black—an emptiness of light. His teeth were iron spikes, his eyes wide and cold, and he gave such a maniacal laugh, Pesha longed to drive his sword through him.

Baliel eyed the monster as well, bored with his theatrics. "Suicide celebrates a premature victory."

Pesha raised his sword. "If only I could—"

"You can't." Baliel lowered it with his hand. "Your ward was overwhelmed. He kept allowing them in, one after the other, kept listening to their lies."

Pesha nodded toward Angelica. "It started when she tried to tell him about the Father."

"Indeed. But in truth, it began only when he considered listening. That was when the dragon sent his warriors to attack. They knew his weaknesses and went straight for them."

Pesha sighed. "And I was helpless to stop them."

"Don't be so hard on yourself." Baliel widened his stance, preparing to fight. "You did all you could. You stood by him, fought off those he did not invite, and whispered wisdom in his ears."

Pesha hung his head. "And now his body will die, and they will drag him to hell. See how Death and the Warden await."

The two angels glanced in the corner where Death stood, fangs dripping in anticipation, beside the Warden who was jotting something down in a large book open in his lap.

"Do not give up yet, my friend. *She* is here now." Baliel smiled at Angelica. "See how bright her light is. She grows stronger every day."

"She is indeed one of the Father's mighty warriors. But what can she do now?"

"Behold,"—Baliel crossed arms over his mighty chest—"see how the demons retreat when she comes near. She is afraid, but she is finally appealing to the Father."

Pesha hoped she would hurry as he watched Death take another step closer.

Baliel pointed to the phone in her hand. "She is finally calling him."

"Who?"

"The one the Father told her to call." Baliel smiled. "Don't you know the Father has a plan for each of His precious children? Do you think this moment took Him by surprise?"

"Of course not. Forgive me." Pesha lifted his chin. "But Greg has not yet been adopted."

"*Yet*. Keep your sword steady, Pesha. The battle is about to begin."

Daniel hated the leap of his heart when Angel's name appeared on his cell phone. He hated the way this woman affected him. Both now and twelve years ago. Like no woman ever had. He had kept his distance after she blew him off at the beach, giving her some space, some time to miss him, to rethink his plea to be more than friends. Good grief, he was offering her the world! A way out of her poverty, a life of ease, and a future for Isaac! Still, she hadn't called him.

Until now.

"Angel, hi." He attempted a nonchalant tone.

"Daniel, I need you." Her voice was so agitated, he immediately stood and headed for the front door of his house, pressing the phone to his ear.

"My friend may be dying. I don't…I don't…can you help me? Please help!"

"Where are you?"

She gave him the address and he hopped in his Porsche, fired up the engine, and sped as fast as he could through the nighttime traffic. What in God's name was she doing in that part of town? Fear gripped him as he pulled onto Sistrunk, past seedy bars and strip clubs, and finally to a ramshackle apartment building that looked more like a no-tell motel. He pulled into a spot and locked the door, praying his car didn't get stolen. Then, taking the stairs two at a time, he halted before a door and knocked, fearing what he would find behind it.

Angel, face white and eyes frantic, ushered him inside. "Daniel, you came." Both relief and surprise rang in her voice. "We've got to get him up. Help me."

The smell of alcohol, dust, and mold blasted him as his gaze landed on a man in his late twenties lying on the floor. Kneeling, Angel grabbed his arm and attempted to hoist him up.

"What happened? Here, I got him." Reaching behind the man, he lifted him to a sitting position, then slid both arms beneath his shoulders and hauled him up to stand. He stumbled beneath the man's dead weight, but caught himself before he fell.

"The lady from 9-1-1 said we've got to keep him walking." Fear strangled Angel's voice.

Daniel glanced at the empty pill container and bottle of booze and figured out the rest. "Are they sending an ambulance?"

Angel wrapped both her arms around her friend and helped Daniel drag him forward. "Yes, but who knows when it will get here."

The man moaned, and Daniel wanted to ask who this was and how she'd ended up in this shady hovel—*in this man's apartment*—but instead he remained silent and lugged the unconscious man across the worn carpet. If they could get him to Daniel's car, he could take him to the hospital. But with only Angel's help, there was no way they'd make it down those stairs.

To make matters even more confusing, Angel began murmuring in some foreign language, her voice cracking, her breath coming hard.

A knock halted her nonsensical mumbling.

With no care as to whether there was a drug dealer or pimp on the other side of the door, she shouted, "Come in!" He would have to speak to her about being safer later.

Two men entered, both of whom he'd seen at her home church meeting.

"Robert! Scottie, thank God!" she shouted with such relief, you'd think they were physicians or even angels sent from heaven.

"Help me get him to your car," Daniel ordered the thick, tattooed one.

"I have a better idea," Robert said. "Lay him on the couch. Is he conscious?"

"He's been moaning, but no."

Scottie, the preacher from Angel's house church, glanced around the room and visibly shivered. "You see them, don't you?"

"Yes, too many to count," Angel replied.

See what? Were these people insane? "He needs to get to the hospital," Daniel announced with authority.

Robert took over for Angel. "Hospital can't help him." He and Scottie tried to lower Greg to the couch, but Daniel remained standing, his grip on the man's back unyielding. "He's going to die. Do you understand? We need to get him to your car."

Angel laid a hand on his arm. "Let them do their work, Daniel. Trust me." She looked up at him with such strong appeal, such sudden peace, that he relented and helped the men position Greg on the cushions.

*This isn't right. This isn't right.* He backed away, anger rising at these fools. He should call the police, have them all arrested before they allowed this poor man to die.

But then Angel would be arrested too.

He hesitated. And in that hesitation, he felt something dark, something sinister pass through the room...a cloud of icy mist that sent a shiver down his spine and made the hairs on the back of his neck prickle.

Greg moaned. Robert and Scottie knelt by his side while Angel stood at the head of the couch, hands gripped beneath her chin, mumbling.

"Greg, can you hear me?" Robert said.

The man moaned again. His eyelids fluttered, and the barest of desperate words squeaked through his lips. "I don't want to die..."

Scottie squeezed his shoulder. "Good. We don't want you to either. And neither does God. He loves you, Greg. So much."

Greg shook his head, his breath coming hard and ragged.

"Do you know how much God loves you? He sent His Son, Jesus, to die for you, so you could be healed, have a fresh start in life, and one day live forever with Him in eternity."

*Give me a break.* Daniel ground his teeth. These uneducated crazies were preaching to this guy when he needed a hospital? "Enough of this!" He stormed forward, intending to hoist the man in his arms and attempt the stairs alone. Better to risk falling than let this man die.

Greg's eyes popped open. They widened as he stared into the empty space above him. "Help me!" His body began to convulse. "They're coming—they're coming for me!"

Daniel froze. Sounds poured from Greg's lips that were not of this world. Groans and gut-wrenching screams, raspy shouts of agony, deep, malevolent voices that were metallic, guttural, male, and female—voices that should not come from a human.

Swallowing a lump of terror, Daniel backed away. *What the heck?* Something very wrong, very evil was going on here. He should leave. Get away from these psychos. The room began to spin around him, and his legs grew weak. He sank into a chair, trying desperately to make sense of what he was seeing, to find a speck of reason on which his thoughts could land.

Robert prayed boldly, "Lord Jesus, cover us all with Your powerful protection."

Scottie added, "In Jesus' name, I command all evil spirits to be silent while we minister to Greg."

The pandemonium stopped instantly, although Greg's body was rigid and tense.

"Jesus died and rose again in power to conquer all evil," Scottie continued calmly. "He has the authority to rescue you. Do you believe this?"

"I... I do..." Greg sputtered.

"Do you repent of your rebellious ways against God?"

Greg coughed and moaned. "I...do...yes." He gasped for air, his chest rising and falling as if he fought a battle within. "Oh, Jesus, please...save me!"

Robert gripped Greg's shoulders. "Demons, I command you to leave this man at once in the mighty and holy name of Jesus."

*What?* Daniel could only stare.

Greg convulsed.

"I said at once, demons!" Robert raised his voice. "He is no longer yours. He belongs to the Father now."

One more convulsion and Greg released such a tormenting scream, Daniel was sure the neighbors would come running. Unfortunately, that was not the end of it. The next twenty minutes passed in excruciating slowness as Robert called out at least five more demons from Greg— Alcoholism, Insecurity, Fear, Hopelessness, and the final one, Despair. Though they resisted at first, each one finally left with either a scream, seizure, or heavy sigh from Greg.

Finally, Greg's breathing returned to normal, color returned to his face, and his eyelids fluttered shut as he whispered, "Thank you, Jesus."

Everyone but Daniel broke out in happy exclamations.

Squeezing the bridge of his nose, Daniel took a minute to collect his thoughts. Surely this was all just an act—a morbid joke in order to get a reaction out of the famous pastor. Why was he even still here? The entire charade was ridiculous. Pushing against his knees, he rose, and lifted his hands to clap at their performance when a flash caught his eye, and he turned to see what looked like the tip of a very large sword— a glowing sword—sweeping through the air. It caught the edge of a shadow...no, not a shadow—a black, empty mass—that instantly dissipated.

Blinking, Daniel rubbed his eyes and stared back at the spot.

Nothing was there.

What was going on? He was more than relieved to hear the faint wail of sirens in the distance.

Pesha and Baliel both shouted a "Hallelujah!", gazing toward heaven where much rejoicing was now taking place.

A skittering noise, like the sound of a legion of cockroaches filled the air, and Pesha watched dozens of demons fleeing Greg's body. They filled the room in a swirling mass of darkness, uttering a cacophony of malicious shrieks and desperate groans, unhappy they'd been cast from their host.

Spotting the angels, the demons drew weapons and advanced in retaliation. Nazare and two other warriors fought them back, away from the humans, sword against sword, blade against blade. The clang of metal filled the room, the grunt of exertion, the groan of pain as blades hit their mark. Soon, the defeated hordes left, licking their wounds and slinging curses and blasphemous insults at the warriors. Only the strongest of them remained—Death, Suicide, and the Warden.

Pesha leveled his sword at Death.

Baliel planted his mighty legs before Suicide, while Nazare blocked the Warden. "You have no hold on him. He is now a prince of the Most High."

"We shall see, mighty warrior, we shall see." Black ooze dripped from Death's spiked fingernails as he drew a curved blade stained red with the blood of the lost. He slashed it through the air, then vanished.

Suicide gave a maniacal laugh and plucked a long knife from his belt... laughing, always laughing, this one...but he fled right behind Death.

The Warden remained behind them, furiously writing in his book before finally disappearing as well.

The angels rejoiced as the room filled with brilliant light, and they joined the joyous sounds of humans praising God for another soul plucked from the darkness and transferred into the light.

*And to her it was granted to be arrayed in fine linen, clean and bright, for the fine linen is the righteous acts of the saints. Then he said to me, "Write: 'Blessed are those who are called to the marriage supper of the Lamb!'"*
*Revelation 19:8-9 (NKJV)*

# Chapter 24

Once again, Daniel stared blankly at the words on his computer screen, unable to gather his thoughts enough to finish his speech. He had to get it done by tomorrow at the latest in order for his staff to be able to complete their edits. He knew this would be the most important speech of his life, a career maker—*or breaker*—Thomas kept reminding him. And he was right. If Daniel nailed this, everyone at the Presidential Prayer Breakfast—which included every important spiritual leader in the country—would know his name. Not to mention the most powerful members of government. And the President himself. A success in that man's eyes would seal the deal of Daniel's appointment as his spiritual advisor.

This was the chance he'd been waiting for. The chance of a lifetime.

But the words he'd just written might as well have been "Jack and Jill went up the hill" for all the impact and charisma they contained. He'd even taken a break and worked out in the church gym, then grabbed a kale salad. Still, his mind found no focus.

Honestly, after the incident last night, nothing else seemed to matter. If what he'd witnessed was true. And that was a big *if* —

A knock on the door brought a welcome interruption. Until he saw Rubio enter in his flagrant, hysterical way. "What is it now, Rubio?" Daniel sat back in his chair.

Rubio extended his bottom lip. "I bother you too much. Of course." He turned to leave.

"No, I'm sorry. I'm just busy today."

"Well, that makes two of us!" Rubio began, clearly seeing Daniel's apology as an excuse to blather. "I simply cannot work with the pianist you gave me. She's immature, catty, and refuses to play the piece the way I suggested."

Daniel would like nothing more than to toss the mind-numbing whiner from his office. Instead, he listened to Rubio's complaint and promised he'd talk to the woman. Thankfully, that seemed to appease him, for after wiping a tear from his eye, he promptly left.

Before Daniel could get back to work, Marley entered. A much more welcome visitor. The man always set Daniel at ease, and this time was no exception as he stood before his desk and studied him. "You look tired, Daniel."

"I am. Have a seat."

"Naw, won't stay long."

And he didn't. Not more than five minutes, during which time he asked Daniel about the youth group taking a possible trip along with Isabel Garcia, the missions director, to give food to the homeless downtown.

"Proselytizing is illegal," Daniel said, leaning back in his chair.

"We're just handing out food. That's it. And offering a smile and a prayer. You know, helping orphans and widows like the Bible says."

*Did it?* Daniel didn't remember that verse. But as Marley continued explaining the trip, he couldn't help but notice the man's excitement, his enthusiasm for showing the youth what he called *pure religion*. Another phrase from the Bible that Daniel didn't remember.

Yet something else was different about his friend. There was a look in his eye Daniel couldn't place—a new passion, or maybe it was just peace. Whatever it was, Daniel envied it.

He finally agreed to Marley's plan and said they'd work out the details later, then sent the youth pastor on his way.

After another hour of staring at the screen, Daniel rose to get a cup of coffee. This wasn't going well. He longed to contact Angel, ask her about what happened, make sure she was all right. The last time he'd seen her she was waving at Greg as they lifted him on a gurney into the back of an ambulance. She, Robert, and Scottie planned to meet him at the hospital, so Daniel decided to go home. He'd seen enough insanity for one night.

And still, he had no idea what it was he'd actually seen.

"Hard at work, I see." Thomas' sarcastic tone grated over Daniel as he poured a cup of coffee.

"I *have* been. Just taking a break."

"Almost done?"

Daniel turned to find Thomas peeking at the computer screen.

"Almost." He lied. "Coffee?"

"Sure." Thomas brushed past Daniel to pour himself a cup.

"Do you believe in demons?" Daniel blurted out.

The cup slipped in Thomas' hand and landed in the sink with a clunk. "What?" He picked it up, thankfully not broken, and re-poured his spilled coffee.

"Demons…you know evil spirits, emissaries of Satan?"

"Oh, come on, man. You don't believe that stuff, do you?" Thomas took his coffee and sat down, a deep crevice forming between his brows. "What's going on with you lately?"

Daniel lowered to a chair across from his friend. "But didn't Jesus Himself cast out demons?"

Thomas snorted. "You and I both know what they called 'demons' in the original Bible were mental illnesses, nothing more. No Satan, no evil spirits lurking around every corner. We know better now."

Daniel nodded. He'd been searching the Scriptures all morning. He vaguely remembered a few references from his early days in seminary, but either he couldn't find them or the word *disease* had replaced the word *demon*. He blew out a sigh and set down his cup. "I don't know. I saw something last night I can't explain."

Thomas sipped his coffee, alarm appearing in his eyes.

Regardless, Daniel continued. "I think it was a demon deliverance." Not to mention a sword and a shadow that shouldn't have been there. But he wouldn't tell Thomas that.

A low growl emanated from his friend's throat as he all but slammed down his cup on the table. "You were with Smokes, weren't you?"

Daniel flattened his lips.

"This is getting ridiculous, Daniel. It's got to stop. Do you hear me? Do you know how hard I fought for you with the board this week? After Harold Jakes and Mrs. Brinkenburg exposed your association with Smokes to them?" Punching to his feet, he began to pace. "I told them you were only trying to help her escape a cult. That you weren't dating her. And because of *me*, they dismissed the charge. And here you are seeing her again!"

"She called me."

"I don't care. Don't pick up the phone. It's obvious she wants your money. Why are you so dumb?"

Anger brewed in Daniel's stomach. He wasn't used to being called dumb by anyone, especially not his friends. He rose to his full height. "Listen, she needed my help and I went. I'd do it again, too. She's my friend. And I won't have the board or anyone else telling me who I can and cannot be friends with."

Thomas shook his head. "After all I've done for you. After what my father did. You're going to ruin us both with your arrogant selfishness." Spinning on his heels, he stormed out the door.

Sinking back into his chair, Daniel rubbed his eyes. Thomas was right. As usual. The logical thing to do, the best thing to do, would be to run as fast and as far from Angel and her friends as he could.

Dreams woke Angelica yet again. They were coming more frequently now, more violent, frightening, and each with an ever-growing sense of urgency. Rising to sit, she crossed her legs, pulled up her covers, and leaned back against her headboard with a sigh. This particular one had started off so beautifully. It was preparation for a party—a wedding, it seemed—in the most gorgeous setting—an exquisite garden filled with lush bushes, majestic trees, and myriads of exotic flowers in vivid colors she'd never imagined existed. A velvet green carpet spread over the ground, and a massive white gazebo sat in the center— ribbons of flickering white lights twinkling around the top. Servants rushed to and fro, setting plates of painted china and shimmering silverware on white-clothed tables. Silver-laced candles, surrounded by red roses, sat in the center of each table. Beside the gazebo, a white carpet led to a canopy positioned before a cascading waterfall that glittered in light that came from neither moon nor sun. The place was buzzing with joy and excitement as an orchestra began playing and a choir started singing.

The scene switched to a woman sitting by a window. Friends surrounded her, each one holding a lamp—the only light in the house. She wore the most beautiful wedding dress

Angelica had ever seen, and her face was glowing as she watched for what Angelica assumed was the arrival of her groom.

Another scene flashed of the same woman in another room, alone. Her dress was torn, ragged, and only half sewn together. But instead of fixing it, she flipped on the TV, grabbed pizza from the fridge, and picked up her cell. A man's voice came over the speaker, and the two began saying things only illicit lovers would say in private.

Angelica wanted to call out to her, to help the woman get ready, but she could only watch from afar as the bride sat in her dingy room, in her tattered gown, eating cold pizza. She had no idea of the extravagant wedding her groom was planning for her. She had no concept of the incredible life he would provide, for it was obvious he was of royal blood—a prince or even a king. Instead of getting ready, she chose to indulge herself with instant gratification, even going so far as to betray her fiancé with another.

Darkness swept away the vision, and the same man Angelica had seen in another vision returned—the one speaking on stage before a cheering, worshiping crowd. He spoke with the same eloquence, stirring up the mob with his words and promises. Behind him, the two lizard-like creatures grew bright red. Flames spewed from their mouths.

Yet no one in the crowd seemed to notice.

Angelica's screams of warning must have been what had awakened her.

Drawing her knees up to her chest, she replayed the dreams in her mind, knowing they were significant for some reason. "Father, I don't know why You are showing me such horrible things. What can I do with this information?" After several minutes of waiting in silence, peace settled on her, and she knew God would reveal His purpose in time. She continued praying, thanking God for Greg's salvation and deliverance, for Melody and Sal—yes, even Sal—and for others she had waited on at the Mermaid Den last week, others she had told of God's love. She prayed for Leigh and Joel. And, of course, for her beloved Isaac, as she always did—fearfully and tearfully begging God to watch over him, to keep him from the evil in the world and from the coming deception.

Which led her thoughts to Daniel. What did he think of the deliverance he'd witnessed? At the very least, he'd stayed when she'd thought he would run. But she feared from his expression of shock and disbelief that the miracle of God's power and love hadn't opened his eyes any further. Now, she had no idea what to do with him. Leave him be—as her mind was telling her—or rush to see him as her heart was screaming? *Lord, help me know Your will.*

She finished off her prayer with a song of praise, then got dressed and made her way to the kitchen where she flipped the TV to her Internet news station.

An Islamic Cleric was shouting something in Arabic from behind a podium.

"In today's news, history in the making, the Islamic Caliphate has been officially resurrected. A Caliphate, which is an Islamic kingdom, has not existed since the early twentieth century, and it has been a dream of many Muslims that this day would come."

Taking all this in and wondering at the significance, Angelica turned on the coffee maker.

The news continued.

"Several citizens reported seeing a large metal disk in the sky above Rachel, Nevada. Reports are coming in from California and New Mexico as well. The Pentagon is neither affirming nor denying these sightings but—"

The screen went black. Grabbing the remote, Angelica tried switching channels and found the regular channels still worked. She flipped back to her Internet station. Written in bright white letters across the screen, it read, "This station is no longer transmitting."

*What?* Angelica grabbed her phone and went to the website that broadcasted the station. She got an error message saying "address unknown."

*Great.* The GIFP finally shut it down. They'd been threatening to do so for years, labeling various news sites—the ones who didn't propagate their lies—as broadcasting fake news that was harmful for humanity.

Harmful to their agenda was more like it.

After waiting for the coffee to finish, she poured a cup, sat at the table, and dropped her head in her hands. A thousand questions spun through her mind, but the one that clambered for attention the most was the formation of a Caliphate. What did it mean? She'd read about Muslim end-times beliefs long ago…something about a messiah who would come during chaos and war after a Caliphate was formed. And what about those disk sightings and the aliens in her dream? "What does it all mean, Father? What do you want me to do?"

*Go tell Daniel.*

"Tell him what?"

*What you have seen. Time is short.*

"Are you coming for us soon, Father? At least tell me that." She was so tired. So very tired.

*Tell him he is not ready.*

She wanted to remind God that *that* particular message hadn't worked the last time she'd given it. But, of course, He knew that. "Okay. You got it, Lord." Then putting on her best pleading look, she glanced up to heaven. "Then will you stop asking me to see him?"

*Let us be glad and rejoice and give Him glory, for the
marriage of the Lamb has come, and His wife has made
herself ready.*
   *Revelation 19:7 (NKJV)*

# Chapter 25

A ngelica hurried down the road toward Daniel's
church. She was almost there when she noticed her
gas light was on, but every station she passed had a line of
cars that stretched endlessly for miles. The recent gas crisis
had caused people to panic and fill up whenever they spotted
an open station. She would have to deal with it later.

Once again, she entered the main sanctuary of the Fort
Lauderdale Church of Grace. And once again, she wondered
what she was doing there. She hadn't gotten too far down the
maze of halls before she reached a set of locked doors and
one of Daniel's bodyguards stopped her and asked who she
was.

He put her under watch of another guard while he took
her name to Daniel. Within minutes, he returned and escorted
her into the opulent room Daniel called an office.

Daniel stood in the center awaiting her arrival, wearing
jeans, a T-shirt that showed every muscle, and a smile that
took her back twelve years to the boy she had once adored
beyond reason.

"Angel, wow, it's good to see you."

He crossed the rug and drew her into an embrace before
she could protest—before she could avoid the rush of warmth
covering her in waves as he cocooned her in his strength. Oh,
how she had missed his hugs, his caresses, the confidence

and depth of his voice … all of which made her feel like nothing in the world could ever hurt her.

But *he* had been the one to hurt her. In the worst possible way. She must remember that.

Pushing from him, she turned around so he wouldn't see the flush on her face.

"How is Greg?" he asked.

"Good. Great, in fact. They are releasing him today." She faced him. "Thank you for your help."

One brow lifted. "I didn't do much but stand there." He sighed and studied her, his blue eyes more intense than she'd seen them in a while. "What the heck was that, Angel?"

*Seriously?* How could he not know? "Demons, fallen angels, possible offspring of Nephilim. You know, our *enemy*? Greg was fighting a losing battle with them. He almost lost his soul. Thank God he called out to Jesus before it was too late." She drew a deep breath. "But I didn't come to talk about them."

He frowned as if he were disappointed, then gestured toward a leather couch that looked comfier than her bed. "What, then?"

She sank into the cool cushions, wondering at her nervousness with this man. "Daniel." She swallowed. "I don't know exactly how to say this."

Sitting beside her, he reached for her hand. "Please tell me you're not breaking up with me again."

She laughed. She couldn't help it. The man was incorrigibly confident or maybe just vain. She was about to remind him that he was the one who had broken up with her, but then that charming dimple of his appeared, and she didn't want to sour the mood.

"How can I break up with you when we aren't even together?"

His lips slanted and he raised her hand for a kiss, just like in one of those historic romance novels. "Can't a guy hope?"

Feeling things she shouldn't, she retrieved her hand and scooted away. "Okay. This is the thing. I have dreams sometimes…well quite often lately. Most of them I believe are from God. He shows me things that will happen, warnings—like premonitions, sometimes visions of the future."

He gave a skeptical sigh.

She might as well just blurt it out. "The end of this age is near. I mean, *really* near."

Groaning, he leaned back into the couch and rubbed his eyes. "Angel, we've been through this before."

"I know. Hear me out. I had this dream last night of a bride waiting for her groom. Two brides, really. One was so excited, dressed in a gorgeous wedding gown, sitting at the window with great expectation. The other had on a half-made gown and wasn't looking for her fiancé at all. In fact, she seemed more interested in food and entertainment and talking with her boyfriend on the phone."

His curious look made her continue.

"I believe this is God's way of saying that Jesus is only coming for a bride who is ready, who's been faithful, who's excited for His return."

His brows collided. "Are you talking about the rapture here? C'mon Angel! There are so many theories about that event. I'm not even sure I believe it's biblical. I mean, believers soaring up into heaven? A little far-fetched, wouldn't you say?"

*Drat.* This was going to be harder than she thought. "It *is* biblical, quite biblical. I can show you the verses." She said a silent prayer for help. "For argument's sake, let's just say it's real and it's happening soon. Wouldn't it be right to warn people about it? Like I'm trying to do to you?"

"Why would you need to warn me?" He huffed. "I'm a believer just like you."

"But you *don't* believe like I do. What if it takes more than a generic belief in God to be part of the rapture? Even the demons believe in God and tremble, right? But they won't make it to heaven."

"Huh?"

"James 2:19 says, 'You believe that God is one. You do well; the demons also believe, and shudder,'" she quoted. "Don't you remember anything from the original text? Back in seminary you had such a love for the Word."

"Coffee?" Standing, he grabbed his mug and started for his mini-kitchen.

Angelica sighed. "No, thank you. Think of it this way. Let's say you're engaged, and you had spent an entire year planning the most elaborate wedding to show your bride how much you love her. Not only that, but you had bought a magnificent mansion for your new wife, filled it with grand furniture and all the latest appliances. Then on your wedding day, you excitedly anticipate seeing your beautiful bride waiting at the end of the aisle for you. But she isn't there. When you find her, she isn't ready at all. She has no gown, no jewelry, and not only that, she's been cheating on you. Would you still want her?"

"Of course not." He poured coffee into his mug.

"That's all I'm saying. We believers are the bride of Christ. Think about it, Daniel. If we—"

"I'm not sure what you're implying here, Angel." He spun and sipped his coffee, staring at her over the rim. "And I'm not sure I want to know. Sounds blasphemous to me. We aren't saved by works, but by grace. We cannot earn a trip to heaven."

"Absolutely! And I thank God for that. But I'm talking about an issue of the heart." She paused to collect her thoughts. "If that second bride had truly loved her groom, had truly committed herself to him, if she couldn't wait to finally be his wife, then she would have done those things the other bride did to get ready. But she didn't truly love him, wasn't committed to him, and she sought her satisfaction elsewhere. Her lack of works proved her lack of love, whereas the other bride's love was displayed in her efforts to do everything she could to please her groom."

Daniel continued sipping his coffee, staring into space as if he hadn't heard a word she said.

Frustration rising, she rummaged in her purse and pulled out the book. "Here, take this."

He glanced at it, then took a few tentative steps forward before halting as if it were contaminated. "You dare bring *that* in here?"

Rare anger fired in his eyes, but she'd come too far to back down. "Take it home. Read it. Remember your first love, Daniel."

"What are you talking about? I love God."

"The Antichrist is almost here. I've seen him in my dreams."

Setting his mug on his desk, he crossed arms over his chest. "Antichrist, monsters, meteors, the sea turning to blood, that's all from Revelation. It's allegorical, Angel, all allegory." Though his tone lacked the usual conviction. "Okay." He rubbed his chin. "Yeah, I remember being into this stuff. Some of what you're saying makes sense. And I know the world has gone crazy around us."

She slipped the tiny Bible onto the table and stood. "I've got to go. Leigh's watching Isaac."

He walked toward her. "Hey, when can I see you again? Next Friday I'm going to D.C. for a few days. How about before that? Dinner? I can take you and Isaac out."

She appreciated that he always included her son, but, once again, he'd totally dismissed a critical message from God. "I don't know, Daniel."

"It's just dinner."

No, dinner was never just dinner with this man. "It's not like we can start up where we left off. We're two different people now."

"Not that different, Angel." He approached and stroked her cheek with the back of his hand so gently, she closed her eyes beneath the sensation. "We still love each other, don't we?"

Did she? She could hardly think with him so close. But she already knew the answer. She did love him. But it didn't matter. He was still resistant to God. Sensing his lips descending on hers, she opened her eyes and backed away. "Please read it." Her eyes shifted to the Bible.

"If I do, will you let me take you to dinner?"

"He's so close!" Nazare pumped his fists in the air. "I can feel it." He turned to Baliel beside him, his eyes bright with anticipation.

"You are getting too involved, my friend." Baliel warned.

Nazare sighed, glancing back at Daniel and Angelica, deep in conversation. "How can I not? His light flickers brighter every time she speaks truth and life to him."

Baliel smiled proudly. "It pleases me that she obeys the Father, even when it opens so many old wounds. But her true test is coming."

"And one for Daniel as well."

Baliel only nodded.

The two angels watched as Angelica retreated from Daniel, Fear stalking her in his ever-vigilant attempt to penetrate her shield.

She hesitated before answering, as if she were seeking the wisdom of the Father. "You should want to discover the truth on your own," she finally said. "But I'll consider dinner if you read some of the forbidden passages and wish to discuss them."

Baliel nodded his approval. "She is wise, that one."

"And he is considering it." Nazare rubbed his hands together in excitement. "See how the darkness recedes from his soul."

"Do not get ahead of yourself, my friend." Baliel eyed Angelica as she left the room.

Nazare, more than pleased, watched as Daniel picked up the Bible. "Didn't you say the Father had big plans for him? Perhaps this is the beginning."

"Just remember, the Father's plans are never what we expect. Now, I must go." Grabbing the hilt of his sword, Baliel started for the door. "She is in danger."

Battling a flood of unwanted emotions, Angelica sped down the hall and didn't see Thomas following behind her until he grabbed her arm and swung her about.

"I see you haven't learned your lesson."

Angelica forced back tears. "What do you want, Thomas?"

"I've already told you. I want you to stay away from Daniel. Yet here you are."

"I had something to tell him. Now I'm leaving." She started to turn, but he held her arm fast.

"You are *not* going to tell him about Isaac."

"That's none of your business." Though that would be the *last* thing she'd do.

"It *is* my business. It's always been my business."

She studied him, remembering what a fun partier he used to be, yet at the same time, always so unsure of himself. But a hardness had taken over his expression, impenetrable and permanent. "Twelve years is a long time, and here you are still lurking in his shadow. Maybe you should get a life of your own, Thomas."

He shoved his angry face toward her as if he intended to strike her, but then that plastic grin splattered on his lips again. "You aren't going to ruin this for me."

"I'm not trying to hurt you, Thomas. I'm just trying to do the right thing. Maybe Isaac deserves to know the truth."

He tightened the grip on her arm. "Here's *my* truth," he seethed. "You even consider telling Daniel, and there'll be no son left for him to embrace."

Terror went on a rampage through her heart, leaving her breathless. "What does that mean?"

Releasing her arm with a jerk, he sauntered away. "You figure it out."

She started after him, but the tremble in her legs stopped her. Heart in her throat, she stumbled to the wall for support, trying to find air and feel her legs again. When she did, she ran from the church as fast as she could.

*Thomas threatened to kill Isaac...Thomas threatened to kill Isaac.* The words kept blaring in Angelica's mind as she drove home from the church. Yet even through the fear, pieces began to fall into place. The gunfire at SeaWorld, the car running over her...was that Thomas' doing?

"Father, that's it. I'm done. I can't see Daniel again. And I must keep Isaac away from him. Don't ask me to do anymore." She pulled into her parking spot, leaned her head on the wheel, and began to sob. "Please, don't take my son from me."

Still shaken and unable to sleep, Angel rose the next day, dropped the kids off at school, and spent the day walking along the beach in prayer. Hot and muggy for September, she slogged along the crashing waves in a daze of terror. Even the sounds of sea gulls, people talking, children laughing, and the distant thunder faded into the background as her thoughts focused on her son and his safety. She pleaded and pleaded with God for his protection. For angels to surround Isaac. She could not lose him. Even though God had said time was short, His idea of time and hers were quite different. "Father, help me."

Yet for all her walking and praying and pleading and crying, heaven was silent, and she felt no better by the time she had to pick up Isaac from school. Even so, she pasted on a smile as he leapt in the car and then gave him such a tight embrace, he wiggled from her. "Mom, knock it off. Kids are looking."

"Sorry." She took off down the road. "I just love you, you know."

"Yeah." He smiled. "Me too."

As usual, she asked him about homework and what he learned that day as they rumbled down the road toward Joel's school when a choking sound came from her engine, and the entire car began to jerk. One glance at the gas gauge, and she realized what she'd done. "Drat!"

"What's wrong, Mom?"

"We're out of gas." She pressed on the pedal, but the car continued to choke until it finally sputtered out. She quickly found a place to pull over—an illegal spot, of course, in front of an open baseball field, but it couldn't be helped.

Totally her fault. She'd forgotten about the gas. "Well, come on. Let's get the can and find a station." Hopefully before a cop spotted her car.

Grabbing the gas can from the trunk, she locked the car, and she and Isaac headed down the street. "I better call Leigh." She reached in her purse for her cell to let her roommate know she'd be late picking up Joel when…

An enormous *BOOM!* quaked the air, and what felt like a wall of fists shoved her and Isaac to the ground.

"It's time," Baliel shouted to Zarene as the two angels darted for Angelica and Isaac.

Zarene glanced back at Angelica's car. "Are you sure?"

"Yes. Push them to the ground, then cover them from the blast."

They reached the humans and Zarene did as he was told. He shoved Isaac down while Baliel did the same to Angelica.

Then the two angels stretched out their hands and covered them with an impenetrable spiritual fortress.

An avalanche of heat tumbled over Angelica. Gravely asphalt scraped her cheek. Using what little strength she had, she fought the force holding her down and flung her body over Isaac's. No sooner had she done so, then the scorching heat dissipated. All that remained was the crackle of fire, hot air, and the odors of gas, oil, and burning metal. She knew before she got up what she would see. And that thought— along with the terror it brought—kept her firmly in place over Isaac, shielding him, protecting him.

If only she could do so forever.

But the sounds of people's shouts and voices and Isaac's movement forced her to move off him and stand, hauling him up beside her. They both turned at once to see what remained of her car, engulfed in flames that speared the sky. Grabbing Isaac's hand, she backed them up several feet away from the heat and the chunks of burning metal littering the ground.

She couldn't form a thought, a word, even a feeling as she stood there watching what would have been her and Isaac burning alive.

If not for the empty tank of gas.

She glanced around. The blast had toppled a fence surrounding the baseball field, tossed an empty shopping cart several yards, and lifted one tire of the nearest car onto the sidewalk.

But they were unscathed. Nudging Isaac back, she scanned him to be sure he had no injuries before embracing him again. Something had shoved them to the ground before the blast. Something…or someone. *Angels.* Had to be. Protecting her, protecting Isaac.

Despite the horror filling her, she lifted her thanks to God as she moved and sat on the sidewalk before she passed out.

Smoke billowed from her car, filling the street. People crowded around, pointing. A siren blared in the distance. One man came up to her and asked if she was all right.

The rest was a dream…answering the policeman's questions, watching the firemen put out the fire, she and Isaac sitting in an open ambulance being checked for injuries, and finally the nice cop who gave them a ride home.

Leigh met her at the door. "Where have you been? We've been worried sick."

Isaac—fully recovered from the trauma—ran past her. "Our car blew up," he said nonchalantly.

Angelica's heart stopped for a moment as she scanned the room and spotted Joel. "Thank God. You picked him up. I'm so sorry."

"The school called. I've been trying to call you, but I keep getting your voicemail." Leigh followed her into the living room where Angelica sank into a chair. "Wait." Leigh stopped and stared at her, wide-eyed. "Did he say your car blew up?"

*Her phone!* It had been in her hand. Angelica sifted through the contents of her purse. Not there.

Isaac grabbed a controller and began playing a video game with Joel. "Yeah. It was cool. Boom! The whole thing was on fire."

Leigh gaped at Angelica. "What?"

"Yeah, kinda like that." She attempted a smile.

"Are you guys okay?"

"Not a scratch. Thanks to the Lord."

"What do you mean?"

"We would have been in the car if I hadn't run out of gas, and I wouldn't have run out if the lines weren't too long last night. You know there's always one station along Atlantic that's open. Not last night."

"Hmm," Leigh said. "Well, I'm just glad you're not hurt."

"Minus a car, though." How was she supposed to afford another one? No doubt her insurance didn't cover random explosions.

Leigh slipped beside her on the couch. "Don't worry. You can use mine in the meantime."

Tears burned in Angelica's eyes. "You're too good to be true. Thanks."

"No worries." Leigh smiled. "Why don't you go take a hot bath? I know how that relaxes you. I'll start dinner for the boys."

Neither the hot bath, nor the bubbles, nor her prayers did anything to calm Angelica's nerves. She knew God had saved her and Isaac. But she also knew that if Thomas—it had to be his doing—would go to such lengths to keep her from Daniel, he wouldn't give up easily.

So, by the time she dried herself off and crawled into her sweats, she had made up her mind.

Her decision was confirmed by Leigh later that night when the boys were asleep.

"I have a question for you." Leigh handed her a cup of tea and motioned them to the couch.

Angelica hesitated at the unusually serious look on her friend's face. "Yes?"

"I've been wondering…is Isaac… Daniel's son?" She locked eyes with Angelica.

Angelica gave a half-laugh, sipped her weak tea, and drew her legs up on the couch. Finally, she sighed. "How did you guess?"

"I don't know. Just the way you've been acting lately. And you never told me who his father was."

Angelica lowered her chin, feeling a pinch of guilt. "We broke up before I had a chance to tell him."

Leigh blew out a sigh and shook her head. "Wow. But he's got so much money! You could be sitting pretty, girl."

Angelica laughed. "There are some things more important than money."

"I can't imagine what." Leigh's smile was teasing, but then she frowned. "Oh, of course. Isaac's protection. Are you sure about this Thomas guy?"

"He thinks I'll ruin Daniel's career. He's threatened me multiple times, but I never took him seriously. His last threat to Isaac was pretty clear. Besides, who else would want me dead? I'm nobody."

"But he's a *pastor*!"

"Yeah. Crazy, huh?"

"Either way, Ange, I hate to say this, but I'd stay away from Daniel if I were you. I mean he's a hunk, and he's got loads of money, but nothing is worth this."

Setting down her tea, Angelica hugged herself. "Believe me, I've been trying. But God seems to have other plans."

"God, eh?" Leigh gave her a teasing look. "How dare He force you to spend time with a hunky, rich famous guy."

Angelica thought of their kisses and hoped the heat swirling through her hadn't manifested into a blush on her face. "I know. Poor me, right? But honestly, I have no desire to date a pastor who doesn't believe in the whole truth of God's Word. For Isaac's sake."

Leigh only nodded and Angelica wondered how much of that she understood.

Angelica hugged herself. "I'm so afraid for Isaac. Not just this new threat, but everything. This world, the cruelty, corruption, immorality, twisted ideas, how can any parent raise a child?"

"You can't worry about all that, Ange." Leigh leaned forward and squeezed her hand. "Just take it a day at a time and do what you can."

Angelica stared at her friend, amazed at her faith. Or was it just ignorant bliss? "Well, I know one thing. I'm not going to do anything ever again that puts Isaac at risk."

*There is no fear in love; but perfect love casts out fear.*
*1 John 4:18 (NKJV)*

# Chapter 26

How does one stay away from a man who sends a bouquet of flowers every day along with letters so romantic they should be in novels? How does one stay away from a man when one's son continually asks when they will see him again? And in particular, how does one stay away from a man who sends over a brand-new Mercedes Benz with a big red bow on top as a gift?

Of course, Angelica sent it right back. She knew Daniel wasn't trying to buy her affection and was only trying to be kind, but there's no way she could accept such an extravagant gift, no matter how much she needed it.

And she *did* need it. As she suspected, her insurance didn't cover car bombs, and she had no money or credit to buy a new one.

Honestly, she was still shaken by the near-death event, and the thought of even talking to Daniel on the phone terrified her. She hadn't been sleeping well, her stomach was in a perpetual knot, and even her prayers seemed scattered at best. Now, as she drove Leigh's car to work, she wondered how she'd get through eight hours of serving drinks to inebriated, lusty customers while fighting off Sal's advances.

The one bright spot in her night would be seeing Greg again. This was his first night back, and she couldn't wait to see the difference in him since he joined the Kingdom. With that thought to cheer her up, she parked Leigh's car, locked it, and entered through the employee door. After stuffing her purse in a locker and checking her makeup, she headed out onto the floor, or what she liked to call the "field, ripe for harvest."

She had barely picked up her tray and order pad when Greg popped up from behind the bar and gave her the brightest smile she'd ever seen on the man. "Hey, Angelica!"

"Greg, I've missed you so much." She reached over the wooden bar and took his hand. "How are you feeling?"

"Like I've won the lottery." After a quick glance over her shoulder, he leaned toward her and whispered, "I can't thank you enough."

"I did nothing." She pointed toward heaven. "The big guy had your name in His book, that's all."

He laughed. "Dunno why He'd pick a loser like me, but I'm so grateful."

"What's this? A party and I'm not invited?" Sal's voice stormed over Angelica like a bad dream. "Get back to work, you two!"

"And good evening to you as well, Sal." Angelica flashed him a smile, winked at Greg, and headed out to one of her assigned tables.

Baliel stood against the back wall of the Mermaid Den. On either side of him stood Pesha and Kazich. All three warriors' mouths twisted in disgust at the debauchery of the place, the waste, the empty souls. All three longed to draw their blades and fight off the demon hordes spinning around those present, some entering their souls to set up house, others whispering lies in their ears. All snarling at the three holy warriors, daring them to stop their foul play.

Shifting his stance, Baliel ignored them. So true what the one human atheist, Jacques Vallee, had said even in his own ignorance. "Human beings are under the control of a strange force that bends them absurd ways, forcing them to play a role in a bizarre game of deception."

Fairly astute for one who didn't believe in God. If only these people could see the hideous creatures that controlled them, they'd run with all haste into the arms of the Savior.

But that was not the way of Yahweh. He gave people the truth about Himself and then let them decide either to serve or reject Him. Oh, how deeply it grieved the Father that most of humanity chose the wide and popular path—the one that led straight to hell.

But there were children of the light here, too. Which was the reason the warriors were present—to observe, guard, and protect. Baliel's eyes followed Angelica as she moved about the room, taking orders and talking to customers. The spirit of Fear lingered about her, seeking entrance. The foul demon had already dug a small trench in her armor of light and sought another crack wherein to chisel.

"She's endured much," Pesha said from beside him.

"Indeed. The brightness of her light has not gone unnoticed by our enemy. He has sent extra forces to break through her armor."

"Aye, I see that. And behold the cracks forming in her shield of faith."

"She fears for her son."

"She does not trust the Father," Kazich commented, but his gaze was on his ward, Melody.

Baliel frowned. "She trusts Him. Just not completely in this matter. It is her weakness, and the enemy knows it. But she has many strengths, and it is my hope she will lean on the Father to overcome her weakness."

Pesha's eyes wandered to Greg, whistling a tune behind the bar as he talked with customers, encouraging, uplifting, and sharing his newfound hope. "I quite agree. Her influence has helped to finally bring Greg into the Kingdom. For that, I am very grateful. What a joy to see him serving the Father."

"All of heaven rejoices, my friend." Baliel turned to Kazich. "As they soon will for Melody. She is close."

The short angel nodded. "She has been reading the Bible that Angelica gave her. Her eyes are being opened. Such a marvelous thing to witness. We are privileged, indeed."

A shower of light caught Baliel's attention, and he turned to see Angelica speaking with two middle-aged women on their third round of drinks.

"Ah, she speaks of the Savior." Kazich grew excited as flecks of sparkling light landed on the women, and instead of bouncing off as most did, soaked into their skin and appeared as glints within their souls.

"Indeed." Baliel continued to watch her as she moved to another table and another, bringing the light with her. Darkness retreated before her every step, fleeing even further when she opened her mouth. He longed for her to witness it—to know what a difference she made.

Scanning the room, Pesha crossed arms over his chest. "How many of these will make it?"

"Very few," Baliel answered. "'Narrow is the gate and difficult is the way which leads to life, and there are few who find it.' There's not much time left."

"I look forward to the wedding," Kazich said.

"It will be a grand affair. And oh so wonderful to see our Lord finally wed."

"He has waited long."

"Too long." Baliel sighed. "And His bride is nearly ready." He maintained his vigil, watching Angelica share the love of God while she flitted from table to table, watching her speak to Melody and witnessing the light inside the lady grow brighter, watching the darkness scatter when she and Greg knelt together and prayed in the break room.

And finally watching Sal angrily call her into his office.

Angelica longed to sit down and relieve her aching feet, if only for a moment, but she'd learned the hard way that Sal didn't like anyone to sit in his presence. As it was, he sat behind his ostentatious desk and studied her like a king would a subject. Why did he have to call her into his office now? She had only fifteen minutes left in her shift, and all she wanted to do was go home and crawl into bed.

She waited for whatever tirade was coming, doing her best to cover herself with her tray to avoid those undressing eyes of his.

Releasing a long sigh, he shook his head at her like a principal would a naughty child. "What did I tell you about spreading your Jesus crap in here?"

*Oh, no.* Angelica bit her lip. "I haven't—"

"Don't lie to me. The customers are complaining."

"Who?" Everyone she'd spoken with seemed open to her words.

"Doesn't matter. I told you that if I got one more complaint, you're gone."

Fear stabbed her gut. "Honestly, Sal, all I am is nice to people and tell them God loves them." And that Jesus died for them so they could live with Him forever. Plus a few other things. "What's the harm in that?"

"The harm is, people don't like it." He pushed back his chair and rose to circle his desk. "The harm is they don't come here to hear about Jesus. They come here to watch half-naked mermaids and get drunk."

As he approached, Angelica glanced at the door, planning her exit if he got too fresh. "I just give them hope," she whispered.

"Hope, schmope. There is no such thing!" He halted before her, the gold chain around his neck flashing in her eyes. "I should fire you on the spot."

Angelica lowered her gaze. "You can't. I mean, please. I just lost my car, and I have no money in the bank. I need this job."

She could spot the precise moment in which power took residence in his eyes. He took a step closer. So close she could smell the brandy on his breath and his body odor.

He leaned in to kiss her, and without thinking, she slapped him across the cheek.

Fury raged in his eyes. He rubbed his jaw. "You whore!" He charged her and she backed away. "You're fired! Get out now!" He pointed to the door.

She hesitated, too stunned to move.

"I said, get out!"

Stumbling on her high heels, she rushed out the door. It slammed, sending a tremble through her as she set down her tray. Shock struck her in morbid waves. She wanted to say goodbye to Greg and Melody, but her mind and emotions tangled in a chaotic spin. Instead, she grabbed her purse from the locker, and darted into the night.

Right into Daniel.

His Aqua Vela scent and rock-hard chest gave him away.

After all the bad news, all the chaos, all the fear, instead of pushing back from him, she fell into his embrace and began to sob.

Immediately, those thick arms encircled her in warmth and safety as he pressed her head against his chest. "Shh. Shh. It's all right, Angel. Shh." That deep voice resounded, those words of comfort that swept through her like a warm tide, loosening her nerves, along with her resolve to free herself from this man.

"What's wrong? What happened?" he asked.

"I just got fired," she sobbed, pushing back from him.

"What? Why?" He gripped her arms.

"Sal, my boss…" Should she tell him the truth? No. Daniel would only rush in and punch the guy flat. And that wouldn't solve anything. "I just want to go home."

"Sure." Swinging an arm around her shoulder, he drew her close. "You're trembling."

She was. She could feel it in her legs as he led her to his car, see it in her hands as she held them out before her. It wasn't like her to be this weak. But too much had happened. Too many things had gone wrong.

"I can drive," she said. "I brought Leigh's car."

"Not in your condition. I'll drop you off, and we can get Leigh's car tomorrow."

She wanted to argue with him, wanted to shove him away and run. If Thomas saw them together, he'd kill Isaac for sure! But she could hardly walk, barely form a coherent sentence.

And she needed him. Drat, but she needed him.

She barely noticed the drive to her apartment, barely noticed Daniel leading her up the stairs, unlocking the door with her keys, and settling her on her couch. Flipping on a light, he shut the door, and she heard him rummaging in the kitchen. Minutes later, he appeared with a glass of water and a look of concern.

She sipped the water, then set down the glass, her nerves finally settling.

He slid on the couch beside her. "What's going on, Angel? You're strung way too tight. It's not like you."

Those deep blue eyes of his, so full of love, began to break down her defenses. She longed to pour out her heart to him as she'd done so many times in the past. She wanted to tell him that the world was plunging into chaos, World War III was about to start, her son was being indoctrinated at school, and now, she'd have no money to feed him. And, oh yeah, Daniel's assistant pastor was trying to kill Isaac. But instead, she only said, "Just got a lot going on."

He nodded.

"Why were you at my work?" she asked.

"I missed you. You aren't answering my calls. And you sent the car back."

"I lost my phone when my car blew up. And I can't accept such a gift from you."

He must have noticed her trembling again, for he grabbed a blanket and tossed it over her shoulders. "I was crazy with fear when I heard about the car. I came by here twice and then by your work three times, but always missed you. I was so worried, Angel."

"There's just been so much...too much...." *And if Thomas knew you were here, my son's life would be in danger.* The thought ratcheted up her heart rate again, and she raised a hand to her brow.

"Here, lay down." Scooting from the couch, he tucked a pillow behind her and nudged her down.

It felt good. Especially when he took her hand in his and began caressing it. "So, what happened at work?"

She shook her head and exhaled deeply, finally able to speak. "My boss had it in for me. We've been arguing for weeks. It's not worth talking about."

"How are you for money until you can find something else?"

Last time she checked, she only had twenty NWO notes in her account. "Fine."

"I don't believe you."

She gave him a weak smile.

"I'll help you until you can get on your feet."

"That wouldn't be right, Daniel."

"Course it would. That's what friends are for."

"Is that what we are?" Unsure why she opened that door, she suddenly wished she hadn't.

He rubbed the stubble on his jaw. "You tell me. You know what *I* want."

Feeling suddenly vulnerable, she rose and swung her legs over the edge of the couch. He had told her he still loved her. But she didn't want to hear that. Couldn't hear that. Not only for her heart's sake. But now, for Isaac's. Perhaps if she was mean, he'd leave. "Daniel Cain's love always comes with conditions," she snapped, sending him jerking back in surprise.

"What are you talking about?"

"You've made it quite clear that you only want a relationship with me if I quit my so-called cult."

His brow wrinkled. "For your own safety."

She set stern eyes upon him. "For *your* career."

"I'll admit that's part of it." He ran a hand through his hair. "But not the main part. I simply don't want to see you or Isaac stuffed in a FEMA camp somewhere."

She gazed at him, wanting so badly to reach him. "Yet Jesus Himself foretold that some of His followers would be imprisoned for their faith. If that is His will for me, how can I run from it?"

"But you have a son to think of. For Isaac's sake, I beg you, keep your faith to yourself."

"That's not what the Bible says."

He leaned back on the couch with a sigh. "I know, I've been reading it."

"You have?" She couldn't deny her excitement.

"Bits and pieces." He smiled. "After all, it was the condition of a date."

She squeezed his hand. "I'm so glad to hear that."

"Don't get all excited. I'm not quitting my church and casting out demons on the beach."

She laughed. "Now, *that* is something to hope for."

Rejuvenated by his declaration, Angelica scooted back on the couch and drew her feet up. They spent the next several hours just talking—like they used to do when they were young and in love. They spoke of God, and surfing, fishing, and Isaac. They talked about the state of the world, his goal to advise the president, her hopes for Isaac's future. They laughed over antics they'd done as young adults, the music they had listened to, the beach concerts they'd attended. All the while she watched every spark in his eye, every flex of his jaw, every gesture and movement and the way he squeezed the bridge of his nose when he was uncomfortable.

And it was like twelve years had never passed.

She was falling in love with him again. A wild mix of feelings twisted her insides at the thought, but fear won out—fear for Isaac, fear for risking another broken heart, fear for Daniel's soul. Yet in the midst of it all, hope burst at the thrill of his touch, at the possibility they had a chance...but more importantly that he was slowly turning back to God. The truth was finding its way into Daniel's spirit and evicting the lies. She could sense it. Especially when he brought up his days of beach evangelism and his eyes lit with excitement.

Now, as her own eyes grew heavy and her heart full, he eased beside her, swung an arm around her, and drew her head to his shoulder. "Sleep, my angel. It will be light soon."

He wasn't kidding. In what seemed like only minutes later, she heard Isaac's voice.

"Daniel, you're here!"

Prying her eyes open, she found her son jumping up and down in front of the couch.

She attempted to stretch but quickly found herself wedged between Daniel's arm and his chest. Horrified, she pushed from him and scooted back, squinting at the sunlight streaming in through the window. It landed on Daniel, glinting on the stubble on his jaw, his hair sticking up in a dozen directions, and the puffiness of his eyes.

And she remembered how wonderful it had been waking up beside this man.

"What are ya doin' here, Daniel? I've missed you."

"I've missed you too, buddy." Daniel stretched out his arms. "Your mom and I were talking and we must have fallen asleep."

"Hey," Isaac said. "Can we go catch some waves?"

"Isaac, leave the poor man alone. He just woke up."

"Tell you what," Daniel said. "I'll go pick up some breakfast, and we'll eat on the beach. No surfing yet, though, it's too calm in the morning."

"Yay!" Isaac beamed. "I'll bring my Frisbee. Can I, Mom?"

"Sure."

After the boy ran off to get dressed, Angel faced Daniel and found him gazing at her with such love, she quickly looked away. She must look a mess with her smeared makeup and tangled hair. "You don't have to do this."

"Are you kidding? I want to." Leaning in, he kissed her on the forehead, grabbed his keys from the table, and headed for the door, whistling. "Meet you across the street at the beach in half an hour."

So, this was what it would be like to be married, to have a man around the house, a father for Isaac. She smiled, but instantly wiped it away. She shouldn't be thinking such things.

A half hour later, as promised, Daniel shuffled across the sand, bag of bagels and cream cheese in hand—a half hour in which Angelica had done her best to clean up her face, run a comb through her hair, and wonder what in God's name she was doing risking her and Isaac's lives.

She shouldn't have stayed up all night with Daniel. She shouldn't have allowed him to take her home. And she shouldn't have agreed to this picnic on the beach. But she'd been so distraught last night and everything felt so right.

If not for Thomas' threat.

But what to do? She saw the way Isaac's face lit up when he spotted Daniel heading their way—as if he already knew, somewhere beneath his conscious mind, that the man was his father.

After shoving down their bagels, Isaac dragged Daniel out to play Frisbee, and Angelica more than enjoyed watching the easy companionship between them. Not to mention, Daniel's muscular physique as he ran and leapt across the sand.

She sighed deeply. "Why am I so weak, Lord? Is it okay for me to be spending so much time with this man? What about Isaac? I'm so afraid."

*Trust me.*

The same two words she'd been hearing for the past week. Trust didn't come easy when it came to her son. Fear always won whenever she thought of any harm coming to him. She prayed for him every day, left him in God's hands. But as soon as she got off her knees, Fear returned. She could almost hear the demon chomping on her like a beaver on crack gnawing through wood. The only problem was, Fear was slowly eating away her precious faith.

*Tell him.*

*What?* Angelica was surely hearing things.

*Tell him Isaac is his son.*

"I can't, Father. You know I can't."

If she did, Thomas would certainly kill them both.

*Look at the birds of the air, for they neither sow nor reap nor gather into barns; yet your heavenly Father feeds them. Are you not of more value than they?*
*Matthew 6:26 (NKJV)*

# Chapter 27

Angelica mounted the stairs to her apartment, dreading what she had to do. Fear once more nibbled at her faith...her peace. She needed to pray. She needed to spend time with her Father. To regain her strength. But first, she had to tell Leigh what was going on. She had a right to know.

Closing the door, she dropped Leigh's keys on the kitchen table and found her friend curled up in a chair, reading. She looked up and smiled at Angelica.

What a wonderful friend Leigh had been. Angelica would miss rooming with her. And Isaac would miss Joel. Even now, she could hear the two of them playing in one of the bedrooms.

"Joel got a new set of Legos," Leigh explained.

Angelica smiled. "You have your car back. Thank you. I'm sorry we left it at my work."

"No prob. I told you I didn't need it today." Leigh batted the air.

Angelica dropped to the couch and drew up her legs. "We need to talk."

Leigh's brows shot up, and she laid the book she was reading in her lap. "Sounds serious."

"Well, it kinda is." Angelica sighed. Where to begin? "For starters, I lost my job last night."

Leigh's eyes widened. "Crap. I'm so sorry, Ange. What happened?"

"Stupid me. I pissed off my boss. He had it in for me, anyway."

"The one who kept propositioning you?"

Angelica nodded.

"You probably have a good case to sue him."

"It wasn't because of that. I was telling some of the customers about Jesus."

"Oh." Leigh grimaced.

"Anyway, I don't know when I'll find something else. Or *if*, in this economy. So you might want to put the word out for another roommate."

Leigh shook her head. "Don't be silly. I don't want another roommate. You'll find something."

Angelica's eyes misted at her friend's kindness. "We don't know that, and you can't afford rent on your own."

"We *do* know that." She gestured to the book in her lap and only then did Angelica realize it was the Bible she had given her.

Excitement wiped away her fears. "You're reading it!"

"Of course. How could I not after you pointed out all the prophecies coming true." A new sparkle lit up Leigh's eyes that warmed Angelica to her soul.

"In fact," Leigh continued, twirling a strand of her long black hair around a finger. "I believe God says something in here about supplying all your needs."

Shame etched Angelica's spine at her own lack of faith. "It does."

"Then you will find another job. A *better* job."

Angelica could only stare at her in wonder.

"And it looks like God has sent you a good man as well." She winked.

Along with elation about Leigh, emotions Angelica dared not name battled within her at the thought.

"What happened between you two, anyway?" Leigh asked. "I don't see why you'd ever let a guy like that go."

Angelica closed her eyes for a moment. She had never told anyone the story. It had been too painful. But Leigh had a right to know.

"I was twenty-one, a cocktail waitress, and he was in his first year of seminary." She could still remember their first date strolling on the beach. "We had an immediate connection, and over the course of a year, we fell deeply in love. Or so I thought. During that time, he grew closer to God and really impressed me with his zeal and his efforts to reach the lost. He was amazing back then."

"Apparently, still is. Look at the crowds he draws."

"Yeah, I suppose." She would leave the discussion of true and false religion for a later time. "Anyway, toward the end of our first year together, he told me he wanted to marry me, but we couldn't sleep together anymore. I admired him so much for that. But then I found out I was already pregnant."

"Wow. Why didn't you tell him?"

"I was going to, but we had a big argument that night. Apparently, the dean of the seminary found out about me and advised Daniel—*strongly*—not to see me again. They thought me being a cocktail waitress and a nonbeliever was a bad influence on him." She shrugged. "They were probably right. Although Daniel didn't want to split up, I felt insulted. I said some things against his seminary *and* God that I shouldn't have said."

Leigh set the Bible down on the table and leaned forward. "So, that was it? You broke up?"

"No. I didn't think so. I mean, people disagree all the time. We had already made plans to meet for dinner the next night, but when I went to the restaurant, Thomas was there instead. He told me Daniel didn't want to see me again."

Leigh shook her head. "Whoa. That must have hurt."

More than anyone realized. Angelica pressed her heart where an ache rose even at the memory. "When I told Thomas I was pregnant, he totally freaked. Told me I should never tell Daniel, because we both knew he'd do the honorable thing. But it would ruin his career and his life. He would be tossed from seminary. He told me Daniel was meant for great things, and I would only stand in his way. He actually offered me money to have an abortion and never see Daniel again."

"Did you take it?"

"No. I didn't want his money. But I knew he was right. I was just a cocktail waitress with no future. Daniel was going to be somebody important. We all knew it. Besides, he didn't want me, anyway."

Leigh's eyes clouded with moisture. "So you just left and never told him about Isaac. Wow. And he never tried to contact you?"

"He did. I guess he changed his mind. He called several times and even came to my apartment. But I never answered him. Eventually I moved, changed my number, and he gave up. I couldn't ruin his career. I loved him too much."

Leaning toward her, Leigh placed her hand atop Angelica's. "You poor thing. I'm so sorry."

"I don't think my heart has ever completely healed." She forced back tears, but they came nonetheless. Leigh handed her a box of Kleenex, and she grabbed one and dabbed her eyes.

"Well, I totally get why you don't trust him."

Okay, now the hard part. Angelica drew a breath. "Listen, there's another reason I should leave, besides the fact I can't pay rent."

Leigh sat back and held up a hand. "I don't want to hear it. You're staying, and that's final."

"I'm serious. *This* is serious. I don't want you and Joel to be in any danger. Who knows what Thomas may do when he finds out I've spent time with Daniel again."

Leigh tsked. "You're worried about us? Crazy girl."

"I would die if something happened to you or Joel because of me. Just another reason for you to find a new roommate. Hopefully someone who doesn't have a hit out on them." Her laugh came out more bitter than she intended.

"Don't be ridiculous, Ange." Leigh waved her away. "Besides, I think you should tell Daniel."

"About Thomas?"

"Well, yeah, that too. But more importantly about Isaac. He has a right to know that he has a son."

Just what God had told her to do. Angelica leapt to her feet, heart pounding. "I can't do that. I can't put Isaac's life in even more danger."

Frowning, Leigh studied Angelica, then pointed to the Bible on the table. "You're afraid of one evil man? Where is your faith?"

Angelica swallowed and gaped at her friend.

"Doesn't it say in the Bible"—Leigh picked up a notebook and began flipping through the pages—"that if God is for you, who can be against you? What can man do to you? That He will give His angels charge over you, to guard you in all your ways?" She stopped on a page and skimmed it with her finger. "Jesus said here in Matthew. 'Do not fear those who kill the body but are unable to kill the soul', and Paul said in Romans"—she moved her finger down the page—"For you have not received a spirit of slavery leading to fear again, but you have received a spirit of adoption as sons by which we cry out, 'Abba! Father!'"

Angelica could only stare at her friend. She'd been writing down scriptures already? More importantly, why was her tone, her expressions so full of faith? A faith that seemed woefully absent at the moment from Angelica.

Her gut twisted at the realization of what she had done. Knees wobbling, she sank back to the couch, thoughts whirling, shame trampling her soul. The words of God dismantled her every argument. Leigh was right. Angelica had given into the spirit of Fear. Not just recently with this new threat. But for years. From the day Isaac was born, she had worried and fretted and feared for him, for his physical, spiritual, and emotional safety. Day after day, she had tearfully pleaded with God to watch over her son.

And yet, she hadn't truly trusted Him to do so.

Fear—that tormenting spirit, that foul demon that constantly stole her peace, had a claw-grip on her soul, and caused her faith to dwindle. And she had allowed it. Year after year, her Father had asked her to put Isaac completely in His care, and year after year, she had said no and tried to protect him herself.

And it was Leigh of all people, a new believer—for she could now see the light in her eyes—a babe in Christ, who had revealed her greatest weakness.

"So you *have* been reading the Bible." Angelica smiled. "You put me to shame."

"No shame intended. I have the same problem with Joel, so I looked up fear in the concordance and jotted down every verse dealing with it." Her eyes sparkled.

Angelica breathed a huge sigh, sensing a burden floating off her shoulders. "You know Him now."

Leigh nodded and the two of them stood and embraced so tightly, Angelica thought she'd implode.

Wiping tears from her eyes, she backed away. "I need to go pray. Afterward, if you don't mind watching Isaac, I have something important I must tell Daniel."

Daniel headed toward his front door, hoping beyond hope it was Angel. Last night had been incredible, just talking with her, sharing their hearts, dreams, and memories, nestled together on the couch until dawn. And then morning on the beach, eating breakfast, laughing and playing with Isaac. Honestly, Daniel couldn't remember a happier time.

But it had been the look in Angel's eyes that made his heart soar even now. The look he remembered so fondly from long ago, a look of pure love—a look of connection between them that even time couldn't sever. He'd finally broken through to her. He *knew* it. And he intended to make her his again—marry her like he should have years ago. If only she'd say yes.

And quit her cult.

Surely after she witnessed the masses he brought to Christ through his ministry, she would realize how much more good she could do joining him than hanging around with those fanatics. His church would just have to deal with her past. And the power brokers in D.C.—who surely had more skeletons in their closet than Angel—wouldn't care after they heard Daniel's speech and saw for themselves his value. It would all work out, he knew it. God would bless him for all the good he had done.

Which is why he whistled as he opened the door.

But his whistle soured on his lips. Pushing his way past him, Thomas marched in, a scowl on his face.

"You saw her again." Without turning back, he stomped into Daniel's living room and halted at the glass doors, staring out at the pool.

"I did. Not that it's any of your business." Daniel returned to his seat on the couch and stared at his laptop where he'd been putting the finishing touches on his speech.

Thomas groaned. "I don't know how to get through to you."

"Why not give up, then?" Daniel leaned back, clasping hands behind his head.

Thomas pivoted, his face red. "Give up everything we've worked for? Is that what you're asking?"

"Don't be so dramatic." Rising, Daniel headed toward the kitchen. "Want some juice?"

"No, I don't want juice. I want you to come to your senses."

Daniel poured the remnants of the juice he'd just squeezed into his cup and stared at his friend. "I love her, and it's going to work out. You'll see."

"You *love* her?" Thomas sneered. "Really? A woman who broke your heart, ran off with someone else, and who's been lying to you all these years?"

"What are you talking about?"

"I'm saying you don't really know Smokes at all. You don't know what she's capable of. But *I* do."

Daniel finished his juice and set down the glass, trying to control his anger. Thomas was a good friend, but enough was enough. "Oh, you do?"

"Remember, I was the one you sent to meet her that night."

Of course Daniel remembered. He would never forget. Angel and he had been fighting and he so desperately wanted to meet her as planned, tell her how sorry he was. But at the last minute, one of his professors had demanded he attend a seminar, and he couldn't say no. He'd tried and tried to call her, but she wouldn't pick up, so he'd sent Thomas with his apology and a request for Angel to meet him later at their favorite coffee shop.

"I was the one who bore the brunt of her anger," Thomas continued.

Daniel swallowed a lump of pain at the memory. Angel had told Thomas that she never wanted to see Daniel again, and that she had already hooked up with another guy.

"I was the one," Thomas said, "who had to tell you the truth and watch my best friend's heart crumble before my eyes."

Daniel returned to sit on the couch. "She's different now."

Thomas ran a hand through his hair, messing its perfect style. "But you don't know the entire truth."

Daniel stared at him, growing more frustrated by the minute. "Listen, I need to finish this speech."

The features of Thomas' face softened as he sat across from Daniel. "This may be hard for you to hear, but I see now that you *must* hear it. You have to know what kind of woman she is."

"I know what kind of woman she is. Nothing you say can change that. Now, if you don't mind…" Daniel gestured for the door, wondering if he'd have to toss his best friend from his house.

"That night"—Thomas leaned forward on his knees, his voice sullen—"she asked me for money."

Daniel shook the absurdity from his mind. "Why would she need money?"

Thomas hesitated for a moment before looking Daniel in the eyes. "Because she was carrying your child."

A red-hot skewer drilled through Daniel's heart. "What?"

"Yeah, man, *your* child. She had just found out from the doc."

"*My* child?" Daniel repeated, numbly. Angel had been carrying his child? No, she would have told him. A terrifying thought pierced his brain. "She didn't… she wouldn't…?" He couldn't even say it.

"No, she kept it."

*Isaac is my son!* Daniel jumped to his feet, part elated, part furious, tremendously confused. "You're lying!"

"Think about it, Daniel. Isaac's birthday is November 11th, right? Seriously, for that to even remotely work out, she would have had to have gotten pregnant within weeks after dumping you."

Piece by piece, Daniel's world began to crumble around him. He hadn't even asked her when Isaac's birthday was. He'd just assumed she wouldn't lie to him. He took up a pace, trying to settle his racing heart. "I trusted her. I never questioned...I never thought she'd keep something like that from me."

"She kept quiet because I paid her off," Thomas said. "With ten thousand I got from my father."

"What?" Daniel halted, staring at his friend, wondering if his heart could take another blow. "*You* paid her? How could you...*why* would you?" Arrows of betrayal stung him from all directions.

"So she wouldn't use the kid to get child support." Thomas rose, an appeal in his eyes. "Like she intended to do. She would have ruined you."

"She took the money?"

Thomas nodded. "For her silence."

Anger, betrayal, fear, and most of all pain, battled within him until he felt his heart would explode. He glared at Thomas. "Why didn't you tell me? All these years...*I have a son.*" Plopping down on the couch, he dropped his head in his hands.

"I did it for you, Daniel. You wouldn't be where you are today, *who* you are today, if I had told you."

"Then why are you telling me now?" Daniel mumbled without looking up.

"I could think of no other way to show you her true nature...to stop you from seeing her."

Daniel grunted and closed his eyes. "But surely you know now I want to be a part of my son's life."

Thomas released a heavy sigh. "Yeah, that's what I feared. But I've put some thought into it. We can put a nice spin on this. You know, a real bleeding heart story about a woman who kept you from your son for so many years. And now that you found out about him, you are fighting to be a Dad, to do the right thing."

When Daniel finally looked up, he found his friend pacing, his eyes flashing as he fabricated the tale he would tell the media. "And you slept with her only once. She seduced you...an innocent young seminary student, and she a loose cocktail waitress."

But Daniel wasn't listening anymore. His emotions were on an ever-accelerating roller coaster...soaring the heights when he realized he had a son, and crashing to the pit when his thoughts tumbled to Angel's unconscionable betrayal.

But he would show her.

*And you shall know the truth, and the truth shall make you free.*
  *John 8:32 (NKJV)*

# Chapter 28

"Hi Daniel." Angelica expected his usual bright smile, the normal spark of excitement in his eyes when he saw her. But instead, his face was steel, his eyes cold granite, and his scowl could frighten the bravest of warriors.

Crossing arms over his chest, he leaned against the door frame of his house. "If it isn't the *liar*."

Angelica took a step back, a familiar ache igniting in her heart. "What? What's wrong, Daniel?"

"Thomas told me everything."

She stared at him a moment, her mind reeling. "So you know about Isaac."

"That he's my son?" He speared her with his eyes.

Whispering a prayer, she lowered her gaze. "I was actually coming here to tell you."

"How convenient."

"I was, believe what you will." What she couldn't believe, what she couldn't understand, was why, after all the threats, Thomas told Daniel anyway.

"Why, Angel? Why?" Pain flooded his eyes with moisture. "Why keep something this important from me? Why take Thomas' money?"

"Is that what he told you?" She shook her head—shock, anger, and pain all mixed in one vicious brew. "I'm sorry, Daniel, I did what I thought was best for you."

"For *you*, you mean. All this time, I'm playing with the kid. Not knowing he's my own son. And you just stood by and watched, no doubt laughing at my ignorance."

"I should have told you." She swallowed. "I wanted to tell you." She retreated another step. Hot sun beat down on her. She deserved it.

His eyes narrowed. "I don't even know you, anymore, Angel. And I don't want anyone like you raising our son."

Alarm screeched through her. "What are you saying?"

"Simply that I'm going to get the best lawyers possible and fight you for custody. And guess who's going to win? A prestigious man of God who can provide Isaac with everything he needs or an unemployed, deceiving cocktail waitress?" Stepping back into his house, he slammed the door in her face.

Making it all too clear why Thomas had told him. It was the perfect way to keep them apart.

The drive home was a blur. Everything was a blur through the tears that kept filling her eyes. She parked the car and headed across the street to the beach, needing a moment alone before she faced Leigh. *And* Isaac. The thought of losing him tore her gut into shreds.

Yanking off her shoes, she tossed them aside and dropped to her knees in the sand, oblivious of the people around her, to their chatter, the music, the laughter, oblivious to the waves and sun, oblivious to all but the agony in her heart.

"What am I to do, Father? I've lost everything. My job, Daniel, and now Isaac. I trusted You." She had finally trusted Him, finally committed Isaac into His hands. "I was going to do the right thing and tell him. I *was*! Why have You allowed this to happen?" Dropping her face to the sand, she wept like she had never wept before.

No answer came, just the crash of waves on shore and the stares of curious onlookers who no doubt thought her insane.

Maybe she was.

For wasn't she making the same mistake all over again? Not trusting God with Isaac. Yes, things were far worse than she could ever imagine, but God hadn't changed.

Bowing her head, she watched her tears drop to moisten the sand. "Father, I'm sorry. I'm going to trust You this time. I'm putting Isaac once again in Your hands. Take care of him, protect him, and let Your will, not mine, be done."

Baliel stood alone on the beach, watching Angelica battle three mighty demons—Fear, Hopelessness, and Despair. Snarling and snapping their fangs, the fiends slithered around her, whispering in her ears and poking her amour, seeking entrance.

Gripping the hilt of his sword, Baliel could do naught but stand and watch. Oh, how his fingers itched to put these vile spirits in their place. But the test had commenced, and human will would prevail. Despite its faulty and often devastating choice.

But not for Angelica. Or so he hoped! She had been through too much, walked the narrow path for too long, grown too much like her Savior to lose the battle now.

Yet, she was weakening. He could see it in her eyes, in the darkness creeping into her soul.

*No! Be strong, little warrior, for you shall rule with Him one day.*

Finally, she closed her eyes, tears spilling down her cheeks, and sought the Father's voice within, sought His peace.

The darkness retreated.

She bowed her head and relinquished all to the Father's good keeping.

Baliel smiled as Fear, Hopelessness, and Despair screamed in unison, uttered a string of foul curses, and sped away, leaving a putrid stench in their wake.

A tap on Daniel's office door brought his gaze up to Mrs. Clipton.

"Yes, come in." He motioned her forward as he glanced at his speech displayed across his computer screen. Tomorrow morning they would fly to D.C., and the next day he'd stand up before the heads of state, the spiritual leaders of the country, and the President himself to give the speech of his life. At least he hoped it would be. In all honesty, he'd not been able to fully concentrate on it since he'd slammed the door on Angel.

Was it possible for the same woman to break his heart twice? Apparently so—the pain in his chest a clear indication of that fact. And also of how much a fool he was. He thought she really loved him. He thought she'd changed from the young girl who'd run off with another man all those years ago. But what sort of person keeps a man from his own son? For ten years! And all her playing hard-to-get. Just crap. She'd only been reeling him in, baiting him for the kill.

Luring him into marriage for his money and status.

"Here's the copy of your speech, Mr. Cain." Mrs. Clipton laid the papers on his desk. "And there's a Miss Rollins to see you."

"I don't know any Rollins." He waved her away. "I don't have time now. Have her make an appointment."

"You'll see me. And you'll see me now." The angry woman's voice snapped his gaze up to see Leigh, Angel's roommate.

"I'm sorry, Pastor Cain." Mrs. Clipton gave him a frightened look. "I told her to wait at my desk."

"It's alright. You may go."

The elderly woman scurried out.

He stared at Leigh, her long dark hair tumbling down her blouse to her capris. "I have nothing to say to you."

"But I have *much* to say to you."

"Nothing I want to hear, I'm sure. So, if you don't mind…" He gestured toward the door. "I have work to do."

"You're the biggest idiot ever to walk the earth." She approached his desk. "And God knows what she sees in you, but you *will* listen to me, Daniel Cain, and I'm not leaving until you do."

Sitting back in his chair, Daniel released a sigh. "Did she send you?"

"No. She doesn't know I'm here." Leigh swung hair over her shoulder and gave him a look that would scare a drill sergeant. "Let me tell you a little story, Pastor. It's about a young girl in love who argued with her boyfriend and who was desperate to make up, who waited patiently at a restaurant for him, only to find he'd sent his numb-brained friend to break up with her."

Daniel huffed. "More lies."

"Couldn't even do it in person, could you?" She snorted.

"I didn't—"

"I'm not done." She held up a hand. "She intended to tell you that night that she was carrying your child, but your friend, Thomas, told her it would ruin you. That you'd be kicked out of seminary."

Daniel snorted. "I'm sure the ten thousand helped ease her pain."

Leigh jabbed her finger at him. "You're dumber than you look, Dan. She never took any money. She didn't want it. She wanted *you.* And you broke her heart."

"That's crap and you know it." Daniel tossed down his pen, unwilling to let her lies penetrate his heart. "Thomas told me she wanted to end things. Told me she'd met someone else, and she only wanted to extort money from me for child support." He shook his head. "Yet even after that, I called and called her. Stopped by her place multiple times. If she loved me so much, if she wanted me to know about the baby, why didn't she answer my calls?"

Leigh leaned her knuckles on his desk. "Because she knew it would have ruined your career. And she loved you too much to do that."

"So much that she ran into another man's arms."

Closing her eyes for a moment, Leigh shook her head. "There was never anyone else, you moron. There hasn't been since you."

Stunned, Daniel merely stared at her. Something…some part of what she said rang true deep inside him—rang true to the Angel he knew.

Leigh cocked her head. "It's obvious your friend, this Thomas, lied to you and has been lying to you for years."

Daniel squeezed the bridge of his nose, seeking the truth among so many lies. "I don't believe it." It wasn't possible. Thomas was his best friend. He'd always been by Daniel's side, sticking up for him, encouraging him, helping him with every aspect of the ministry. He would never do something like that. Would he? Yet…hadn't Thomas always put Daniel's career above everything else? He shot angry eyes at Leigh. "You expect me to believe *you*—where do you work, Walmart?—and a cocktail waitress over my own associate pastor?" He waved her away. "Get out."

"Humph. Like I said, I have no idea what she sees in you. You treated her like dirt when she came to tell you about Isaac. Sure, she should have told you before. But she was terrified of losing him. After you broke her heart once, she needed to know she could trust you again. Especially with Isaac. Can you blame her?"

If what this crazed woman was saying was true, then no, he couldn't. But that would mean that the one person he had trusted most in the world had done nothing but betray him for years.

"I knew I was wasting my time." Shaking her head, Leigh started for the door. "Just do me one favor. If there's an ounce of decency in you, if you ever loved Angelica and if you love your son, please don't take Isaac away from her." Then turning, she stormed from the room as quickly as she had come.

Leaving Daniel in a cyclone of confusion.

He sat there, staring into space, trying to sort through all the facts and feelings raging within him when Thomas poked his head in the door. "Got a minute?"

"Sure." Daniel's eyes followed him in like a lion on his prey.

"Great speech." Thomas laid the copy Daniel had given him on his desk. "You're going to wow them. What's wrong?"

"You lied to me. Angel didn't break up with me. She wanted to stay together. She wanted to tell me about the baby."

A flicker of fear tumbled across his friend's face. "Who told you that hogwash?"

"Doesn't matter. Tell me the truth. What did you tell her at that restaurant?"

A slight tick registered at the corner of Thomas' lips. "I told her what was best for you both."

And at that moment, Daniel knew the truth. Pushing back his chair, he stood, resisting the urge to circle the desk and pummel his friend. "You lied to me! All these years." Betrayal ravaged through his gut.

As if sensing danger, Thomas backed away. "And if I hadn't, if you had met her later that night and she told you about the baby, you wouldn't be in this grand office right now, would you? You wouldn't have a church at all, let alone a mega-one. And you certainly wouldn't be invited to D.C. to speak at the annual prayer breakfast or to Belgium to participate in the World Religions conference."

No, Daniel would have married Angel. He would have married her and helped raised their son. But he would have been expelled from seminary. And with no other skills or money, he would have most likely ended up working on the docks like his father.

A loser.

Still, that was *his* choice. And it had been taken from him. "I thought you were my friend."

"I am, don't you see?" Thomas gave him a pleading look. "The greatest friend anyone could have. Everything I've done, I've done for you."

"I'm not so sure." For the first time, he saw his friend in a different light—a greedy, power-hungry light—and it disgusted him.

"You robbed me of ten years with my son…eleven years with the woman I love. How could you do that to me?"

"I'm sorry, Daniel. I really am." Thomas sank to a chair and dropped his head in his hands.

And for the first time, Daniel heard remorse in his voice.

He looked up, his eyes pleading. "Listen, let's go to D.C. tomorrow. Give your speech, and then we'll sort through this when we get back, 'kay? This is too important to screw up now. Especially over *Smokes*."

He spit her name out like it was a blasphemous word.

Daniel wanted to scream, he wanted to yell obscenities at his friend and punch him in the gut. He wanted to run to Angel and take her in his arms. But D.C. stood in his way. He hadn't come this far to give it all up. No, he would concentrate on the trip, give the speech of his life, and when he got home, he'd deal with Thomas.

But more importantly, he would go to Angel and beg her forgiveness.

*For the Lord Himself will descend from heaven with a shout, with the voice of an archangel, and with the trumpet of God. And the dead in Christ will rise first. Then we who are alive and remain shall be caught up together with them in the clouds to meet the Lord in the air. And thus we shall always be with the Lord.*
*1 Thessalonians 4:16-17 (NKJV)*

# Chapter 29

A salty breeze wisped over Angelica's face, caressing strands of hair and tickling her nose. Behind her eyelids, a red hue shoved away the darkness of the night. But she wasn't ready to open her eyes yet. She wanted to savor the astonishing euphoria that was expanding in her soul, a restlessness, an excitement... an incredible joy. So different from the torment she'd endured during her long, sleepless night.

For some reason, even though she'd been trying to keep her distance from Daniel, his rejection had cut deeper this time than it had twelve years ago, marring her soul with bottomless trenches of pain. She'd cried out to God in the long, lonely hours, seeking His comfort.

And found it in His sweet presence.

His words of encouragement, of love, even in the midst of her tears, had smoothed the sharp edges of her agony. He had a plan. A good one. And He would never leave her. He would never leave Isaac. Even if she lost him to Daniel and he became immersed in apostasy, God would not forsake her son.

MaryLu Tyndall

All things were working together for good to those who loved the Father. She knew that and kept repeating it whenever fear for Isaac rose within her. Whenever fear for how she would find a job and provide food began to scrape away her faith, she clung to that truth in Romans 8. And peace returned.

But her heart still ached for Daniel. She'd tried to call him several times, but he was ignoring her. Whether he followed through with his threats for custody or not, she wanted him to know how sorry she was for lying to him, for denying him the pleasure of knowing Isaac all these years.

An odd ray of red sunshine drifted over her eyelids, yet again, as God's breeze stroked her cheek. She opened her eyes, turning her weary head to the window. White cotton curtains waved at her, dancing vibrantly in the strange light. A chorus reached her ears. Outside her window, dozens of birds sang in such crisp harmony they put human orchestras to shame.

Tossing off her covers, she swept her feet over the side of the bed, rubbed her eyes, and made her way to the window. Moving aside the curtains, she knelt and crossed her arms on the sill, staring out onto the most brilliant sunrise she'd ever seen. Ribbons of crimson and gold curled across the horizon as if they were wrapping a beautiful blue present. And in the middle, a bow of golden sunlight rose like a king ascending to his throne.

Her spirit leapt inside her. *Really* leapt. So strong, she felt it in her body. "What is going on, Father?" she whispered.

A blast of wind swept down the street, lifting tree limbs and palm fronds and swirling garbage to the sky, as if everything was praising the Creator. Even the trash. She chuckled, and shifted her gaze back to the ocean, such a gorgeous shade of deep royal blue, made even more beautiful by the golden crowns cast atop each wave by the rising sun.

Cars clogged the street below, horns honked. Music sounded from somewhere down the strip. A baby cried. But Angelica barely heard it all. A peaceful bliss settled on her, as if she were detached from reality...a part of this world, yet drifting farther from it with every passing second.

Despite her broken heart and uncertain future, a mad rush of joy consumed her, and she began laughing uncontrollably. What a grand morning!

She spent the next hour praising her Father before rising to get the kids ready for school.

Oddly, Leigh was sensing something too. She'd awakened with a rare joy and an overwhelming excitement— so much so, she couldn't concentrate on anything and kept smiling for no apparent reason. The children were equally jovial, and Angelica wondered whether she should check the news, even though she didn't trust it. Maybe something weird was happening in the atmosphere.

However, nothing unusual was being reported, except one story that struck her. Several countries had just attacked Israel—Iran, Turkey, Libya, and Russia among them. The screen was filled with tanks, troops, jets, and explosions. Angelica sank to the couch beside Isaac, who was eating his cereal, and called Leigh to her side.

"I think this is Gog-Magog."

"What's Gog-Magog?" Leigh asked, chomping on a piece of toast.

"Ezekiel 38." Angelica ran for the Bible in her room and quickly returned, flipping to the right page. She read the passage to Leigh and then pointed at the screen.

Leigh dropped to the couch and set her half-eaten toast on the table. "Holy cow," was all she said.

Despite the horrors displayed on the TV screen, Angelica could not bring herself to worry. Instead, she flipped it off, looked at Leigh, and out of an understanding borne from being roommates for so many years, they both decided to forgo work and school and take the boys to the beach. It seemed that kind of day.

Of course, Isaac and Joel were ecstatic. The instant their feet hit the sand, they tore off to make a castle near the water, while Angelica and Leigh found a spot for their towels.

Only a pink line remained on the horizon now, but the sky was a brilliant blue—almost turquoise, like the color around tropical islands. And the clouds. Their edges sparkled as if they were braided with diamonds. Angelica turned to Leigh and found her staring as well.

"Have you ever seen a sky like this?" Leigh finally asked.

Angelica shook her head. "I can't stop looking at it, it's so beautiful."

"Yet only a few other people seem to notice," Leigh commented, glancing across the beach. "Most are just doing their thing."

Weird. Though it was early, families with young children and a few teens who should be in school were scoping out the best spots to park their stuff.

"Something's up, isn't it?" Leigh eased a strand of hair behind her ear. "Something important. Spiritual." She glanced at Angelica.

"I have no idea, but I feel it too." She smiled at her friend. "I'm so glad I have you to share God with now."

"Me too." Planting her hands behind her, Leigh stretched out her legs and gazed over the glassy sea, her expression as peaceful as the waves lapping on shore.

But Angelica was restless. A sudden urge forced her to her feet, so strong, she had no choice but to obey. "I've got to go see Daniel."

Leigh nodded and smiled. "Then go."

Angelica mounted the steps to Fort Lauderdale Church of Grace wearing her jeans with the holes at the knees, a T-shirt, her hair a mess, and not a lick of makeup. She couldn't help but smile at the difference from when she'd ascended these same steps to speak with Daniel nearly three months ago. Had it been that long? So much had happened.

She had called his admin and found out he was leaving for a flight to D.C. at 9:00, and since he wouldn't see her, she hoped to run into him as he walked out to his limo.

Just as she had done once before.

Only this time, she had more than a message that was delivered reluctantly and without care. She had an appeal, a *desperate* appeal, that came from her heart. It had nothing to do with her. None of this had ever had anything to do with her, she realized, for the message was the same. But this time, she meant it. She wanted him to hear it and respond to it more than anything.

Sunshine warmed her face, and she drew in a deep breath, a breath of hope and life and anticipation. Above her, swaths of golden light spanned the blue sky. So strange, yet so beautiful. One more step and she saw the limo idling to her left, a man in a suit standing by the passenger door. Another step up and the front doors of the church opened and out rushed Daniel and Thomas, two bodyguards in tow.

Daniel was clean-shaven, his hair neatly combed, and an expensive suit hung perfectly over his muscular frame. His gold cuff links and jeweled tie clip shimmered in the sunlight. But that was all that shimmered. A deep sorrow clung to him as he stared down at the white stone steps. Thomas was silent beside him. One of the bodyguards headed her way.

Taking another step, she halted as Thomas looked up and uttered a curse. "Do we have to get a restraining order to keep you away?" he growled as he approached. "Escort this woman to her car," he ordered the bodyguard.

Before the guard could touch her, she peered around him. "Daniel, I just need a word. Please."

His eyes, shadowed and red-rimmed, landed on hers and instantly came to life.

The guard grabbed her arm.

"It's okay," Daniel finally said. "Step away."

Releasing her, the man took a step back, eyeing her as if she intended to blow herself up and all of them with her.

Daniel approached, tentatively at first, but then he smiled. "It's so good to see you."

"It is?" Shocked, Angelica gripped his outreached hands. "The last time—"

He drew her into an embrace. "Never mind about that. I know the truth now, and I'm so sorry."

She melted against him, longing to stay in his arms forever. Tears blurred her vision, and she backed away, not wanting to stain his nice suit. "Me too. I shouldn't have kept Isaac from you. I'm sorry."

He brushed a tear from her cheek with his thumb. "We were both tricked." He glanced back at Thomas, who looked as though he'd just swallowed a grenade.

"We have to go, Daniel." Thomas urged. "We'll miss our plane."

Feeling the pressure of time, Angelica said a silent prayer. "Remember what we talked about? The wedding, the groom, and the bride who made herself ready? Remember the—"

"Yes, of course. But, listen." He squeezed her hands. "I have so much to tell you. So much time to make up to you. But, I've got to go. We'll talk when I get back. Promise."

"Come with me, Daniel. Don't go to D.C.," she blurted out.

Thomas groaned. "Daniel, come on. The plane won't wait for us. You'll see her in a few days."

Yet Daniel remained, staring at her, his blue eyes so full of pain and love. Shadows consumed him from above, and he gazed up to find a bank of white clouds rolling over the sun.

No, not white… brighter than pure snow, their edges frosted in silver. They rippled when they moved—like waves crashing on shore. In the distance, darkness rose on the horizon, thick, tarry clouds boiling higher and higher.

The bodyguards, driver, and even Thomas stared up at the unusual sight.

Angelica blinked and spotted four angels standing on the steps to her right, her angel among them. His glance briefly took her in before his gaze returned to the proceedings, but she thought she spotted a tiny smile on his lips.

Releasing her hands, Daniel planted a kiss on her cheek. "He's right. I'll call you from D.C." Then turning, he walked toward the limo.

"Daniel," she called frantically, and he looked back at her. "It's almost time. Turn away from the things of this world, the fame, the money, man's version of the truth. Give your whole heart to God. All it takes is one turn, one step of your heart in the right direction—just one, before it's too late."

Thomas moaned and snapped hate-filled eyes her way. "Give me a break, Smokes. Do you know who you are talking to?" He grabbed Daniel's arm. "Come on, you promised."

Daniel tugged from his grip, his eyes remaining on Angelica, a battle waging within them.

*Help him see, Father.*

Wind blasted over them, so strong it nearly pushed Angelica from the step. But she planted her feet even more firmly.

The angels drew their swords, the eerie chime like nails on a chalkboard. Only then did Angelica see the horde of demons thundering toward them from within the church—dark, hideous creatures, some armed with knives and spears, others with only their claws, all foaming at the mouth to grab as many as they could and drag them to hell.

Above her, a brilliant speck of light appeared at the center of the sky, growing larger and larger, pushing the blue aside as it went, and circled by a rainbow of glittering colors.

Yet the horizon remained a frothing cauldron of black.

The angels engaged. The ring of metal on metal filled the air, the curses of the spirits, the wails and grunts of battle. Yet no one heard it but her.

The stench of rotting flesh and sulfur pinched her nose.

A shout thundered across the sky. A command, loving yet strong. "Beloved, come forth!"

Everyone stared at the speakers framing the front doors of the church. Everyone but Angelica. She looked up, smiling.

Her prince was calling her home.

A trumpet sounded, loud and long. The confused men looked around for its source. The bodyguards drew their guns.

For the first time, fear appeared on Thomas' face.

"Daniel?" Angelica held out her hand. "Please!"

Baliel, Nazare, Arithem, and Ethos made quick work of the putrid swarm that had attempted to pervert the will of the two yet undecided.

Baliel had been warned by the Lord of Hosts there would be great resistance in these last minutes, and hence, he and his friends had been fully armed and prepared for battle.

Now, as the holy warriors turned to face their charges, swords still drawn, they spotted the demons who had slithered through their defense—invited by those whose fates still lay at stake. Greed, Pride, Fame, Confusion, and Anger attacked Daniel, spearing him with lances and shooting him with arrows.

Nazare started to charge, but Baliel held him back. "Not until he resists them. We cannot."

Grimacing, Nazare remained, though Baliel could see the distress on his face. He ached for his friend. He knew well the pain of watching a human that had been under one's protection since birth struggle at the crossroads between death and life. Baliel had been there when Angelica had faced that trial. And he'd been elated when she'd chosen the right path. And kept on it.

But Nazare had been forced to endure Daniel's constant betrayal of the One who died for him. Even now, when he'd been told the truth, when the signs were all around him, he faltered beneath his own pride and anger.

They had but minutes left.

Angelica held her hand out to Daniel.

The demons who were attacking him retreated, but only to a short distance.

Light began to spark within him. Nazare drew in a gasp of hope.

Angelica smiled and nodded her encouragement.

Thomas called to him. "What are you doing? You'll lose everything." He stepped toward him. "You can talk to her when we get back. But right now, you have to get in this car!"

The demons assaulted Daniel once again.

The light within him dimmed.

And slowly...ever so slowly...he turned and looked back at Thomas.

No sooner had Daniel glanced at Thomas than a charge of electricity crackled the air so loudly, pain etched through his bones. Power surged through his being, and he faced

Angelica again. The desperate appeal was still written on her face, luring him to abandon everything—his past, present, and future—to give all to the God he claimed to serve.

Somewhere deep within him, he desperately wanted to. But...

A bolt of lightning struck right where Angel stood, so bright, Daniel had to turn his face away. The metallic smell of electricity charged the air, prickling his skin. Before he even opened his eyes, he groped for his phone in his pocket, intending to call 911. *Dear God... Angel's been struck by lightning!*

Drawing the phone to his ear, he opened his eyes.

And blinked.

Angelica was no longer there.

He spun, scanning the stairs, the church building, the parking lot—she was nowhere in sight.

"Tank's gone," one of his bodyguards shouted as he combed the area, gun drawn. "What's happening?"

Light faded. Daniel gazed up. Churning, black clouds rose from every direction, swallowing up the sun. Then it was gone and darkness covered the earth. Thunder roared, trembling the stairs beneath their feet.

Oddly, he heard weeping in the distance.

The phone slipped from Daniel's hand.


Baliel bid Nazare farewell. "He will need you now more than ever. Be strong, my friend."

A tear spilled from Nazare's eye.

*Behold, I tell you a mystery: We shall not all sleep, but we shall all be changed—in a moment, in the twinkling of an eye, at the last trumpet. For the trumpet will sound, and the dead will be raised incorruptible, and we shall be changed. For this corruptible must put on incorruption, and this mortal must put on immortality.*
*1 Corinthians 15:51-52 (NKJV)*

# Chapter 30

Angelica floated upward through transparent light. Through it, she could see stars, gazillions of them, galaxies, supernovas of every imaginable color. So beautiful! So clear. Perfect. The colors and shades so vibrant and alive.

Other people—many others—smiling and laughing, surrounded her.

The ache in her feet was gone, the familiar exhaustion faded, her sleep-deprived eyelids suddenly felt light, and her tummy no longer growled from hunger. She felt strong and full of energy, and she glanced down to see she had a new body—looking much like her old one, yet different, glowing, powerful, more beautiful in its strength and magnificence.

*The rapture!* It had actually happened! She could hardly believe it. Elation soared through her.

Her angel appeared by her side, staring down at her in approval. He looked just as he had on earth—tall, muscular, long white hair, intense eyes, and strapped with a dozen weapons. But here he looked more solid, more filled with light, more real.

"What is your name?"

"Baliel."

"You've been with me from the beginning, haven't you?"

"I have."

Her thoughts shifted to her son. "Isaac!?"

"He's well. You'll see him soon."

"Daniel." She glanced behind her and saw the earth in all its blue beauty growing smaller and smaller.

Baliel shook his head.

If it was possible to feel sad in such a glorious state, Angelica felt a twinge in her heart. "I failed him. I failed the Father."

"Never fear, little one. You did the Father's will."

"I don't understand."

"It was your job to tell him the truth, to open his eyes. Otherwise he would have fallen for the deception coming upon the entire world." Baliel glanced down at the planet swirling through space, and she sensed his sorrow. But then he faced her again. "Because of you, he knows." He smiled. "Never fear, he will do great things for the Father during the most difficult time the world will ever experience. He will bring thousands into the kingdom."

*Thousands?* Angelica swallowed a lump of emotion she couldn't describe. *Daniel?* Daniel would finally turn back to God! Such glorious news. Such wonderful news. And yet, he would endure so much tragedy, so many horrors.

"You will see him again soon."

Just then Angelica remembered her final vision of Daniel, the only one that hadn't yet happened—she, Daniel, and Isaac walking hand in hand through that amazing field of flowers.

Baliel ushered her onward. "When he has completed his task, he will be martyred."

"Martyred?" Angelica gulped.

The angel nodded and gestured ahead to a light so bright, she could see nothing else. "But now, your Prince awaits."

Turning, excitement buzzing through her, she continued upward and emerged onto an enormous platform of light floating in space. Rainbows made of more colors than she knew existed encircled the stage in a dome of vibrant light, while each step she took was upon shimmering glass. Mobs of the happiest people she'd ever seen dashed here and there, embracing, laughing, and bubbling with joy. Everything was so vivid, so real and gorgeous. It was as though a shadowy veil had been lifted from her eyes, making everything on earth now seem like a mere shadow when compared to this far greater reality.

Isaac ran into her arms. "Mom!" Embracing him tightly, she kissed the top of his head as Leigh appeared, hand in hand with Joel, huge smiles on their faces. Greg rushed up to her, then Melody, Robert and Anna, Scottie, and all the others from her church. They looked the same, yet different—so very magnificently different!—stronger, younger, better versions of themselves without the extra weight, the haggardness, the ravages of disease, and the lines of age, pain, and heartache on their faces.

More people emerged from the bustling crowd—people whose names she didn't know, but whose faces she would always remember. People she'd told about Jesus at the Mermaid Den, people she'd thought had not listened, had not cared. One by one, they came and stood before her. Some thanked her. Others kissed her cheek. Many others had tears of joy flowing down their faces. Hundreds of them! *There were hundreds of them*! Humbled, Angelica could hardly believe what God had done through her.

Music danced past her ears, the sound of a full orchestra from instruments she'd never heard before. It was the sweetest melody she'd ever heard, the notes so alive and bubbling with joy, they reached down into her very soul. People began singing and swaying to the music when a light appeared near the center of the platform, brighter than the sun.

"It's Him! It's Jesus!" someone shouted.

Isaac looked up at her. "Mom, we're going to finally see Him face to face."

"Yes, we are, son. Yes, we are. And we will be with Him forever more."

*And they overcame him by the blood of the Lamb and by the word of their testimony, and they did not love their lives to the death.*
Revelation 12:11 (NKJV)

# Epilogue

D aniel rubbed his eyes, heavy with exhaustion, and stared up at the flat-screen on the wall in his office as he'd been doing for the past few days. Scenes of chaos and mayhem paraded across his vision—riots, violence, anarchy all over the world as both citizens and governments struggled to deal with the sudden disappearance of millions.

The war in the Middle East raged on, both sides sustaining heavy casualties. A meteor had crashed into Spain, leaving half the country in flames. Others landed in the sea, sending tsunamis careening toward shore, wiping out entire cities.

And in the midst of it all, a single man stepped into the limelight. He was good-looking, tall, and as smooth as a polished gem. Behind him stood the newcomers, silent watchers of mankind. Words of "world peace" and "cooperation" slid from his lips like silk and floated over throngs of adoring crowds, entrancing them into a state of comatose adoration.

*The Antichrist.*

Daniel had learned all about him during the past three days. He'd not eaten. He'd not slept. Instead, he had read the entire Bible that Angel had given him. And he'd prayed. Oh, how he had prayed! Flat on his face most of the time. Sobbing and groaning in repentance of what a fool he'd been, how deceived, how selfish, ambitious, and greedy he'd become.

And sweet, sweet Angel had done her best to wake him up. Even after all the pain he'd caused her. Even after his rejection, she'd come one last time to plead for his soul.

Now, she was gone. And his son with her.

Not only her, but Marley and Isabel, and dear Mrs. Clipton, along with several of his staff.

Sometime during the second night of his agony, Jesus had appeared to Daniel. He'd walked right up to Daniel and touched his head, commanding him to rise.

"The time to grieve is past. You have work to do." His voice was strong, yet so full of love that Daniel could only stare as tears sped down his cheeks.

"I love you, son. Be strong and courageous. I am with you always," He'd said.

And then He was gone.

Daniel had melted into the carpet, overcome by the presence of the Holy Spirit and an intense love that had saturated his soul.

He flipped the TV off. He had read the book. He knew what would happen next.

And it wasn't going to be pretty.

Thomas poked his head in. "Man, you look terrible." He stepped inside. "All this because Smokes is gone?"

Daniel shook his head. Though he'd tried to explain everything to his friend, Thomas still didn't get what was happening.

"Of course, I miss her and Isaac, but it's not just that. I told you, they were taken in the rapture. And we are still here. Doesn't that make you even slightly nervous?"

"Come on, the rapture?" Thomas snagged an apple from a bowl and took a bite. "You heard what they said. Those creatures—the watchers from another planet—said the missing people are perfectly fine, safe, and are being reprogrammed. You have to admit those crazy Christians were getting a bit too zealous." He finished his bite and sat on the couch. "I mean, their archaic ideas were holding back civilization. Think of what we can do now without them? The sky's the limit." He pointed at Daniel with a smile. "And you're going to be a part of it."

Daniel squeezed the bridge of his nose. "They aren't being reprogrammed, Thomas. They're in heaven."

Thomas frowned. "Don't worry, you'll see her and the boy again. When she's back to normal."

Daniel released a heavy sigh, troubled that his friend was so deceived. He'd been praying for Thomas and would continue until the man saw the light.

Thomas leaned forward on his knees. "Listen, you gotta stop this crazy talk. They've rescheduled the D.C. breakfast. We're back on. Nothing's changed."

"Except the world has gone mad and aliens have landed."

"I think it's kinda cool. Makes sense. They were the ones who put Adam and Eve here and have been watching humanity evolve ever since. Man"—he whistled—"who would have thought? It's almost too incredible to believe."

"I'll agree with that," Daniel said.

"They're so much smarter than we are. Amazing. Besides, all they want is to help us save our planet and our people."

How could Thomas believe such nonsense? Daniel glanced at his watch. "I better get out there." It was Sunday, and although people had been stumbling into the church ever since the rapture—terrified and confused, begging to see Daniel—he hadn't spoken to any of them. He first had to spend time with the One who had the answers before he could help anyone else.

Grabbing his Bible, he headed for the door.

"You're preaching in your jeans? At least comb your hair." Thomas followed him down the hall.

"I doubt anyone will care." Daniel navigated through the maze of halls and finally entered the backstage area where he greeted the musicians warmly, noting the fear on their faces. He glanced at Kimberly and two of his other pastors as he climbed the steps to the stage.

Shame assaulted him. His pastors, church members—people under his discipleship—still here.

But it was out on stage where he got his biggest shock.

Half the auditorium was filled. Half of the people who had listened to his sermons week after week, half of the people he counseled and taught, had not made it.

He stood there, frozen, scanning the terrified faces of his flock as a hush fell over them. He had prepared nothing. No sermon, no message. He had no grand, eloquent words to say. But at that moment, he felt power buzz through him ... the power of the Holy Spirit.

Clearing his throat, he made his way to the podium when Thomas clutched his arm and spun him around, his angry gaze focused on the book in Daniel's hand. "Is that what I think it is?"

"If you think it's a Bible, then yes."

"An original one?"

"Absolutely. Angel gave it to me." Jerking from his friend's grip, he continued forward.

"You'll be arrested. *We'll* be ruined. What do you think you are doing?"

Grabbing a microphone, Daniel glanced at him over his shoulder and winked. "Finally preaching the gospel."

# About the Author

AWARD WINNING AND BEST-SELLING AUTHOR, MARYLU TYNDALL dreamt of pirates and sea-faring adventures during her childhood days on Florida's Coast. With more than seventeen books published, she makes no excuses for the deep spiritual themes embedded within her romantic adventures. Her hope is that readers will not only be entertained but will be brought closer to the Creator who loves them beyond measure. In a culture that accepts the occult, wizards, zombies, and vampires without batting an eye, MaryLu hopes to show the awesome present and powerful acts of God in a dying world. A Christy award nominee, MaryLu makes her home with her husband, six children, three grandchildren, and several stray cats on the California coast.

For a peek the characters and scenes from the book, visit my When Angels Cry Pinterest Page!

If you enjoyed this book, one of the nicest ways to say "thank you" to an author and help them be able to continue writing is to leave a favorable review on Amazon! Barnes and Noble, Goodreads, Kobo, Itunes (And elsewhere, too!) I would appreciate it if you would take a moment to do so. Thanks so much!

Comments? Questions? I love hearing from my readers, so feel free to contact me via my website:

http://www.marylutyndall.com

Or email me at:

marylu_tyndall@yahoo.com

Follow me on:

FACEBOOK:
https://www.facebook.com/marylu.tyndall.author

TWITTER: https://twitter.com/MaryLuTyndall
BLOG: http://crossandcutlass.blogspot.com/
PINTEREST: http://www.pinterest.com/mltyndall/

To hear news about special prices and new releases that only my subscribers receive, sign up for my newsletter on my website or blog! http://www.marylutyndall.com

# Other Books by MaryLu Tyndall

THE REDEMPTION

THE RELIANCE

THE RESTITUTION

THE RANSOM

THE RECKONING

THE FALCON AND THE SPARROW

THE RED SIREN

THE BLUE ENCHANTRESS

THE RAVEN SAINT

CHARITY'S CROSS

CHARLES TOWNE BELLES TRILOGY

SURRENDER THE HEART

SURRENDER THE NIGHT

SURRENDER THE DAWN

SURRENDER TO DESTINY TRILOGY

VEIL OF PEARLS

FORSAKEN DREAMS

ELUSIVE HOPE

ABANDONED MEMORIES

ESCAPE TO PARADISE TRILOGY

SHE WALKS IN POWER (BOOK 1 OF THE
PROTECTORS OF THE SPEAR TRILOGY)

PEARLS FROM THE SEA DEVOTIONAL

CENTRAL PARK RENDEZVOUS

TEARS OF THE SEA

WESTWARD CHRISTMAS BRIDES

Made in the USA
Middletown, DE
28 September 2017